MESSA

I slid the barn ~~door open~~ and peered into the shadowy space. With the gunmetal sky outside, little light made its way in the high windows, but I thought everything looked like I'd left it. Except . . .

On the rough wooden floor a couple of yards in sat a piece of paper folded in half and propped up like a tent, as if whoever left it wanted it noticed. That paper definitely hadn't been there when I'd locked up yesterday. I pushed the door wide open, glanced there, to make sure no one was lurking behind me, and stepped in far enough to snatch the paper, then hurried back out before opening it.

In typed capital letters it read: BETTER LAY OFF ASKING QUESTIONS ABOUT THE MURDER. YOU WOULDN'T WANT TO BE NEXT.

Books by Maddie Day

FLIPPED FOR MURDER

GRILLED FOR MURDER

WHEN THE GRITS HIT THE FAN

Published by Kensington Publishing Corporation

When the Grits Hit the Fan

Maddie Day

KENSINGTON PUBLISHING CORP.
http://www.kensingtonbooks.com

KENSINGTON BOOKS are published by

Kensington Publishing Corp.
119 West 40th Street
New York, NY 10018

All Kensington Titles, Imprints, and Distributed Lines are available at special quantity discounts for bulk purchases for sales promotions, premiums, fund-raising, and educational or institutional use. Special book excerpts or customized printings can also be created to fit specific needs. For details, write or phone the office of the Kensington special manager: Kensington Publishing Corp., 119 West 40th S New York, NY 10018, attn: Special Sales Departr Phone: 1-800-221-2647.

Kensington and the K logo Reg. U.S. Pat & TM Off.

ISBN-13: 978-1-61773-929-3
ISBN-10: 1-61773-929-4
First Kensington Mass Market Edition: April 2017

eISBN-13: 978-1-61773-930-9
eISBN-10: 1-61773-930-8
First Kensington Electronic Edition: April 2017

10 9 8 7 6 5 4 3 2 1

Printed in the United States of America

33614080818187023

*For Annie Tunstall and the late Richard Gale,
the most inspiring eighty-somethings I've ever known.
Richard was one of my Hoosier consultants
for this series, and they have both encouraged me
every step of my author journey.*

Acknowledgments

I'm grateful, always, for the entire team at Kensington Publishing, and to my agent, John Talbot. The Wicked Cozy Authors continue to support and inspire: Jessie Crockett/Jessica Estevao, Sherry Harris, Julie Hennrikus/Julianne Holmes, Liz Mugavero/Kate Conte, and Barb Ross. I love you ladies. I thank Sherry particularly for continuing to suggest that my protagonist Robbie is nicer and stronger than my earlier drafts portray her. She's right, of course.

Thanks to Joan Emerson for the idea about bacon-cheddar-chive scones, and fellow author Kelly Cochran for the brilliant book title. My son JD lent more bicycle consulting for this book, and DP Lyle's *Murder and Mayhem* helped with several forensic details. I hope I got them right.

I recently reconnected with a friend from my Indiana grad school days. As The Original Grit Girl, Georgeanne Ross grinds and sells pure stone-ground corn grits and other ground corn products every week. After I tasted them, I had to include her grits in this book. You should order some at http://gritgirl.net/. She graciously allowed me to include a version of her recipe for creamy cheese grits, too. Another friend, the super productive and successful author Sheila Connolly, was nice enough to let me adapt her recipe for Irish Pork Chops for this book.

Caveat #1: The fictional professors and graduate students in this story bear no resemblance to the actual members of the Indiana University Sociology Department, and particularly not to those who specialize in medical sociology. I am quite sure their interactions are entirely respectful and productive, in contrast to those portrayed in this book.

Caveat #2: I realize that with climate change, a winter cold enough for ice fishing in Brown County is ever more rare, so indulge me in imagining one of those freak frigid-weather winters that still pop up once in a while in southern Indiana.

As always, I want to thank my sons, my sisters, my beau, my fellow Friends, and my many author friends for having my back, cheering me on, and putting up with me. I love you all.

Dear readers, including librarians: I'm awed and blown away by how much you love this series! Thank you, thank, you thank you. A gentle reminder that a positive review of a book you read goes a long way in helping the author. I would be ever grateful to see your opinion on Amazon, Goodreads, Facebook, and elsewhere if you liked my story (and check out my other author names: Edith Maxwell and Tace Baker).

Chapter 1

Who knew people could be so nasty to each other?

I'm Robbie Jordan. While I cleared dinner plates, I watched and listened as a mix of grad students and professors from Indiana University discussed medical sociology during their bimonthly dinner meeting at my restaurant, Pans 'N Pancakes. It wasn't pretty. I'd served fifteen of them Chicken Ezekiel on rotini, with garlic bread and winter greens from a local farmer harvesting even in February. The air still smelled deliciously of Kalamata olives, garlic, and roasted tomatoes, and from the empty plates, it sure looked like the meal had been a success.

The conversation? Not so much. Half the terminology went right over my head. But when Charles Stilton glared at my friend Lou Perlman, the meaning was unmistakable.

"It was unethical of you to take the ideas in my paper and present them as your own," Lou went on, the silver rings on her fingers flashing as much as her eyes as she pointed at him across the wide table. "You agreed to sponsor me, but I sure didn't agree to give up my original research."

"You're a doctoral student," the diminutive professor said, his bright green shirt a spot of color among the more muted shades worn by his colleagues. He picked up his glass of red wine and sipped. "I'm a tenured professor in the same field. I can't help it if our research is pursuing parallel ideas. I didn't steal a thing." He studied my shelves of vintage cookware and blinked as if the conversation was over.

I'd met Professor Stilton in the preceding weeks. He'd been polite and friendly to me but had gotten into tiffs with the others at a few of the gatherings. I'd have to ask Lou what was up between them.

A woman I hadn't seen before pushed back her chair. She stood and set her hands on the table. "That's enough, you two. These meetings were supposed to be congenial intellectual gatherings, not some mudslinging sessions."

Charles stroked his tidy black goatee. Ignoring the woman, he turned to the man on his right. "How about them Pacers?"

I watched Lou fume, nostrils flared, lips pressed together. She pushed her chair back and stalked to the restroom. We had met in the fall when she'd come in for breakfast with a group of cyclist friends. She'd helped me find my father and we'd become good friends. I'd never seen her so mad.

The woman who'd admonished them had come in late and I hadn't been introduced to her. Shaking her head, she picked up her plate and brought it to where I stood at the sink in the kitchen area that adjoined the rest of the space.

"Thanks." I wiped my hand on my apron before extending it. "Robbie Jordan, proprietor here."

She set down the plate and silverware and shook hands with a firm, vigorous touch. "I'm Professor Zenobia Brown. But just call me Zen." A wiry woman, she stood a couple of inches shorter than my five-foot-three, and was at least two or three decades older than my twenty-seven years. Her salt-and-pepper hair was cut in a no-nonsense short do with the top a little bit spiked. She smiled, her skin crinkling around blue eyes. "My mom thought with a last name like Brown I needed a unique first name. Anyway, I'm a new professor in the department. The chair, actually. I live halfway between South Lick and Bloomington and I've been meaning to get over here for one of your famous breakfasts. Still want to."

"Not so sure they're famous, but you're welcome to come and sample what we serve."

"Whole wheat banana walnut flapjacks? That's my kind of breakfast." She glanced back at the group. "Sorry about the commotion. It's like wrangling cats sometimes to get these people to act civilly."

"It's okay. As long as I get paid and people don't start a food fight, I don't really care how they get along." I'd happily agreed to Lou's idea of the dinner meetings. I'd only opened my country store breakfast-and-lunch place in October and hadn't realized how slow business would be during the winter. It was cold and often snowy in the hills of southern Indiana, but most years not snowy enough to bring a winter tourist trade. Even the locals seemed to be staying home instead of eating out. I'd reduced the days I stayed open to Wednesday through Sunday to save money on my assistant Danna's pay. It also kept me from ordering food that spoiled because it didn't get used. The boost of a nice flat sum from this group every other Friday night was definitely helping the bottom line. I served the same menu to everybody, changing it up each time, and so far no one had complained.

I loaded up two platters of brownies and took them to the table, which I'd created by shoving together smaller tables into a conference-table-sized surface they could all sit around. "Coffee or tea, anyone? Or decaf?"

"I'm sticking with wine," Charles said, pouring the last of his bottle of Merlot into his glass. "I can because I'm walking home," he added in a defensive tone.

I knew he lived half a mile away right here in South Lick. I thought most of the other faculty and students, like Lou, resided nearer the sprawling flagship Indiana University campus fifteen miles away in Bloomington.

"It's so great you got permission for us to do the BYOB thing, Robbie," Lou said, back in her chair, pouring a half glass for herself from a bottle of white. "Dinner's not really civilized unless you can drink wine with it. And I'm having more because I caught a ride with teetotaler Tom here."

Tom, Lou's fellow grad student, grinned and waved.

"As long as I'm not a licensed alcohol establishment, which I'm not, it's apparently legal. And as long you pour your own." I'd purchased a supply of stemless wine glasses and a few corkscrews when I'd learned I could allow customers to bring bottles of wine. Nobody had asked yet if they could carry in beer or hard alcohol, which was good, because my research hadn't extended that far. I didn't advertise the BYOB option, and I wasn't usually open for dinner, anyway, but several times a group of ladies had brought their own wine for a special luncheon, as had an elderly local couple celebrating their sixtieth wedding anniversary with lunch out instead of dinner.

Lou had been talking with Tom and Zen. She tilted the bottle at Zen's glass. "More?"

I noticed Lou was carefully avoiding any inter-action with Charles, wisely so. He was still deep in conversation with the man next to him.

Zen covered the glass with her hand. "Not for me, thanks. One glass is my limit. I'm training for a marathon. But I'd love a cup of decaf, Robbie."

So running was why she was that wiry. I was a serious cyclist, myself. It was how I'd met Lou and Tom, who also loved riding for miles up and down the scenic hills of Brown County. But my cycling habit was offset by my love of eating. Nobody would ever call me wiry and I didn't care. I was healthy, and I did have a nicely defined waist to offset my generous hips.

I took the rest of the hot drink orders. After I delivered the mugs, I busied myself cleaning up. It was already eight-thirty and I still needed to prep for tomorrow. We'd agreed on a finish time of nine o'clock for these gatherings. I was up every morning by five-thirty to open the doors by seven, so I didn't want Friday nights to turn into an open-ended session of wine sippers sitting around talking abstractions.

The discussion had turned to the topic of public health, which apparently wasn't as controversial as the conversation between Lou and Charles had been, and didn't seem abstract at all. Snippets of talk about social change in women's paid and unpaid work and the consequences of these changes for women's health floated my way. Zen seemed to be leading the discussion, while Charles sat back with his arms folded, a little smirk on his face. I carried the remains of the rotini and the salad into the walk-in cooler. When I came out with butter and flour in my arms for tomorrow's biscuit dough, the mood had changed.

Zen stood with her hands on her hips. "How dare you say that to me?" Her eyes narrowed and nearly shot daggers at him.

Charles shrugged then grabbed his coat. "You can take it. You're our esteemed *chair*, aren't you?" He sauntered toward the front door. "Have a nice night, fellow sociologists."

The cowbell on the door jangled his exit, but it looked like Zen's nerves were a lot more jangled.

Chapter 2

By nine the next morning the restaurant was blessedly not in a slump. For once, every table was full and a party of three women browsed the antique cookware shelves as they waited for seats to open up. *Good.* I'd much rather be too busy than sitting around waiting for customers. The air was full with the rich aromas of sizzling sausages, sweet maple syrup, dark coffee, and freshly flipped pancakes. Bits of conversations were punctuated by the clink of silverware and the occasional jangling of the cowbell on the front door marking exits and entries.

Between hurrying from table to table, taking orders and clearing, I glanced at Danna, the best nineteen-year-old co-chef I could imagine. Tied with an orange band, her titian dreadlocks hung down her back as she flipped pancakes, turned sausages, and expertly ladled gravy onto hot biscuits. The girl was tireless, nearly always cheerful, and had contributed plenty of innovative ideas for extras to accompany our usual menu. She'd made creamy grits with cheese last Saturday and we'd sold out. Today the Specials chalkboard read, WARM UP YOUR TOOTSIES OMELET: ROASTED RED PEPPERS AND PEPPER JACK CHEESE SERVED ON A WARM CORN TORTILLA AND TOPPED WITH FRESH JALAPENO SALSA. It was Danna's invention, even though as a native Californian, I might have thought of it myself.

"You good?" I called to her.

She returned a thumbs up, so I continued on my trajectory to three men with the ruddy faces of those who spent a lot of time outdoors. I didn't know if they were farmers, construction workers, or even electrical linemen like my new sweetie, Abe.

"Refill, gentlemen?" I held out the coffeepot. One covered his mug with his hand, but another smiled and lifted his mug. The third had pushed aside a plate empty except for a small pool of gravy and was engrossed in the *New York Times* crossword puzzle. He was doing it in ink. My radar went up since crosswording in ink was my favorite downtime occupation, bar none—even more than cycling.

"Today's?" I asked him, sidling around to his side of the table. "I haven't gotten to it yet." I smiled when he glanced up.

"Know what the biggest Channel Island is?" He frowned at the paper. "I don't even know what channel they're talking about."

"How many letters?"

"Nine. Could be the British Channel. How do you spell brek-how?"

"You mean Brecqhou? That's only eight letters. I'll bet it's Santa Cruz. Try that."

He added those letters, nodding as he did.

"That's it." He glanced up at me. "So it must be the California Channel Islands. How did you know?"

I laughed. "I grew up across from Santa Cruz Island, in Santa Barbara. Santa Cruz is definitely the biggest island of the archipelago, and it's gorgeous on a clear day. It's like seeing the top of a mountain range push up from the ocean. Which I suppose it is. They're all gorgeous—Anacapa, Santa Rosa, San Miguel, even tiny Santa Barbara Island."

"Sounds like you miss them. Well, thanks, miss. I appreciate the help." He chuckled. "Thought I was only coming in for biscuits, gravy, and bacon."

"My pleasure. Will that be all today, guys?"

He looked at his tablemates, who nodded. "Yes, I do believe so. It was all very tasty."

"I appreciate that." I slid their ticket facedown onto the table and headed for another table. The cowbell on the door jangled and I turned my head to see Maude Stilton holding the door for her tiny mother, Jo Schultz. I'd bet Jo was all of five feet when she stood up real straight, although Maude was a good five or six inches taller.

"Come on in, ladies," I called, and headed that way, instead.

Jo, the former owner of my building, handed her wool coat to Maude and sank onto the bench. "Hi, there, Robbie. How's my store?" She smiled, further creasing her lined face. She always wore her white hair in a bun on top of her hair, giving her an even more old-fashioned look than her almost seventy years would suggest.

"It's good. And busy this morning, as you can see." I gestured behind me. "I'm sorry you'll have a short wait, Jo, but I'm glad to see you." I greeted

Maude, too. "There are two parties before you. Breakfast usually turns over pretty fast, though."

"Not a problem, Robbie. Glad you're busy." Maude, a successful local architect and Professor Stilton's wife, didn't look a bit old-fashioned. Barely a line showed in her face, even though she had a nearly twenty-year-old son. Every time I'd seen her, her streaked chestnut hair was freshly colored and cut in an elegant layered style that fell between her ears and her shoulders. She slid out of a stylish cardinal-red coat and hung it on the coat tree with Jo's.

"It's looking real good in here," Jo said. She might look like an older lady, but both her mind and her eyes were clear and sharp. "You done a good job with the renovations. And I'll bet you're glad not to be involved in any more murders."

"You can say that again." I shuddered inwardly at the memory of being face-to-face with a killer right here in my store at the end of November. "It's been nice and quiet for three months, and I'm planning on it staying that way."

"Say, you ever get a chance to work on the upstairs like you said you were wanting to?"

Danna dinged the little bell indicating an order was up. I swiveled my head in her direction and caught an annoyed look. Busy like we were, I had no business chatting up a customer even if we were connected through this building.

"Gotta run, Jo," I told her. "I'll catch up with you later."

I ran my tush off for the next half hour, clearing, taking orders, and serving up platters of tasty, filling breakfasts. By the time I delivered an egg white omelet with dry toast and a bowl of fruit for Maude and a half order of banana-walnut pancakes for Jo, it was almost thirty minutes later and the crush was over. Three tables were empty and four others already had their checks.

"Whew. Sorry that took so long," I said, setting down their food. "Can I top off your coffees?"

"No thanks," Jo said

"Please," Maude said. "I ought to take some to Ronnie. He's out ice fishing all day. At nineteen, did he think to take a thermos of something warm to drink? No, he did not."

"That's one cold way to have fun," Jo said. "But he's my grandson. I expect he has a mind of his own, and right that he should."

"I helped him take his equipment onto the lake this morning when I dropped him off. You wouldn't catch me sitting on a bucket all day long hoping to catch a couple perch or bluegill." Maude raised perfectly arched eyebrows and shook her head.

"Jo, you were asking about the upstairs. I've been working on it this winter." I'd done all the renovations on the downstairs myself. My mom had had a successful business as an artisan cabinetmaker in California and had taught me carpentry. When she'd died suddenly a year ago, the money I inherited from her, together with my savings from working as a chef in nearby Nashville, Indiana for the three years prior, had helped me buy the property from Jo. But I'd rather still have Mom alive. "So far I'm still in the demolition phase."

Maude looked worried as she glanced at her mother.

Jo seemed to shrink into herself, but she mustered

a smile. "That's nice. I know you want to make the place into an inn."

"I'm sorry." I cringed at my thoughtlessness. "That's not very nice of me to mention the demolition. You both used to live up there. It's just that I wanted a configuration of walls different from the previous ones." And insulation. And modern wiring. And a myriad other improvements.

"Don't worry about it," Maude said.

Jo's smile brightened. "I'm glad you're going to improve it. The place got pretty run down, I admit."

"That striped wallpaper I put up in my room was pretty bad, as I recall," Maude said. "But hey, I was a teenager."

"And you did it all yourself, don't forget." Jo smiled at her daughter. "You did a good job."

"If you need a consult on the new design, my office is right above the bank." Maude's mouth smiled, but not the rest of her face. "I'd be happy to take a look one of these days." She kept smiling as she talked.

I don't know why it was, but people who smiled while they were talking had always struck me as insincere. "I'm finding some interesting things in the walls," I said.

Maude, who had a bite of omelet halfway to her mouth, halted her fork and tilted her head and eyes toward the ceiling.

"Oh?" Jo asked. "What have you found?"

"Some coins, a newspaper, an old cup. Things like that."

"Can we see them now?" Maude asked. "I was away on sabbatical with my husband last year when the store was sold. I never got to do a farewell walkthrough of the old place." She smiled wistfully.

Danna motioned to me as a party of eight pushed through the door.

"I have to get back to work. I'll bring them by for you to look at one of these days, shall I?" I asked Jo.

"Please, dear. Please do." She glanced at her plate. "Oh, don't these flapjacks look yummy, Maude?"

Maude blinked a few times, and stared at her own plate. "Absolutely, Mom. They sure do."

Chapter 3

Lou and I clipped our snowshoes onto our boots at the back of her little SUV in the Crooked Lake lot off Route 135 at three-thirty that afternoon. She'd picked me up at the store twenty minutes earlier. Only one pickup truck sat in the lot, likely a late-day ice fisherman. I'd driven by in the morning on one of my days off last week and the lake had been full of guys sitting on low stools watching the flags they'd set up to indicate a nibble. Others were twisting giant augers to drill new holes or hauling up a wriggling fish. I should see if I could buy a supply of catfish or whatever they were catching for next week's IU dinner or even for a lunch special.

We still had three hours of light before sunset at six-thirty, and I needed to get out and stretch my legs in the fresh air. When I'd called Lou to propose an outing after the store closed, she was as eager as I was. Winter can be a long season for cyclists when ice and snow make biking outdoors a real pain.

"You can almost taste spring," she said with a

grin. "Look how much light is in the sky." She wore a cone-shaped purple and pink knitted hat with ear flaps along with a breathable pink jacket and stretchy black pants.

"It's only a month until the equinox." I tugged my own striped knit cap down around my ears. My jacket was green but my double-layer pants were the same style as hers. "Funny how in late August this much light just seems sad, like summer is over. But now? It means the snow's going to be gone one of these days."

The main path down to the lake had been trampled flat by dog walkers and fishermen. I grabbed my poles. At Lou's direction we set out to the left on the five-mile trail around the lake. I'd only been out there once in the winter. Other hikers and snowshoers had broken trail, so we weren't floundering through two feet of white stuff. We both wore modern metal and plastic snowshoes instead of the traditional ones made of wood with the long point at the back. I didn't see any point in not having good gear.

"You lead the way." I pointed with a pole. "Your legs are a lot longer than mine and I don't want to hold you up." I followed her as we trudged into the woods. It was a little tricky not to step on my own shoe, especially with my short legs. I had to adopt a wider stance than I normally walked with. Lou wasn't using poles for extra balance, but I liked the extra stability they gave me. Swinging poles also added more of an upper body workout.

"I already had one run through here this morning," Lou said over her shoulder. "It's a great place to exercise."

"You went running in the woods?" I asked.

"Sure. Didn't see a soul except when I did a loop on the lake."

"It's so pretty in here."

The sun filtered through the trees and scattered sparkling light on a set of tracks that paralleled our trail for a few yards. The sharp clean air tickled my nostrils and made my lungs happy.

"We don't have snowy woods in California. At least not in my part of the state."

"Yeah, but you have the Pacific Ocean. And great wines."

"I'll say." Which I wouldn't mind a glass of when we were done.

"Want to sprint?" Lou flipped a grin over her shoulder, then set off running, the snowshoes *fwapping* behind her.

"Are you kidding?" This was only my second time out on the contraptions. But hey, I didn't have strong cyclist's quad muscles for nothing. I gave it a try, lifting my knees and pushing off. I'd been at it for only a couple of minutes before I tripped. I yelled on the way down and nearly face planted. "Yo, Perlman," I called.

Lou stopped, turned around, and *fwapped* back to me. She extended her hand. "Here, pull yourself up." She was clearly trying not to laugh, but a snort slipped out.

"It's not really that funny." My own giggle made a liar out of me as I managed to get vertical again. I brushed the snow off my jacket and legs. Leaning on my poles, I shook the white stuff out of first one snowshoe then the other. "Okay if we walk? My legs aren't as long as yours."

"Wuss." She stood there grinning.

"Show-off."

"Scaredy-cat."

"Jock." I tramped around her. "I'm going to lead now."

"Whatever you say, Shorty."

As we tramped along, I spied a Pileated woodpecker through the trees and pointed out its tall black and white body and its distinctive red crest to Lou. She talked to me about her plans to attend an academic conference in Sweden in April. I told her about how glad I was the restaurant had been full all day. We continued in idle chat until we fell silent, the only sounds the noise of our footwear and the crunch of the snow underneath.

"What was up with you and Charles Stilton last night?" I finally asked.

"He's unscrupulous and unfair. When I came to IU, I thought I could work with him. He's very charming on the surface. We collaborated on some research. That is, I researched my idea and wrote it up, but I met with him once a week to talk about it. He steered me in a particular direction, and that was fine. It was a good tip. Then I saw in the department newsletter that he's about to publish my work under his own name." Her voice was filled with disgust. "He outright stole it."

"That's terrible. Can you do anything about it?"

"Not really. I talked to Zen, but the paper has already been accepted by a major journal, and I can't really prove that he robbed me. What I can do about my studies is change them. I'm switching topics. I'm never working with that jerk again. My coursework is finished, so I won't have to study with him, either."

"Sounds like a plan."

"It'll take me longer to get my degree now, but one good thing is that Zen is going to be my adviser."

"I liked her."

"She's very cool," Lou said. "I'm glad she joined the department. Our former chair recently retired about ten years after he should have."

"Did you know I bought my store from Charles's mother-in-law?"

"Really?"

"Jo Schultz. She's a very sweet, very sharp older lady, but she hadn't been keeping it up at all. The place was kind of a wreck, even upstairs where she lived."

"It isn't a wreck now. You've done a fabulous job with it."

I thanked her. "I'm working on the second floor, so it's even more of a wreck, but it won't be for long."

We kept going until we came to an opening with a clear path leading off the trail to the right.

"Want to check that out?" I asked, pointing with my pole. "It might lead down to the lake. We can watch the ice fishing."

"Sure. That's the direction of the lake."

I took a right. The snow was deeper and didn't look like anyone else had taken the same turn. I lifted my knees and pushed down, breaking trail for Lou until my thighs and calves burned. After a minute we came to a small frozen stream with a couple of wide logs laid over it as a bridge. We crossed and trudged along as the path sloped downward, soon opening up to a clearing at the edge of the lake. The bank was only a foot high, so I figured out how to maneuver myself down. The poles came in handy. When Lou caught up, she simply jumped onto the lake.

"Wow, what a beautiful sight." I leaned on my poles and surveyed the expanse as a cloud blew over the sun. The lake was covered with snow, of course, but the wind had carved drifts in places and swept it clean down to the ice in others. The whole scene had a bluish tint, even the trees at the far edge. A figure sat on a red stool across the way near a clearing at lake's edge. Behind him, I could spy the truck we'd seen in the parking lot.

"Come on. We can work up more of a sweat on the flat," Lou said.

"I'm already sweating." I unzipped my jacket halfway down and ran a finger around the neck of my sports turtleneck.

"It's good for you."

"You think it's thick enough to walk on?" It had taken me, the coastal Californian, years to trust that it was okay to walk on water. Frozen water, but still it had made me very, very nervous the first time I walked on a solid lake three years ago. It just didn't seem right.

"Uh, yeah. You think ice fisherpeople would sit on it all day long if it wasn't? The paper said it's been ten inches thick all winter. Okay, Wimpy?" Lou didn't wait for me to answer and set out at a fast walk. "We can get back to my car in a straight line," she called back.

At least she wasn't running again. When a gust

of wind chilled my chest, I zipped up again and followed. I wasn't a wimp. I was from the Southwest.

Lou started singing out loud, a goofy lighthearted sound. Smiling, I caught up and walked next to her, but I couldn't quite match her energetic pace. We were about a third of the way across when I spied a dark hole in the snow ahead. As we drew nearer, I saw that footsteps led away from the hole in the direction of the guy on the stool.

"Seems far out on the lake to be drilling a fishing hole," I said.

"Avoiding the competition, I'd guess." She detoured around it and kept going.

I paused at the hole. It was a couple of feet across, and the water on top had iced over again. I leaned over and peered in. It seemed odd, with all this cold, that happy fish were still swimming around down there, carrying on their simple lives as if it was June or October. Maybe I could spot one. I saw something move and squatted to get a better look.

I stared at something and scooted a little closer. What the heck kind of fish was that? I was curious but didn't want to get too close to the edge. A gust of wind blew snow over the opening and up into my face. I wiped my face clean, then used my gloved hand to wipe off the thin layer of snow covering the ice.

I fell back on my rear. No fish was that brightly colored green. I grew cold, not from the wind but from dread. No fish on earth sported a tidy black goatee.

Chapter 4

"Lou," I called to her, but my voice came out no more than a croak. I tried again. "Lou! Come here. Hurry." I stood and waved with my pole. Not that hurrying was going to help Charles Stilton. Not anymore.

She turned around and joined me. "See a crappie in there, or a bass? We can have fish for dinner." Her tone was still joking.

"Look." I pointed to the hole. It was if the world had frozen, too. I heard no sound, no rustle of branches, no thudding of my own heart.

Lou spied Charles's head. Her gasp was loud. The color went out of her face. She shifted her focus to me and stared, eyes wide. "That's Charles," she whispered. "Oh, my God."

I nodded mutely. "What do we do now?" I whispered, too.

She swore and took another look down. "He's beyond help, right?"

I dropped my poles and retrieved my phone. I grabbed the fingers of one glove with my teeth to pull it off. "As far as I can tell." I snapped a couple of pictures, making sure to hold on tight to my phone so it didn't join Charles down there.

"What are you doing?" Lou's voice sounded panicked.

"I want to be able to send a picture to the police." I pressed 911, but all I got were a series of beeps. I examined it and let out a curse of my own. "No bars. No reception out here. We have get somewhere where we can call the police."

"Do we just leave him here? What if he floats away underneath the ice?"

"We can't do anything about that. Or"—I stashed my phone in my pocket and slid my glove back on—"I guess I could break the coating of ice with my pole and snag his shirt or something." The thought made me shudder. "No. He hasn't floated away yet. Maybe part of him is frozen to the top." I caught sight of the fisherman across the lake. "Hey!" I yelled, waving my arms.

Lou did the same, but he must not have noticed us. He sat there without moving.

"Listen, you're the sprinter," I said. "You head for the parking lot. You have your phone, right?"

Lou patted her pocket. "Yep."

"Drive somewhere if you don't have reception in the parking lot. I'll stay here."

Relief crossed her face. "You sure?"

"I am." Somebody had to remain there.

"But why not come with me?"

I shivered. "I don't know. It just seems right to stay with him."

"I'll go fast." She tugged her hat down as a gust of wind swept by. "I wonder how he got there."

"I don't know. But, Lou? Don't walk in those tracks, okay?" I pointed. "They might be evidence."

"Evidence? For what?"

I scrutinized the hole. "I doubt he went for a swim. It was either an accident, a suicide, or—"

"Or murder," Lou whispered again. She glanced around with wide eyes.

I looked around, too. "I'm afraid so. But make sure you tell the officer who shows up about the tracks. And hurry, okay?"

Lou nodded and headed out, her long legs lifting and planting in a sprint worthy of an Olympian, laying parallel tracks to the ones leading to the hole.

I pulled my hat farther down and snugged my collar around my neck. Charles didn't seem to be going anywhere, so a piece of his clothing or a body part must be frozen into the ice underneath. I skirted the hole several feet away and peered at the footprints leading to it. There were two lines of tracks, but the snow was stirred up as if they'd trudged on an unbroken path. I doubted the police would get anything useful from them, but you never knew. Maybe they could. I pulled out my phone and took pictures of the tracks, too.

I had a feeling this wasn't an accident. And Charles seemed too full of himself to want to end his own life. Had he walked with his killer, chatting, unsuspecting? Was he already dead and had been carried out there? It was far from the shore. The killer would have had to be awfully strong to do that. I didn't see signs of anything being pulled through the snow, like a sled or a bag that might have carried a body. When could it have happened?

Surely not during daylight hours or other ice fishers would have seen the crime.

Wait. Maude had said her son Ron was out fishing this morning. How terrible if his father was already dead on the same lake. I drew in a sharp breath. What if Ron . . . ?

"Don't go there, Jordan." I shook my head and went back to the position where I'd first come up to the hole. I backed up a few steps and began to lift and lower my knees as fast as I could to stay warm. Out here in the open and wind, the sweat from our tramping through the woods was cooling. I felt bad worrying about trying to keep my body temperature up when Charles would never be warm again.

I checked Lou's progress. She'd paused at the red stool for a minute and seemed to be talking with the guy sitting there before jogging on past him.

Let her get reception in the parking lot. Please let the police come soon and relieve me from this dreadful vigil.

Chapter 5

I was chilled through by the time I heard a siren approach the lake. It had seemed like forever, but when I checked my phone it had only been twenty minutes since Lou had taken off. Two snowmobiles roared onto the ice from the parking lot. I'd been hopping around, sprinting to the woods and back, doing whatever I could to stay warm, but it wasn't working. As I watched, one of the snowmobiles, which towed a type of sled behind it, stopped at the guy on the red stool, then followed the other snowmobile. The guy stood and looked like he was packing up.

As the snowmobiles grew closer, I saw Lou straddling the back of the one being driven by a tall figure. It had to be Buck, otherwise known as Lieutenant Buck Bird, the second in command on the South Lick police force. The snowmobiles skirted the two original tracks as well as Lou's and pulled up a few yards away from the side of the hole where Charles floated. The smell of exhaust tainted the clean air.

I hurried over to them. Buck removed a helmet and hung it on the snowmobile. Under it he wore a navy watch cap with a South Lick Police insignia. The dark cap made his thin face look even narrower.

"Thanks for coming, Buck." My teeth chattered so much I could hardly speak.

"Hey, Robbie." Buck spoke slowly as usual, dragging out the first word into almost three syllables. "Heared you found yourself another body."

I pointed to the hole, then wrapped my arms around myself again.

"You're freezing." Lou put her arms around me and hugged, rubbing my back. "Buck, do you have a blanket or anything for her?"

The other snowmobile clattered up. Officer Wanda Bird, Buck's cousin, sat in the driver's seat.

"Robbie needs a blanket, Wanda," Buck said. "Robbie, go and sit on my machine, now. The engine's still warm and it'll get your feet off the ice."

I bent down and fumbled with the clips on my snowshoe bindings, failing with my stiff fingers to release them. Lou knelt and undid them for me while Wanda opened the container on the sled behind her snowmobile.

"I feel terrible," Lou said. "I called the police from my car and then sat in the lot with the heat on until they came." She helped me get settled on the snowmobile seat. "Buck tried to make me stay on shore, but I told him I had to direct them around the tracks."

"Here." Wanda draped a foil blanket over me. "Hold on to that in front. It's what you call one of them space blankets. Reflects your own heat back." She wrapped a thick wool blanket around me next, draping it over my head, and expertly tucking it into itself so it didn't fall off.

"Thanks, Wanda." My shivers were already receding. Although she'd been gruff and officious in the past, I appreciated her kindness when I really needed it.

Buck was snapping pictures. Of the hole. Of the original tracks. Close-ups of the area around the ice hole. He straightened. "Good thing he ain't floating away like a piece of flotsam. Wanda, some measurements." Buck turned to Lou. "You say his name is Charles Stilton?"

"He's a professor at IU, but he lives in South Lick," she said. "I think he might be from here."

"You're a student over there in Bloomington, ain't ya?" Buck watched her.

"Right. He and I are . . . I mean, we were in the same department," Lou said.

"Huh." Buck rubbed the top of his cap.

Another siren wailed up and cut out at the parking lot. I saw an officer stretch yellow tape across the entrance to the lake as static erupted from under Buck's winter jacket.

He unzipped it part way, pulling out a clunky device, then tapped something on it. "Bird here." He listened, squinting down at the hole, then over at me. "Yes, ma'am." He listened some more. "No, ma'am."

I'd bet a California sushi roll that was Detective Octavia Slade on the other end.

"Got it. Over." He clicked something and resecured the radio under his coat again. "The detective is tied up. She said to go ahead and let you ladies get off the ice. Be dark in a hour or three. She'll want to get your statements later tonight after y'all have warmed up."

So I was right. Detective Octavia Slade, who'd basically made off with my boyfriend, Jim, back in November. *Great*. I knew she was a competent state police detective, but the last thing I wanted to do was spend any more time with her.

"I thought she was on temporary assignment to Brown County," I said, struggling to keep my teeth from chattering as I spoke.

"Seems to be a pretty darn long temporary. She's still the lead detective in these parts." He frowned. "Now how in blazes are we going to run you both back to shore?"

Wanda pointed to the parking lot at the same time as I heard another engine come to life. Sound traveled so well across the open expanse the noise seemed like it was only yards away instead of way across the lake. Another snowmobile roared onto the ice and headed in our direction.

"She musta sent reinforcements," Buck said. "Good. Whoever it is can ferry you two back. And your gear, of course."

"Buck, what do you think happened to the professor?" I asked, still clutching the blankets around me.

"Welp, since I'm seeing two sets of tracks, I'm thinking it wasn't no suicide. And it'd be harder than Chinese arithmetic to jest fall into a hole of that size. Yep, I'm guessing it was murder, plain and simple."

I didn't know what Chinese arithmetic was. But I did know that murder was neither plain nor simple.

Chapter 6

Lou followed me into my apartment at the back of the store. We'd agreed, since she lived in Bloomington, it made more sense for her to warm up and eat something at my place before we were summoned to the police station for our statements. Maybe we could convince Octavia to interview us right there. Either way, I was glad for the company after seeing a dead body in the ice. I hung Lou's jacket on a hook next to mine before turning up the thermostat.

"How does beef stew sound?" I asked her after checking the contents of my refrigerator. "I made it a couple days ago. Or we could have the leftovers from last night. They're in the restaurant cooler."

With a shudder, Lou sank into a chair at the kitchen table. "I don't even want to think about last night. How can a person be alive and then just be . . . dead?"

"You've never seen a body before?" I'd seen one

murder victim, and that was one too many. "It's really a shock."

"I have not, and it is a shock. I can't stop seeing Charles under the ice. The poor man."

"The poor man, is right. And his poor wife and son. Maude was in the restaurant this morning." I carried over wine glasses and a bottle. "A glass of red?"

"Only one. Don't want to be a tipsy testifier."

"For sure." I poured for both of us, and set out a piece of Brie and my favorite crackers, a seed-dotted crisp made with brown rice flour. I poured the stew into a pan and put it on to simmer, then joined her at the table. Warm air blessedly blew up from the grate above the baseboard.

Lou reached down to pet Birdy, the black-and-white long-haired cat who'd adopted me in the fall. Glancing at me, she said, "I'm afraid, Robbie."

"Why?" I sipped my wine.

"Everybody knows Charles and I had problems. And I'm bigger than he was. What if they think I killed him?"

I *tsked*. "That's ridiculous. You don't murder somebody simply because you had an academic tiff with them."

"Of course not." She straightened, bringing a mew of objection from Birdy. "But they might think so."

I stood, opened a can of wet food for Birdy, and plunked a spoonful into his treat bowl. It always made him happy. At the moment, doing anything happy was a welcome relief from the horror of the afternoon. I watched him lap it up, then asked Lou,

"Did Charles have that kind of conflict with a lot of people?"

"He did. Mine was only the most recent. And most public."

"If he was a horrible man, he probably had enemies right here in South Lick, too."

"Maybe."

"I wonder when he was killed. Everybody was gone from here by nine last night." I frowned at her. "Where were you last night?"

"You're thinking about my alibi. That's the next problem. I live alone, you know that. After I got home, I went to bed. I stayed home in my pj's in the morning and worked on the paper I'm going to present in Sweden. I didn't get dressed, go out, or talk to anyone until I came out here to run at about ten. Charles must have been dead by then. I was alone. No alibi, Robbie." She tapped her index finger on the table, her heavy silver rings gleaming against her skin, which somehow stayed tan all winter.

"Neighbors. A neighbor might have seen that your car didn't budge."

"Maybe." She hugged herself.

"You look cold. Let me find you a sweater." I rummaged in my bedroom closet until I found a fleece sweatshirt that was too big for me, and I pulled on my own IU hoodie, too. In the kitchen, I tossed her the fleece.

"So you didn't go out on that part of the lake this morning?" I asked her.

"No, I went all the way around on the trail, then I did a loop on the lake from the parking lot. I didn't reach where we found him. He must have already been there, don't you think?"

"Were there lots of people ice fishing?"

"Yeah."

"That means if somebody didn't see him, he must have been killed during the night. I tilted my head. "Do you hear something?" A faint tune was playing.

"Phone, maybe?" she said, pulling the fleece over her head.

I snorted. "Doh." I headed for my jacket pocket and pulled out the phone. The call had discontinued, but I smiled when I saw the name. I sent a quick text to Abe saying I was home but missed his call, then I took the phone back to the kitchen with me. Almost immediately he texted back.

Can I stop by?

I tapped out a reply. Sure. Lou is here. We're in the back. I set the phone on the table and glanced up to see Lou studying me.

"What's that little smile?" Lou asked.

"It's Abe. He's going to stop by."

"And now you're blushing." Lou pointed at my face.

"Hey, I like the guy. So shoot me."

She made her hand into a gun. "Bang." Her grin slid away. "No, let's not go there."

I stirred the stew, lowering the heat. "Do you think I'm making a mistake, getting involved with him?" I set the wooden spoon on the stove and sat again.

"A mistake? Why, because you don't want to get dumped again?"

"Yeah." I wrinkled my nose. "I'm really happy hanging out with him. But what if I let myself get too close and get hurt?"

"Is that how you want to live your life, holding back in case someone hurts you? You're tough, Robbie. If that happen, and I don't think it will, you'll survive. Anyway, third time's a charm."

"I guess. I know I'm tough. And I have a good life, a successful business. But I like Abe. I want to have children and have a family life one of these years." I took a sip. "Then I hear that little voice saying *What if?*"

"Tell it to shut the ef up, then." She grinned. "Here's to this one working out for you." She lifted her glass and clinked it with mine.

When knocking sounded from the back door, I got up and let Abe in. His big brown eyes beamed at me under curly hair peeking out from a bright green watch cap. He planted an enticing kiss on me.

"Come on in." I led the way to the kitchen.

Lou raised a hand in greeting. They'd met when I'd thrown a small Christmas party in my apartment, and at least one other time, I thought.

Abe said hello and slid into a chair.

"Have you eaten?" I asked.

"No. But I need to pick up Sean at seven and we're going to cook dinner together. I'll take half a glass of wine, though."

I handed him a glass. "Help yourself. Fun that you and your son cook together." Abe was a divorced and still fully involved father, sharing custody and being part of his thirteen year-old's life.

"Agreed. My dad taught me to cook, so I'm just passing it on. How's it going, Lou?"

"Good. Sort of. You?"

He swirled the wine in his glass. "Heard you two had an adventure on the ice today."

I stared at him. "How in heck do you already know that?" I sat, too.

He scratched his jaw with a grin. He'd let a full beard grow over the winter and the trim brown growth suited him. Luckily, it didn't hide his delicious dimple. "Haven't you learned yet what a small town South Lick is?"

Lou tilted her head to the side. "I'll say."

"Rotten for Charles." Abe shook his head.

"We were saying the same thing. Did you know him?" I asked Abe.

"Not well, but I had a few dealings with him out at his house. The last time was after that big storm we had in January and we were fixing a line. The power to the neighborhood had been off for a few hours and Professor Stilton was not a happy camper."

"You're an electrician, right?" Lou asked.

"Sort of. I work for Brown County REA, so I work on the electricity outside houses, not inside."

"What's REA?" She kept tapping her finger on the table, beating out a rhythm of some kind.

"Sorry. Rural Electric Association. It's the electric company around here, except it's a cooperative. Eighty years old now."

"So Charles was acting badly when the power was down?" I asked.

Abe nodded. "He made it seem like I'd done it to him personally. Said he had a big lecture to prepare. You'd have thought he was King of Indiana or something, the way he was acting. People down the street were in worse shape, a mom home alone with three little kids. She wasn't out in the street yelling at me, and when the lights came back on she brought out a plate of cookies for us."

"Takes all types," I said.

"It must have been tough for you to discover the body, hon." Abe stroked my hand where it lay on the table. "And that makes twice."

I didn't speak for a moment, picturing Charles's face in the ice. I'd thought finding a body in my restaurant last November would be the first and last time I would ever encounter a corpse outside of a funeral home. I was wrong. "Very tough. Lou and I were out for fresh air and exercise, which snow-shoeing sure is. I definitely didn't expect to come across a dead person on the lake. And someone I'd met, who was alive right here last night."

"Last night?" Abe looked from me to Lou and back. "That's right, you have that study group thing. I forgot."

"Unfortunately I argued publicly with Charles during dinner last night." Lou pressed her lips into a line.

"It'll be fine, Lou," I said. "They'll find who did it. I'm sure they will."

"You guys are thinking it wasn't an accidental death." Frowning, he looked from Lou to me and back.

"That's what Buck said after he showed up. There were two sets of tracks, so it wasn't suicide, and he didn't think somebody could simply fall into an ice fishing hole that size."

"Ouch," Abe said.

My phone trilled on the table, with SOUTH LICK POLICE registering as the caller. I groaned. "Guess I'd better get that."

Chapter 7

Lou and I bolted our stew after Buck told me we were needed at the station to give our reports. I asked him if we could do the interviews in my kitchen, but he said the detective wanted us down there right away. Detective Octavia, that is.

"Do we need lawyers?" I asked

"Up to you," Buck replied.

Lou looked worried, but we decided to just go in and get it over with.

I was glad I'd eaten, because I'd been sitting in an interview room for half an hour with nothing happening. The last time I'd been here was early October. I'd been under suspicion for a brief time, and Jim had come with me. Green-eyed real estate lawyer Jim Shermer. Dancer Jim, and my former beau, my first since my divorce in California almost five years ago. He'd decided to resume a decade-old relationship with Octavia when she'd been sent to work on the murder in late November.

Being dropped had stung, but truthfully, I'd started to question our relationship even before he'd rejected me.

I'd kept my head up and moved on, which turned out to be a very pleasant path, since Abe and I started hanging out. I ran into Jim around town occasionally, although we never really talked. I hoped he was doing well.

What a depressing space the room was. Painted a mustard yellow, the lower half had a glossy finish so they could hose down the walls if a prisoner threw a cup of coffee or punched the wall and bled, probably. Despite the glossy paint, scuff marks and a few dents marred the walls, and the table in front of me had seen better days. The air smelled of spilled soda and tired plastic. A camera lens poked out of the wall, aiming straight at me. It was almost enough to make me feel guilty, even though all I'd done was almost literally stumble over a body.

I glanced at my phone, but there wasn't any reception. It was seven-thirty. I had prep to do for tomorrow's breakfast. Was I ever going to get out of here?

Finally the door swung open, and Octavia strolled in carrying a tablet device as well as a paper notebook. A uniformed Wanda followed her in and stood by the door.

Octavia was dressed the same way she'd been almost every time I'd seen her—knit top, a muted blazer, dark pants, and black sneakers. Her silvering hair was cut in the same no-nonsense short cap. It was her look and she was sticking to it. She extended her hand. "Good to see you again, Ms. Jordan."

She was going all official on me. She'd called me Robbie in the fall.

I shook her hand and murmured something polite in return. It wasn't exactly good to see her. "Is this going to take long? I have work I still need to do at my restaurant tonight to get ready for tomorrow."

"I hope it won't," Octavia replied as she sat across from me. "We will be recording the interview." She tapped something into the tablet and set it between us then stated her rank and the date and time. "Officer Wanda Bird is also present. Roberta Jordan, do you agree to this voice recording?"

I nodded.

"Excuse me. You need to state it verbally for the record."

I sighed. "I agree to the recording."

She asked me to state my name and address, which I did.

"Please take us through the events of this afternoon at Crooked Lake," Octavia said. "Describe who you were with and exactly what transpired."

"It was about four o'clock and I was snowshoeing in the woods around the lake with Lou Perlman."

"Is that Ms. Perlman's full name?" Octavia looked up from the small notebook she'd been writing in and peered at me over dark-rimmed glasses.

"It's Louise." Surely they already knew that, but I humored her. I continued telling her about our tramping through the woods, finding the path that led to the lake, and taking it.

"Did Ms. Perlman suggest taking the path to the lake?"

I thought back. "No, I did." *Why did she ask that?*

Octavia narrowed her eyes at me as if she didn't believe it. "Go on."

"So we got down to the lake and headed across."

"Did you stay together?"

"She was often ahead of me. Her legs are a lot longer and she walks faster."

"Did you see anyone else on the ice?"

"Only a guy fishing over by the parking lot."

"Then what happened?"

"I came to the ice fishing hole and was curious if I could see any fish down there. I bent over to look. I saw Charles Stilton, instead."

"Ms. Perlman didn't look into the hole, too?"

"No, she'd gone right by it." I folded my arms and regarded Octavia. She'd probably already asked Lou the same questions and was trying to see if we would relate identical stories. Not that it was a story. I was only telling the truth.

"What happened when you glimpsed the deceased?"

"I called out to Lou to come and see. She turned around and joined me."

It was Octavia's turn to gaze back at me. "I'd like you to think carefully now. Exactly what did Ms. Perlman say when she saw the body? How did she act? No detail is too small."

"Let's see." I pictured the scene again, unpleasant as it was. "Lou recognized him. She said something like, 'That's Charles.' We both agreed he was beyond help and that we needed to call the police."

"And did you?"

"Well, obviously." She must already know that Lou had called. "Right, Wanda?"

She didn't meet my eyes, instead examining a

corner of the ceiling. Nice Wanda had reverted to officious Wanda.

"Just answer the questions, please," Octavia said. "Did you call from out on the lake?"

I waited a moment to get my suddenly flared temper under control. "There was no reception out there. Lou is faster than I am, as I said, so we agreed she would go for help. She took off for the shore and I stayed near the hole. It was about twenty minutes before she came back with Buck on a snowmobile. And Wanda on another one." I glanced at Wanda but she still avoided my eyes.

"Did you remain at the scene?" Octavia asked.

"Essentially. I walked around a bit to try to stay warm, but the ice fishing hole was always in sight. Then Buck and Wanda showed up and you must know the rest."

"Tell me what happened last night in your store."

I went through the evening until I came to the part where Lou accused Charles. "She said something like he essentially had stolen her work and published it as his own."

"What was his response?"

"He said he was pursuing parallel research. That he was a professor and she was a lowly graduate student."

"Did he use that word? *Lowly*?" Octavia asked.

"No. It was in his tone of voice, though. You know, like he was better than her."

"How did the evening go after that?"

I pictured the gathering in the restaurant for a moment. "Lou and Charles didn't interact again as far as I saw. It went fine. Well, until Zen—"

Octavia held up her hand. "Hang on." She flipped

through her notebook. "That would be Professor Zenobia Brown, chair of the sociology department?"

"Yes. Charles apparently said something offensive to her. I didn't hear what it was. He added that she could take it because she was the chair. The way he said the word *chair* made me think there was conflict behind it."

"What happened next?"

"Charles left. The event wound down after that."

"How did Professor Stilton leave? Did he drive, get a ride?" Octavia tapped on the tablet.

"I didn't see him after he went out the door, but he'd said he could finish his bottle of wine because he was walking home."

She glanced up sharply. "I didn't know you had a liquor license."

"I don't. And because I don't, customers are allowed to bring in their own wine. Don't worry, it's legal. I checked."

"All right." Octavia looked reluctant to accept my story, but she didn't press me. "What time did Ms. Perlman leave your store?"

"Everybody was gone by nine. Lou caught a ride with a guy named Tom, but I don't know his last name. Are we almost done?" My rear end was not appreciating the hard chair seat and my breakfast prep was calling me.

"One last question. You're Ms. Perlman's friend. Do you think she is psychologically capable of murder?"

I stared at her. "Are you kidding? No, of course not. She's not a suspect, is she?"

"Do you have anything else to tell us?"

Of course she wasn't going to answer me. I thought for a second. "Charles's wife Maude was in the restaurant with her mother this morning. She said her son Ron was out ice fishing." I closed my mouth before I started speculating. Octavia could do whatever she wanted with that piece of information. Come to think of it, if Charles hadn't gone home last night, Maude wouldn't have been calmly having breakfast out. Would she? Maybe he made a practice of not going home.

Octavia nodded and made a note before she pushed back her chair. She dictated the time into the tablet, said, "This interview is concluded," and tapped something. "Thank you for your time, Robbie. I appreciate your cooperation. If you think of anything else, no detail too small, you know where to find me. I ask you not to discuss the specifics of your discovery on the lake with anyone until further notice."

"Fine."

We'd already talked about it with Abe, but Octavia didn't need to know that. What harm could it do? Besides, he and the rest of the town already knew most of the story.

I stood, too. "You can't think that Lou would have killed Charles. All they had was an academic disagreement. And why would she go out on the lake with me if she knew he was dead right there?"

Wanda opened the door.

"Thank you, Ms. Jordan," Octavia said. "Officer Bird will show you out."

"I'm assuming you're done with Lou, too," I said. "I need to give her a ride back to her car at my store." I followed Wanda into the hall.

"We have not concluded our interview with her, no," Octavia said. "We'll be responsible for returning her to her vehicle. You are free to leave."

"You're not keeping her here." I was about to continue my protest with, "You can't," but of course they could do whatever they wanted.

"You're free to leave, Ms. Jordan." Octavia turned away, her sensible shoes taking her silently down the hall.

"Wanda." I faced her, setting my hands on my hips. "How long is she going to keep Lou? Does she need a lawyer?"

"Not at liberty to say." Wanda gestured toward the door leading to the front. "After you, Robbie."

Chapter 8

I got back to the store before nine, but barely. Lou's car sat forlorn in one of the diagonal parking spaces in front of Pans 'N Pancakes. I drove my van past it, around the left side of the building, and into the barn where I kept it in the winter. After slamming the car door, I kicked the nearest tire. For my good friend to be suspected of murder, even for a minute, was ridiculous. Outrageous. And frustrating.

I let myself into my apartment, locking up tight after myself, and then went through to the store. I flipped on the lights. I hated the thought that once again a murderer walked free at the same time the detective was questioning my bright, funny, loyal friend.

"Come on, Birdy. Keep me company tonight, okay?" I called, leaving the door ajar. He raced in. Any normally closed door was a magnet to him when it was open. He always seemed delighted to get away with sneaking in where he wasn't allowed.

The health inspector would have a cow if Birdy was in here during operating hours, but I occasionally let him prowl the place at night as long as he stayed off the counters and tabletops. He was a lot more interested in the old part of the space and the artifacts Jo had left in the store—an antique scale, an old icebox, a hundred-year-old red metal tricycle. Jo had volunteered to junk it all, but I'd insisted I wanted to keep the flavor of the country store, which included the somewhat dusty fixtures like the vintage cash register I used for cash transactions and a treadle sewing machine I'd repurposed as a display table.

Birdy also loved exploring the vintage cookware, some of which I'd acquired but much of which had come with the store. Nesting metal canisters sat on the shelves alongside an antique corn popper, and cast-iron muffin pans rested next to a heavy meat grinder. There were cake pans, a red-handled beater, whisks galore, and a few objects even I wasn't sure what they were used for. As long as I ran the duster over the shelves after Birdy had been exploring, I figured I was safe from violating health regulations. It wasn't like these were gleaming new objects, anyway.

Before I got to work, I wrote a note for Lou. *Stop in if you want to talk. No time too late. Hugs.*

I went out and slid the note under her windshield wiper. I stood in the cold for a minute, arms wrapped around myself. Stars glittered in the sky like silver celestial sequins on a black velvet gown. I hoped Lou would get out tonight. They had to let her go. Didn't they?

By now I could prep biscuit dough for a hundred in my sleep, so I set to work back inside. My busy hands let my mind wander free. *How can I find out who Charles's real enemies were?* I measured flour into my industrial-sized food processor and added a bit of salt, then dropped in cubed butter and mixed until it resembled peas. Maybe someone had seen Charles go out on the lake. I quickly stirred in the eggs, poured in the milk, and pulsed until it just came together on the blades. He must have been killed either late last night or early this morning. He couldn't have been shoved into that hole in broad daylight with a dozen ice fishermen on the lake. I patted the dough into three big disks, wrapped them, and stored them in the walk-in.

Charles's own son Ron was ice fishing yesterday morning. Maude had said he was nineteen, so maybe Danna had gone to high school with him. She might know of a mutual friend who could ask him if he'd seen anything. It would be hurtful to quiz either Maude or Ron about Charles's death while they're grieving. Octavia surely would, no matter what.

Pancakes were next on my list. I assembled the dry ingredients for the whole wheat batter so it would be ready to mix up in the morning. Or maybe we'd do waffles instead. I used the same essential recipe, only varying the amount of milk. I'd acquired a big vintage waffle iron that cooked eight waffles at once. Unfortunately it had come with old and frayed wiring. I was a skilled carpenter, but rewiring wasn't among my talents, so I'd asked Abe for help and luckily he'd been happy to oblige.

I could serve waffles with a choice of vanilla yogurt or sour cream, and maple syrup or a frozen fresh strawberry sauce I knew was in the freezer.

All this cooking brought my seventy-one-year-old Aunt Adele to mind. She'd brought me here a year ago to see all the vintage cookware to console and distract me after my mom, her little sister, had died suddenly. When we'd found the store was for sale, Adele had encouraged and supported me every step in my project to buy and renovate the property. In October, I'd realized my dream of opening my own restaurant, due in no small part to her enthusiasm. She was currently helping set up a school library in India with her eighty-something boyfriend Samuel MacDonald. She was to be gone for a month, and I missed her.

Since Mom's death, during tough times the first person I thought to talk with was always Adele. I couldn't do that now, but I could send her an e-mail. As former mayor (and fire chief) of South Lick, she would want to hear about the murder. Maybe she'd even send back some tidbit of information about Charles that would prove useful. I washed my hands and headed to the store computer at my desk tucked in a corner behind the open kitchen area. I used my phone for plenty of Internet surfing, but there was something satisfying about typing on a real keyboard and reading on a screen bigger than ten square inches. Using a big laptop set me apart from most of my peers, but I didn't care.

I didn't see any messages from Adele, although a new one from my father sat in the In-box. I smiled. It was still strange to think those words—*my father*.

For twenty-seven years I'd thought I didn't have a
father. My mom had never told me about him. It
was soon after I opened the store when I'd learned
about Roberto, and Lou had helped me find him.
I'd nervously contacted him in Italy and discovered
he hadn't known about me, either. What a joy it was
when he welcomed me into his life.

We'd shared a wonderful visit at his home in Pisa
after Christmas, although his daughter Graciela, my
half sister, had not been as welcoming as my father,
his wife, and my teenaged half brother. It must have
been shocking for Graciela to learn that her father
had an American child. I hoped someday I could
develop a closer relationship with her.

First, I typed my message to Adele and sent it,
then I opened Roberto's e-mail. He sent news of a
trip he and his wife, Maria, had taken to Greece,
and asked about my business and about Adele. I
frowned reading the next part.

> I tried to make Graciela see she should love
> you, but she is still angry with me. I apologize for
> her childish behavior when you were here, *cara.*

I couldn't do anything about my half sister. I'd
never had a sibling and had been looking forward
to getting to know her and my half brother, Alessandro. He'd been fun, but Graciela not so much. It
certainly wasn't Roberto's fault. Graciela was twenty-
four, a mother to a darling little boy, and wife to a
very nice man who didn't speak a word of English,
unlike Graciela.

Roberto ended by saying he and Maria wanted to
come and visit in the spring. I clapped my hands at

the thought. I would welcome them with arms wide open. Which meant I'd better get the rooms upstairs done in a hurry. The new space would be perfect not only for paying bed-and-breakfast customers, but also as a guest suite for my step-mother and *Babbo*. My father.

Chapter 9

Awful as the idea was, a murder in town was clearly the antidote to the recent winter slump at my restaurant. Danna and I hadn't been this busy since before Christmas. The restaurant had been full up, with more than a dozen people waiting at any given time, ever since I'd unlocked the doors at eight.

The old wall clock chimed nine as my friend Philostrate MacDonald pushed his way in the door. He whistled, sidestepped the hungry group in line for tables, and sauntered to my side at the grill. "Looks like you could use a bit of extra help." His amazing blue eyes shone in his dark face. He leaned in and added, "It's too bad, but murder sure gets folks up on a Sunday morning."

"Shh. That's a terrible thing to say, not that I haven't been thinking it," I whispered, glancing around. No one seemed to have heard, thank goodness. "We'd love your help, thanks," I said in a normal voice. "You know the drill?"

"Of course." He headed to the sink. "Wash up, apron up, clean up."

"At least for now. You can swap out serving with Danna, or even take the grill for a while. Plenty of work for three."

Phil, Samuel's grandson, was a good friend. He also baked the brownies and cookies on my lunch menu when he wasn't at work as the IU Music Department secretary or rehearsing his latest part in an opera or musical comedy. He was a few years younger than me and I could barely remember how we'd met. Somebody must have introduced us. Didn't matter. He'd saved my bacon, almost literally, by pitching in a few times, and I'd gotten to at least try to return the favor when he was accused of the murder last November.

I flipped open the lid to the waffle maker and gently lifted out all eight waffles in one piece, then separated them. Two went on a plate ready with bacon and one egg over easy, and the rest I slid into the warmer. They wouldn't stay there long. I dinged the bell for Danna and closed the lid to the waffle iron so it could heat up again.

"Want to switch?" I asked her. I'd been cooking for an hour, and I liked to get out and schmooze with my customers.

"Sure."

We donned clean aprons before I carried the waffle order and one with a Kitchen Sink omelet and hash browns to a table of two gentlemen, one thin and white-haired, one stout and bald.

"The waffles?" I asked. When Bald raised his hand, I set down his order and then the other. "More coffee?"

"No thanks, hon." Thin looked at me. "Quite the discovery yesterday, young lady. Stilton dead on the lake. Have you recovered?"

I swallowed. "I feel very bad for his wife and son."

Bald snorted. "Not sure the son feels so bad."

"Oh?" I asked.

"Them two got along about as well as two weasels in a sack," Thin said.

"Yup," Bald agreed. "They was shouting at each other in public last week. Showed poor taste, if you ask me. No disrespect to the deceased, you understand, but airing your dirty laundry like that? Should oughta've taken their quarrel inside where it belonged."

I was dying to ask what they'd been fighting about, but Danna had dinged the bell and I had no business lingering. "Enjoy your breakfast now," I said before heading for the grill, wondering what Charles and Ron had been fighting about.

Phil was busy busing—clearing tables, cleaning them, setting them for the next round of customers—and loading the dishwasher. He whistled a melodic warbling tune as he worked. With his help, the tables started turning over faster at the same time fewer customers streamed in. We usually, at least in the busier season, got a second rush on Sundays after church services let out, with folks still wanting breakfast at eleven or even twelve. But it wasn't even nine-thirty.

I delivered four more plates to two couples who were regulars on Sunday mornings. One couple was Sue and Glen Berry, whose adult daughter I'd found murdered in November.

Sue looked up at me with worried eyes. "Robbie,

we heard what happened. How terrible for you to . . ." Her voice trailed off and she studied the table, kneading her hands on top of it.

"I'm okay, Sue. I mean, it's not okay Professor Stilton is dead, of course."

"Of course not," Glen said. "I think it brings up sad memories for us both."

"I'm sure it does," I said. The murder had hit their family hard, and at a time when their other daughter was well along in a pregnancy.

"I always said Stilton was going to come to no good, though," Glen went on. "Chuck was not easy to like."

"God rest his soul," Sue added in a hurry.

"Chuck?" I tilted my head at Glen.

"Everybody around here called him Chuck. Always did," Glen said. "Once he started over at the college, he said he was Charles. As if."

"In what ways wasn't he easy to like?" I asked.

"Went around acting like he was in charge. Because he was a professor and some of us in South Lick never even went to college, maybe. I'll bet I earn four times as much in my business than what he got over there at the university, and my only degree is a high school diploma," Glen said.

The man of the other pair bobbed his head up and down like he completely agreed. "Chuck grew up right here in South Lick. He wadn't no better than the rest of us. We all put our pants on one leg at a time."

"That time he tried to tell me how to draw in more customers," Glen said, shaking his head. "I said I could manage fine on my own, thank you very much."

56 *Maddie Day*

"Now let's not speak ill of the dead." Sue laid her hand on her husband's.

I cleared my throat. "How's the grandbaby?"

Sue brightened. "She's a real dear. Nursing like a little champ despite being born a couple three weeks early. Paulie's real happy to have her, you know, after everything that happened."

"Named her Susannah, after Sue here." Glen's pride was written all over his face.

"I'm really happy for you guys."

Sue beckoned me closer. "I heard a student in Charles's department is under arrest for the murder." Her eyes widened and her eyebrows went way up, almost like she was excited about the prospect.

"No, that's not right." I shook my head fast. "The student is my friend Lou. She was with me when I found Charles on the lake, but she's not under arrest. The authorities questioned both of us last night. And we were each released to go home." I cleared my throat. Except all I really knew was that her car was gone this morning. She hadn't come in to talk and I hadn't stopped to call her yet this morning so I had no idea what had gone on in her interview. Surely if she'd been arrested her car would still be out front. "Now, who has the waffles?"

If gossip like Sue's spread, the town would have Lou locked up for the murder in a New York minute. But only in their minds, thank goodness.

The next time the cowbell jangled I saw Buck coming through the door, his uniform looking more rumpled than usual once he removed his coat.

"It'll be a couple minutes yet, Buck," I called out.

Phil gave a quick rising and falling whistle like a cardinal's and pointed. At the far end of the restaurant was a small table, all cleared and set.

I laughed. "I was wrong. Right over there, Buck. Thanks, Phil."

Buck ambled to the table with his hat in his hand, greeting townspeople as he went. I wanted to ask him about Lou, but I was way too busy. I took a few more orders, made change for a family, and delivered two plates of biscuits, gravy, sausages, and scrambled eggs before I had time to get to Buck.

I carried the coffeepot over and poured when he nodded. "What can I get you?"

He glanced at the Specials board. "Double order of waffles, please, and three eggs over easy with bacon. Can I get a side of biscuits, too?"

The guy was so tall and skinny I thought his foot might leak food. I'd never served him anything smaller than a meal that would double my weight if I ate that much.

"Coming right up. Hey, any idea how long Octavia kept Lou last night?"

"It was purt' late. Maybe midnight?" He stretched his legs out halfway to Kentucky and yawned, bringing his long thin fingers to cover his mouth. "That Octavia is one taskmaster."

"I don't get it. Why in the world would Octavia think a smart grad student would kill her professor? Lou would never do something like that."

"How long you knowed this Louise, anyway?"

"I met her in the fall." I scrunched up my nose. "We go cycling together once in a while. And she helped me find my father."

"Not exactly a lifetime acquaintance then, you two.

Being able to ride a bike ain't much of a character reference. Who don't know how to ride a bike?"

I stared at him. "I'll put your order in." I turned around way too fast without looking and bumped smack into Phil with a tray full of dirty dishes. The sound of them crashing to the floor echoed the crashing of Lou's life and the disturbance, once again, of our peaceful little town.

Chapter 10

As full as the restaurant had been, at ten-thirty it suddenly was equally as empty. The cowbell jangled as Buck followed the last customer out, and then the only sounds were the quiet churning of a full dishwasher and two last pieces of bacon sizzling on the grill in front of Phil. The air held the aroma of toasted waffles, sweet strawberries, and grilled fat. It was the smell of a dream come true—my dream— which was not supposed to include mystery and mayhem. Once I'd calmed down from Buck's implied accusation, and after I'd helped Phil clean up the broken dishes, I'd tried once more to convince Buck of Lou's innocence. He'd said only that it was Octavia's job and he was letting her do it.

I took a moment to text Lou, saying I hoped the experience at the station wasn't too awful, and that I'd call her after the restaurant closed this afternoon.

"You were right, Phil," I said. "A murder does bring them out. It's an awful reason, but it's true."

"I'll bet we get a lunch rush, too." Danna swiped

a table clean and set it with new paper placemats and silverware rolls in the blue cotton napkins I'd splurged on. She moved on to the next table, which was cleared but not ready for customers.

Danna and I had talked about the murder only briefly before we'd opened the doors. She'd uncharacteristically shown up for work late, at only a few minutes before eight. She'd apologized but not explained her tardiness.

She glanced at me with a sympathetic look. "Too bad you had to find another body, Robbie."

"You can say that again." I straightened the pile of paid tickets on the counter and set the miniature cast-iron skillet I used as a paperweight back on top. I dug into my apron pocket, extracted a pocketful of change and small bills I'd cleared from tables, and dumped the money into the Tips jar next to the antique cash register.

"Was it totally bad?" Phil asked as he flipped the bacon onto a plate.

"Sure it was. I saw him through an ice fishing hole when Lou and I were out snowshoeing on the lake. He was floating right below the ice." A shudder rippled through me like a California earthquake aftershock and I hugged myself.

Danna shuddered, too.

"Sorry. So did anyone else hear gossip about Charles?" I asked. "Seems like everybody in town had something bad to say about him this morning."

"Well, yeah. Nobody liked that guy." Danna stretched her arms over her head, then stifled a yawn. "And his son Ron? He must have inherited the unpleasantness gene or something."

"You know Ron?" I asked Danna.

"I went to school with him from kindergarten until we graduated last year. He was always getting in trouble."

"You two sit down," Phil said. "I have to run soon, but can I make you a bite to eat while I'm still here?"

"I'd love a couple scrambled with some hash browns. And that bacon." I poured myself a mug of coffee and sank into a chair next to the kitchen area. I was suddenly famished and exhausted. "We really needed your help this morning, Phil. I owe you one."

"Thanks, dude," Danna said. "Got any waffles in the warmer?" She cleaned and set the last table, grabbed a tall glass of orange juice, and then joined me.

"Coming right up." He busied himself at the grill, singing what sounded like a bit of opera.

"What sort of trouble did Ron get in?" I asked Danna.

"You name it. Rude to teachers. Got in fights with other boys. Stole a couple beers from the market when he was fifteen. He barely stayed out of jail for that one, but Officer Bird let him off."

I sipped my coffee, which went down hot and dark, exactly how I liked it. I stocked only a good French roast in caf and decaf. None of those mild breakfast blends for me. So far, I hadn't heard any customers complain. "Somebody this morning mentioned that Ron and Charles were arguing in public only last week."

"They butted heads big time," Danna said.

"Do you know what Ron is doing now? Is he in college?" I asked.

"I think he's taking classes at Ivy Tech, but I don't know what in." Danna retied her scarf.

Phil brought our plates over and set down one for himself—a cheese omelet and a couple of pieces of wheat toast. We each tucked into our meal like we'd been in the wilderness for days. Working on our feet at such a pace burned up calories like an intense three-hour hill ride on my road bike.

"Ivy Tech. That's the community college, right?" I asked. "I thought the closest locations were Bloomington and Columbus." Columbus was only a few miles farther than Bloomington was from here, but it was due east instead of west.

"They offer classes in Nashville, but not administration and other stuff, I think," Phil said.

Nashville, the county seat, was only about five miles from South Lick. "That's got to be a much more convenient location than either of the other campuses. Any word from Samuel lately?" I asked Phil.

"Radio silence. I'm not worried. He's doing work he loves, in a place he loves, with the lady he loves. It's all good." Phil wiped his plate clean with the last piece of toast and popped it into his mouth. He stood. "I'm outta here. Have a rehearsal at noon. You girls stay out of trouble, now."

"We'll try." Although if I needed to get into trouble to clear Lou's name, I would.

Chapter 11

Sure enough, the lunch crowd rushed in on us like a gaggle of teenage boys—hungry by definition. They were hungry for food and news, or maybe gossip was more like it. Word of my involvement in Charles's death must have spread during the churching hours.

Danna and I repeated the morning scene, but we didn't have Phil to ease our burden. Instead of clearing and serving, I spent much of my time fending off questions. Saying yes, the police had the situation under control. Telling the townspeople fixing their curious eyes on me that I'd been asked not to discuss the details of my discovery. Asserting that no, Louise Perlman wasn't a killer.

I was grateful Danna and I had eaten during the lull. We hadn't had a minute free since. And right when the lunch crowd seemed to be lessening, the bell jangled again and I groaned silently.

"Yo, Jordan."

I glanced at the door and relaxed. My pal

Christina James stood in the entrance with her girlfriend, Betsy.

"Look who the cat dragged in," I called, then thought how I was starting to sound like a native. "Come in, both of you." I gestured with a big smile and hurried toward the door.

Christina, a chef at a new restaurant in South Lick, was a good friend. Our schedules had overlapped so she'd never had the time free to eat at Pans 'N Pancakes. The color was high in her cheeks and for the first time since I'd met her, she wore her long light hair floating loose on her shoulders instead of in a ponytail hanging out the back of a ball cap. She wore a streak of purple down one strand of hair, also new for her. The two women made their way in, Betsy holding the door for the person behind her as she said something over her shoulder.

I greeted Betsy. My eyebrows went up when I saw who she was talking to.

Zen Brown came in, followed by another woman, and waved to me. "Told you I've been wanting to come here for breakfast." Her tone was friendly, but she didn't smile. New lines had deepened around her eyes that I didn't think I'd seen Friday night.

"Glad you could make it," I said. Had she heard about Charles's death? Bloomington with a university population close to fifty thousand, plus the additional thirty thousand other people who lived and worked in town, wasn't exactly the village South Lick was. On the other hand, an academic department could serve as a village. I'd bet it had the similar ability to play the telephone game, passing news from one person to another and misrepresenting it anew each time.

"This is my . . . friend, Karinde," Zen said. A Nordic-looking woman, tall with two long white-blond braids, raised a finger in acknowledgment.

"Welcome. I'm Robbie Jordan. I own the place." I looked from Zen and her friend to Christina and Betsy. "Wait, do you all know each other?"

Christina laughed. "From way back. We'll take a table for four if you have one."

I surveyed the place. "People are leaving that one over there. Give me a minute to clean and set it. You can check out the cookware if you want or take a seat on the bench."

"Cookware." Christina strode in the direction of the shelves.

Betsy, a lean woman who worked as a welder, followed her. "Always the cookware." She rolled her eyes and tossed back curly black hair but looked fondly at Christina.

Before I turned away, I saw Zen murmur something to Karinde, who pursed her lips and shook her head.

A few minutes later when the table was ready, the four of them headed that way, Christina and Betsy holding hands. Two silver-haired women stared as they walked past.

One of the ladies said, "That's just plain disgusting." She didn't whisper, either.

"Right out in public, too," the other one chimed in.

I ignored it, as did my friends. I was sure they'd heard it all before. I took over menus along with the coffeepot. "Coffee?"

Betsy shook her head and pulled a bottle of Moët champagne out of the bag on her lap. She set it on the table, the moisture on the cold glass glistening. "Forget the coffee. We're drinking this."

"Celebrating?" I asked.

Christina looked up at me with a face-splitting smile. "We're getting hitched." She laid her hand on Betsy's. "Now that we can."

"Awesome." I high-fived her and then Betsy. "Good for you. I'm really happy for you both." Indiana's challenge to same-sex marriage had only recently been defeated. I glanced at Zen and her friend. Zen looked pleased for them, too, but Karinde frowned.

"Thanks," Betsy said.

"I'll bring wine glasses. Sorry I don't have champagne flutes." I headed for the shelf of glasses.

One of the two ladies stopped me. "Are you sure you want that type in here, hon?" she asked, tilting her head toward Christina and gang.

"Do I want my friends in here? Of course I do." I kept my tone friendly. "I serve everyone who wants to eat here, who can pay, and who behaves themselves."

She cleared her throat, glanced at her dining companion, and back at me. "Well, bless your heart. What do we owe you today?"

I laid their ticket on the table and kept on going.

Chapter 12

"Whew," I said to Danna five minutes later. "The bank account is going to be happy, and my feet are, too, when this day is over." Besides my friends, four other tables were occupied. They were already served and nobody new had come in.

"Totally." Now that things were easing up for the moment, her hands were immersed in sudsy water, scrubbing a couple of pots in the sink.

I flipped the burgers for Christina and friends—two beef, one turkey, and one veggie—and added a slice of cheese on the beef patties. I ladled out three cups of Abe's Mulligatawny soup, filled one cup with creamy carrot soup, and carried those to the table.

"Let's see. Who was the vegetarian?" I surveyed them as Zen pointed to Karinde. "Got it. Creamy carrot for you, chicken for the rest." I distributed the soup and was about to turn to get back to the burgers when Zen pushed back her chair.

"Be right back," she said to the other women. "Robbie? Can I talk to you for a second?"

I glanced toward the grill. "Come with me. I don't want the meat to overcook."

She looked in the same direction and rubbed the back of her neck. "I'd rather talk where it's a bit quieter."

"Danna, can you finish up those plates, please?" I called, waiting until she nodded before leading Zen across the room to the area near the door. I faced her. "What's up?"

"Charles, that's what. I heard you found him." She studied my face.

So I was right about the academic village. "I did. Lou and I were out on snowshoes."

"The police have been leaving messages on my cell. I haven't called them back. I understand you've helped solve a couple crimes around here. Why do you think they want to talk to me?" With a worried look on her face, Zen rubbed the back of her hand over and over.

"I wouldn't worry about it. I mean, you didn't kill him, did you?" I kept my tone light. I didn't know anything about her other than her position as department chair.

"Of course not." Her worried look turned to horrified. If she had killed him, she also possessed talents as an actress.

"Then call them back. You're the head of Charles's department. I'm sure they only want to learn more about him."

"But we had words Friday night. Everybody heard." She kept rubbing her hand as if that would erase the problem.

"I didn't. I was in the walk-in. What did he say to you?"

Her head turned and I followed the direction of her eyes. She was focused on the table where Christina, Betsy, and Karinde sat talking, sipping champagne, and tasting soup.

I was pretty sure Karinde was the only one Zen saw.

She looked back at me. "He said a—" She clapped her mouth shut as the bell on the door jangled.

Buck ambled in and doffed his hat. "Ladies." He hung the hat on the coatrack and cupped his hands, blowing into them. "It's dang nippy out there."

"Hey, Buck." I snuck a glance at Zen.

She'd gone pale and her head was swiveling as if she was looking for a place to hide. Too late for that. But what she was worried about? "This is Professor Zenobia Brown. She's—"

"The chair of the sociology department," Buck finished. "I know. Howdy-do, Dr. Brown. I'm Buck Bird, with the South Lick Police. Funny, we been huntin' high and low for you. Even been over to your house early this morning, but you didn't appear to be in residence."

Zen straightened her shoulders before extending her hand. "How are you, Officer? I'm afraid I was away overnight. What can I help you with?"

Buck shook her hand. "I don't suppose you've heard the news? About the murder of one your professors? A Dr. Charles Stilton."

"I have heard, and it's a terrible tragedy for Charles to die so young and violently," she said, her voice level. "We'll be arranging a memorial service for him on campus, of course."

"A decent thing to do. It's just that the detective

on the case wants to talk with you. Has your cell phone been away, too? 'Cause we been leaving messages, asking you to call us."

Zen lifted her chin, which she pretty much had to since Buck's face was a foot above hers. "It was turned off. I only now saw those messages and was planning to call in. May I finish my lunch first?" She waved toward her table.

"Why, surely, ma'am. I come in to get some lunch for myself, as it happens. When we're done, I'll tell you what. I'll just escort you over to the station. Wouldn't want you gettin' lost here in South Lick, now," he drawled with a friendly smile, an expression which did not hide his keen eyes.

"Fine," she said through lips that barely moved for their tension. "Excuse me." Still with erect posture, she made her way back to the table.

Buck looked at me. "You was talking in private with her, looked like from outside."

"Did you follow her here?"

"Let's simply say we've been looking for her. So, was you all talking about the murder?"

"Just briefly."

"You didn't tell her none of the details about finding him, I hope." He studied my face, the smile now gone from his.

"Of course not. I was told not to."

"She say where she spent last night?"

"No." I shook my head. "She came in about half an hour ago with that tall blond woman at the table. She introduced her as her friend Karinde."

Zen had hesitated before the word *friend*. Maybe she and Karinde were a couple, too. I didn't care, but she might have reasons she didn't want to go public about it—her family, her position as an academic, or some other reason.

"Welp, we found her now. And, like I said, I need me some lunch. Can I get—"

"Bowl of soup, double cheeseburger, fries, coleslaw, and a brownie?" It was my turn to smile. "Coming right up."

"Heck, Robbie. I guess you're getting acquainted with my hollow leg, now ain't ya?"

"That I am, Buck. That I am."

Chapter 13

At a little after four o'clock, I sank into a corner of my sofa with a pint glass of beer, a bowl of almonds and cashews, and my phone. The day's considerable take was securely locked up in the small safe in my apartment. I accepted plastic from customers, but most locals almost exclusively still used cash for meals like breakfast or lunch. Danna and I had cleaned up the tables and kitchen, and I'd locked the door after her. Birdy had bounded up and was nestled into my lap. The late afternoon sun warmed the wide pine floorboards, making the old wood glow golden. It was still cold outside, but the days were blessedly lengthening on a regular schedule.

As I stroked my kitty's smooth long fur, I said, "That was quite the day, Birdman."

He purred his chirping purr in agreement, his tail lazily swishing, his eyes happily shut. I doubted Zen was as happy, with Buck following her to the police station. I'd heard the interaction between Karinde and Zen before they'd left and it had seemed contentious. Karinde hadn't seemed happy, either about Zen going to the station or about having to catch a ride home with Christina and Betsy. Since Zen had driven, Karinde didn't have much choice. Christina and Betsy had said they were fine with providing taxi service.

Relationships. Why were they so fraught, I wondered, munching a few nuts. Even two lovebirds like Christina and Betsy were sure to have conflicts now and then. I knew they'd been a couple for several years, and sealing it with marriage must mean the good times outweighed the bad. Maybe I was wrong about Karinde and Zen. Maybe they were, in fact, merely friends and not lovers. I shook my head and sipped my IPA. I was sure Abe and I would have conflicts, too, sooner or later. Speaking of him, I checked my phone. He hadn't called, but Lou had, and I saw that I had an e-mail from Adele.

First, see what she had to say. I opened the e-mail and scanned it. Adele expressed dismay at the murder. Told me to stay safe. Asked me to convey her sympathies to Maude. The last line caught my eye:

Chuck was almost universally disliked. I'm only surprised he wasn't killed before now.

Interesting. If that was true, Octavia was going to have a full roster of suspects to investigate. Speaking of suspects, I pressed Lou's number.

After she connected and we greeted each other, I said, "How'd it go last night?"

She didn't speak for a moment. "Robbie, they

really seem to think I killed Charles. It's ridiculous. They kept me there until twelve-thirty, asking me the same questions over and over. Why had I accused him of stealing my work? Had I met with him privately yesterday morning or at any time prior? Hadn't I seen him on the lake in the morning? Was I aware of how much taller I was than him? And on and on."

"Sorry. It doesn't sound like much fun."

"I was totally wiped when they finally let me go. I saw your note, but I needed to get home and pass out."

"Maybe you should get a lawyer." I took a sip of beer.

"I spent the morning hiring one. My dad's best friend is a law professor at Purdue. He found me somebody good in Bloomington." Lou's father was a professor at Purdue University. She paused. "But if the police are jumping on me as a suspect, Robbie, what does that mean for the person who actually killed Charles? He or she is walking around out there free as a bird."

I could hear the wobble in her voice even as it rose. "I know what you mean. If it's any comfort, I think Octavia Slade is a good detective. It's her job to ask you questions. It means she's also interviewing other people. I'll bet they've had Charles's wife Maude in. Friends of his. Today Buck came into the restaurant while Zen was having lunch. And afterwards he escorted her to the station for an interview."

"Zen Brown? I don't get that at all."

"She was Charles's chair," I said. "Which means she was his boss. He said something to her Friday

night that she found outrageous. Did you hear what
it was?"

Lou groaned. "Bar none, that guy was talented at
rubbing everyone the wrong way. He said, and I
quote, 'You're a dyke. Of course you study women's
health. You and all your lesbo friends are the only
people who care.' It was definitely outrageous."

"That's nasty. That's super nasty."

"You bet it is."

"Is Zen gay?" I asked, thinking again of the way
she looked at Karinde.

"I kind of think so. But if she is, she's not open
about it. I mean, she never talks about her personal
life, and she never brings anybody to department
functions like our annual picnic. She lives out in
the woods somewhere, so she has the privacy to do
whatever she wants. Which of course, she has every
right to. We're all just people."

"Totally." My phone buzzed, meaning another
call was coming in. I glanced at it. ABE. I could call
him back. I wasn't going to interrupt Lou at a time
like this. "Can you think of anyone else in the department Charles butted heads with? You could
give Octavia some leads."

"I did exactly that last night. He got nasty with
a few others, students and professors. I hope
Ms. Slade follows up." She yawned. "Sorry. Once I
got home it was so hard to fall asleep. I tried warm
milk with brandy, reading a boring sociology text,
counting backwards from a thousand. Nothing
worked until almost dawn. This sucks. I have a lot
of work to do, but I can't concentrate. And I teach
a section of Intro tomorrow morning."

"Just write the day off, then. You can wing it in class, can't you?"

She laughed. "Yeah. I'll put my hair up and wear my power suit and my highest heels. They won't even notice I'm not prepared."

"You in a power suit? I might have to audit your class tomorrow to see that." Tall athletic Lou in a skirt, jacket, and heels? I usually saw her in exercise clothes of one kind or another, and a few times, like Friday night, in a grad student outfit of jeans and blazer. I'd never been with her when she was dressed up. "You probably look like a CEO."

"Maybe not quite, but I've been told I do clean up pretty good."

I was glad to hear her voice steady and amused. Back to normal. "For now, go make some popcorn and put on an old movie. Eat chocolate. Have more brandy. You're going to be fine," I assured her.

"Yeah, probably. Thanks, Robbie. You've lifted me out of a dark hole."

"Happy to. I'm sure you'll return the favor when I need it."

"Any time."

"Not to put a damper on your good mood, but make sure you lock your door, too," I urged.

"I'm way ahead of you. Triple locked. Hope the building doesn't catch on fire." She laughed lightly and disconnected.

I slid Birdy off my lap. Time to check my own locks. I was pretty sure I'd secured the door, but it never hurt to check.

Chapter 14

I opened my apartment door when Abe knocked at a few minutes past five. "Ready for some wrecking?" I stretched up and kissed him.

"Demolition never sounded so good." Appropriately, he wore old clothes—a soft flannel shirt thin at the elbows, faded jeans that seemed like they knew his body, and scuffed work boots. He held a yellow and black carrier that looked like a small gym bag, but by the way he hefted it, it probably held tools, not tennies and exercise clothes.

"I really appreciate the help. Follow me." Dressed in a nearly identical outfit, except mine sat on my curves entirely differently than his did on his muscular build, I led the way into the store and unlocked the door to the stairs.

"I've never even noticed this door," he said, pausing.

The door was tucked in the back corner of the east wall beyond the cookware area. A tall shelving unit half hid it. "I don't advertise it. For one thing, these stairs aren't ready for the public yet." I flipped on the lights, revealing a steep and narrow set of stairs. "Up here isn't exactly finished, either."

We clomped our way up.

"I'll say. But what a great space."

I'd already removed all the interior walls except the one that was weight bearing. Like I'd done downstairs, I'd installed super-strong laminated veneer lumber to support the weight so I could take out the last wall. Up here was indeed a nice big space, as large as the entire restaurant. My apartment was an early 1900s single-story add-on to the original 1870 structure, so the back windows upstairs looked out onto the gently sloping roof of my living quarters.

The tail end of the day's sunlight poked in through the western windows. The front of the building faced south and got plenty of light throughout the day.

"You didn't carry all the rubble down those stairs, I hope," Abe said.

I waved him over to a window on the eastern side, pushed up the sash, and pointed down to a big rectangular container. "Took the easy way out and tossed it."

"Smart." He stood behind me and wrapped his arms around my waist, resting his chin on my shoulder.

"Mmm, that feels way too good." I swayed with him. "But you did offer to help, didn't you?"

He pressed his lips to my ear, sending a zing of heat through me.

I turned to face him. "Seriously. If you keep that up, I can't be held accountable for my actions." I smiled. "Come on, let's tear out some lath and plaster."

He rolled his eyes, pretending to mock me. "I love it when you talk dirty to me," he said, finally dropping his arms.

"We're going to get dirty all, right." I'd tied a hot pink bandana over my hair to keep the dust out. I closed the open window and picked up a heavy flat pry bar from the pile of tools I'd laid on a drop cloth in the corner. "You can use this or a crow bar."

He dug his own pry bar and a pair of work gloves out of his bag and held them up. "Always come prepared. And yes, I was a Boy Scout back in the day."

"Let's start over there." I grabbed a hammer, too, and headed to the back wall, the one overlooking my apartment. "It's a shame to take off this wallpaper, but it has to go." The paper featured a background of tiny pink flowers with larger puffy bouquets at regular intervals. The covering was faded, stained, and torn, and I needed to rewire and insulate before installing new sheetrock. I pried off the window trim and then went to work on the wall. The wallpaper covered crumbling plaster that had been pressed into the inch-wide slats called lath. The screech of nails pulling out from the studs behind the lath grated on my ears.

"Any idea how the murder investigation is going?" he asked.

"No. Only that they kept Lou at the station questioning her until after midnight last night. What seemed like the whole town came in to eat and gossip today. Buck took Lou and Charles's department chair in for an interview after lunch, too. She was eating with a few friends when he came in. He told me she'd been evading their search for her, like not answering her phone."

"That must be routine, checking out everybody Chuck worked with or knew."

"Right, although it seems like Lou is under extra scrutiny. Charles said something insulting to Zen, the chair, Friday night and she got justifiably angry with him. The whole group witnessed it and somebody must have told Buck, so maybe she's under suspicion, too." I hammered a section to break up the plaster. "I don't know Zen at all, but she seems smart. And nice."

"There have been killers in the past who people described like that. You never know." Abe worked on the other side of the window. He'd pulled the six-foot ladder over and was attacking from the ceiling down.

"I guess. We can swap places once you get that top section done." I could reach the ten-foot high ceiling with the ladder, but it was easier for Abe, who at five foot nine was half a foot taller than me.

"You got it, Shorty."

"Hey!" I lobbed a piece of plaster at his head, missing, of course. "Let's show some respect for the proprietor here."

"Yes, ma'am," Abe said, drawing out the *ma'am* in exaggerated respect. "*R-E-S-P-E-C-T*," he started to sing, then launched into the rest of the song.

The guy could carry a tune, I had to admit. I chimed in with the "Sock it to me," refrain until we were both laughing too hard to keep singing. A wide swath of plaster and lath came off all at once and I jumped back to avoid getting hit by it. As it fell, I saw an object drop down into the wall between the studs. Something black and odd-shaped, neither plaster nor lath. I peered into the cavity but couldn't see it.

"What are you looking for?" Abe asked.

"I don't know. Something got dislodged and fell down. I'll find it when this section is cleared." I kept prying and pulling, working down, even though it made more sense to work horizontally. When a coughing fit interrupted me, I went back to my tool tarp and grabbed a couple of white cupped face masks. I handed one to Abe.

"We should've been wearing these from the start. Plaster dust isn't good for anybody's lungs." I slid the elastic over my head and pinched the little metal strip on the bridge of my nose, then resumed work. When I got down to about a foot off the floor, I peered in again. Part of the plaster had fallen into the cavity, so I dug that out and dumped it on the growing pile of refuse. Finally I reached in and felt around.

"Aha." I straightened, holding a ladies shoe in my hand. It was a small size, maybe a five, but definitely a shoe for an adult woman. A high heeled black shoe with a chunky sole, cutout toe, and squared off three-inch heel that made me think of an elegant woman in a tailored suit swanning down a street. In 1947.

Abe pushed his mask down to his neck. "That looks sort of high fashion, doesn't it?"

I pulled my own mask off my nose and mouth, too. "Yes, but fashion from a long time ago. I wonder if there's another one." I reached back into the cavity. What I came up with was an entirely different kind of shoe. Two, in fact. I dusted them off and showed Abe my find—two miniature pink moccasins, complete with a tiny star of beads sewn onto their tops. Baby's first shoes. The leather, once smooth, had stiffened and the side of one was brown from water damage or another trauma. "I found a few other objects when I took down the interior walls." I pointed to a small table in the middle of the room where I'd set a page from an 1870 newspaper, a few tarnished coins, and a rusty screwdriver.

"How'd they get into the walls?" Abe climbed down from the ladder and took one of the moccasins.

"Good question." I frowned, surveying the wall. "The shoes are way too modern to have been left when the outer walls were put up in 1870. And these are definitely original walls"—I examined the window itself more closely—"but this window isn't original. In fact, it looks like an old double pane. Somebody, most likely Jo, must have paid to have new windows put in. These have aluminum triple track storms on the outside, too, and the combination would have been a lot warmer and tighter than the original sash windows with removable storms."

"If the old window was taken out, the wall would have been open." Abe folded his arms. "Can you identify how old the new window is?"

"Maybe. I'll ask Don what he knows."

Don O'Neill owned the local hardware store a few blocks away.

"Good idea. My big brother has all kinds of useless information knocking around in that head of his."

"Be nice, now. He's a good guy."

"I love the dude, you know that. He's just kind of, well, goofy."

I laughed. "True enough. Has he ever gotten over feeling guilty about hanging out with Georgia?"

The local library aide's husband suffered from advanced dementia. She and Don cared for each other deeply, but Don's faith caused him angst about the relationship.

"Not really, but the guilt isn't enough to stop him. He and Georgia give each other a lot of tenderness, and they both need it. I sure don't judge him."

"Me, neither." I carried the shoes to the middle of the room and set them on what I thought of as my artifact table. "Ready to get back to work?"

Abe whistled as he climbed up the ladder again. "You're a brutal taskmaster, but yes, ma'am. Back to work it is." He pulled his mask back up.

"I'm not that brutal," I protested. "You're going to get dinner out of the deal. And maybe something more." I pulled up my own mask and glanced at him.

He winked one of those big brown eyes at me before turning to the wall.

Chapter 15

I stretched in bed the next morning. Abe had left for work before dawn, but we'd spent a nice evening and had had a thoroughly enjoyable sleepover. We'd demolished much of the wall before knocking off for dinner, although we hadn't discovered any new artifacts. Even though I had plenty of work to do—shoveling the rubble out the window—I let myself luxuriate in the relaxed pace of a day off.

Birdy leapt onto the bed. I wiggled my foot under the covers and watched as he pounced on this sudden prey. I played footsie with him until he tired of it and jumped down to prowl elsewhere in the apartment. Now that I had time for my mind to wander, my thoughts remained on hunters and prey. *How had Charles's murderer attacked him? Had Charles been pounced on?* The two sets of footprints haunted me. Charles must have walked out on the lake willingly. Or maybe not. His killer could have pressed a gun to his ribs under cover of winter coats. It was a puzzle I'd like to solve, but Octavia had the unenviable task of working out the clues and connections, not me.

I didn't bother to shower, as Abe and I had shared one last night, washing off the plaster dust in the most delightful of ways. I hummed an aria as I dressed and put the coffee on. My mom had taught me to love opera, but I hadn't figured out why until I discovered my Italian father.

Once Birdy was fed and I'd set a chocolate biscotti and a nice hot mug of dark java in front of me, I sat at the kitchen table to check what was going on in the world. I thumbed through my e-mail. Nothing particularly urgent there. A text from Abe containing only an icon of a big-eyed smiling head with red lipstick kisses all over his yellow face. I was smiling, too. Maybe it was okay not to worry about getting hurt again.

I turned to the weather report next. "Uck." We were supposed to get a snowstorm tonight. I'd better get that rubble out the window before the snow fell. I checked the local news site, but the only story about Charles's murder said the authorities were continuing to follow up on leads, and if members of the public had seen any suspicious activity on Crooked Lake to report it to the South Lick Police. In other words, they didn't have a clue who'd killed him.

Since I was so cozy in the apartment with my furry slippers and my coffee, I decided to try to find information about the upstairs windows online instead of venturing out to ask Don at Shamrock Hardware. I had no idea when aluminum triple-track storms were first used, or double-pane windows, for that matter. Maybe during the Carter administration with its emphasis on energy conservation, which would put the date during the late nineteen seventies. If I couldn't find anything, I'd text a picture of the window to Don.

It didn't take me long to read that double-pane windows were invented in the early 1950s, with aluminum triple-track storms around the same time. *Wow.* So that shoe—no, those shoes—could have been dropped into the wall as early as sixty, sixty-five years ago. *Huh.* I sat back in the chair and laid my phone on the table, picturing Jo Schultz. I did the math in my head. No way she was old enough to have owned the store in the 1950s. I didn't think she was older than seventy, although come to think of it, I wasn't sure why I thought that. If she was seventy, she was at most ten or so when those windows were invented. Of course, the technology wasn't necessarily widely available at the time of its invention. I also didn't know the history of the store before she'd owned it, other than that it'd been built by one of the founders of South Lick back in the second half of the nineteenth century.

I drained my coffee. The whole day stretched out in front of me for shoveling out debris but that could wait a little. While I was still clean, I was going to go see Jo.

Chapter 16

I approached Jo's house, a classic cottage of the region with a wide overhang on the front porch and a gabled roof. She lived only five blocks from the store, so I'd walked over. As a grievance offering, I took a loaf of banana nut bread I'd retrieved from my freezer.

As I neared the front walk, Ron Stilton emerged from the house and shut the door behind him. I paused, watching him, since he hadn't seen me yet. He sank onto the porch swing and buried his face in his hands, his shoulders shaking in a red IU hoodie. I didn't know what to do. Interrupt what looked a lot like grief or abandon my visit? He'd come into the restaurant a few times, either with his mother or a group of his friends, but we'd never really had a conversation. Maybe I shouldn't have come at all. Jo must be grieving for her son-in-law, too. I could just give her the bread, express my condolences, and leave. Or I could go home.

I hesitated a moment too long and must have

made a small movement. He lifted his head and saw me.

I headed up the walk. "Good morning, Ron."

His hair, growing out after a bleach job, straggled over his sweatshirt, and his eyes were rimmed in red. "Is it good?"

"I suppose not. I'm so sorry for your loss." That phrase always seemed so trite, like a person had lost their pen or their glasses. Didn't death deserved a richer expression?

He stood, his clothes not hiding how skinny he was. I'd forgotten he wasn't much taller than me, but of course, neither was his father.

"Thanks, I guess. Dad and me, you know, we had our problems. But he was still my old man." He sniffed and swiped at his eyes with his fists, then jammed his hands into his pockets. "You here to see Grandma?"

"Yes."

"She's in there. She'll be happy you came. Catch you later." He trudged down the steps.

That was the push I needed. I climbed the stairs and rang the bell.

Jo's face lit up when she opened her front door and saw me. "Why, Robbie, come on the heck in. It's awful nice of you to visit. But shouldn't you be over at the store flipping flapjacks?" Dressed in black stretchy pants and a fluffy fleece the color of her cornflower blue eyes, she stood back and gestured me in. She didn't act like she was grieving.

"I'm always closed on Mondays." I followed her into the living room of the small house she'd bought after she sold me the store. "I brought you some banana bread. I wanted to say how sorry I am about Charles." I handed her the loaf, wishing it wasn't still frozen.

"How sweet. Now you sit right there, hon. Can I get you a cup of coffee? Milk and sugar?" she asked.

"Thanks. And yes to both."

She bustled off toward the back of the house with a lopsided gait. The room was sparsely furnished and brightly decorated. The modern but comfortable couch was covered with a rainbow-color woven blanket, and the matching armchair wore a tie-dyed slipcover. A colorful woven wall hanging decorated the space between the two front windows and a wooden loom stood in the sunlight. The old wooden floor was clean, although it could have used a sanding and new coat of poly. A braided rag rug in the middle looked new, with its shades of purple and turquoise not faded or worn in the least.

I knew Maude was an architect. She must have gotten style genes from Jo.

I'd never seen the upstairs in my store while it was occupied. Jo had moved out before she'd put the building on the market. The downstairs hadn't shown much style except for that of an old dusty country store, but I knew she'd run out of funds after her late husband's long illness. Starting fresh in a manageably small house must have been a big relief to her.

Jo returned holding two mugs of coffee. She set hers near an armchair, then selected a coaster depicting a Parisian scene and set it under my mug on the flat wooden arm of the couch. She sat in the armchair at right angles to the couch. I'd never noticed before that one of her legs looked shorter than the other, and her thigh looked thinner, too. That would explain the lopsided gait. Maybe she'd been a polio victim as a child.

I thanked her for the coffee. "Looks like you're a weaver. Do you sell your work?"

"I do, from time to time. I still have a number of small pieces I made for a holiday craft fair. They serve as wall hangings or table centerpieces or whatever."

"That one on the wall is beautiful." I pointed.

"Thank you. It's one of my favorites."

I took a sip of coffee. "How are you doing with Charles's death, Jo? I'm so sorry for your loss." There it was again, the impossibly clichéd expression.

She stared at the wall hanging for a moment, and then back at me. "I don't mind telling you that my unfortunate son-in-law was a very difficult man, Robbie, may Chuck rest in peace. He gave my daughter a great deal of hardship. And he treated my grandson Ronnie the same way. You must have seen Ronnie leaving, come to think about it."

"I did. He seemed pretty shaken up by his father's death."

"You're right. Go figure, as mean as Charles was to him. Anyway, I am not actually grieving Charles's passing. I know it sounds cold, but I've never been one to sugar coat life."

That explained why she'd said "unfortunate son-in-law" rather than "unfortunate death."

I sipped my coffee, which was a dark roast with an unusual but fabulous flavor that made me think of Turkish coffee. I sniffed the coffee again and decided cardamom was the delightful culprit.

"I made no secret of my opinion of him around town," Jo went on. "I think the detective is considering me a 'person of interest.'" She surrounded the last words with finger quotes.

"Really?" Well, of course Octavia would. She'd have to look at a mother-in-law who had a dislike for the victim. Opportunity would be a different equation, though. No way tiny Jo—who walked with a limp, no less—could have hauled Charles into the ice hole.

"Really. We'd had a disagreeable encounter downtown recently, with a number of witnesses." She searched my face. "But you're the one who found Chuck's body. That must have been awful for you." She rubbed a turquoise ring with her thumb.

"Not my favorite thing to happen when I'm out snowshoeing, no."

"Tell me. Did he have an expression on his face? Scared or surprised? I keep thinking about who could have killed him, and whether he knew them."

I tried not to shudder visibly as I thought back. He'd been face up in the ice fishing hole, but had I noted an expression? "There was ice over the hole, so I can't really say, and . . ." I let my voice trail off. I wasn't supposed to be talking about the details. I was pretty sure Jo hadn't murdered Charles, but she'd told me he hadn't treated his own wife and son well. "It seems like there were a lot of people Charles didn't get along with."

"I was one of them. He never liked me trying to protect my Maude. She's adopted, you know. My husband was shooting blanks, as it turned out, so we found a baby to adopt. But she's still my girl. She had a bit of a rough patch in high school but then straightened herself out. At least until she married Chuck."

I didn't know what *rough patch* meant but didn't figure it was a good time to ask.

Jo went on. "I shouldn't say this, but good riddance to him. The man was psychologically abusive. In a serious way." She brushed a snowy wisp of hair off her forehead and tucked it back into the bun on top of her head.

"I'm sorry to hear that."

"You don't need to be sorry to hear the truth." She looked into her mug for a long moment. "So," her voice brightened again, "tell me what's new with you. How is the renovation coming along?" She smiled at me. "You mentioned you were going to bring some things for me to look at."

I picked up the cloth bag I'd brought along. "I found a couple interesting things in the wall last night. I wanted to bring them by and ask if you wanted to keep them." I glanced at her before digging into the bag, and thought I saw a look of panic pass over her face, a quick widening of her eyes and a flash of flared nostrils that lasted only the briefest of seconds.

She blinked and smiled. "How fascinating. What did you find?"

I pulled out the black shoe. "I found this, but only the one." I handed it to her. Of the artifacts, I'd only brought the shoes. The rest of the items I'd found didn't seem personal.

She turned it all around and stroked the now-rough leather. "This was Mother's. She used to wear these when she and Daddy went out on the town. She'd put on her black dress and pearls, dab Woodhue behind her ears, slip on these heels." She glanced up at me. "My mother was a very stylish woman. No taller than me, but every inch a lady."

"Any idea how it got into the back wall upstairs?"

"I grew up in that building, you know." Jo snorted. "I put the shoe there myself. I miss my mother now that she's gone, but we experienced a great deal of conflict at one point. I was so mad at her when I was a teenager." She shook her head at the memory. "My parents were replacing all the windows upstairs. One night when they were out and the walls were still open, I shoved her shoe into the cavity. But just one. I knew how much she liked this pair. She took very good care of them, so they lasted. She couldn't figure out for the life of her where that one shoe went."

"That explains it," I said.

"You ever do anything like that to your mom?" Jo asked, setting the shoe gently on the sleek coffee table.

I laughed. "Believe it or not, I didn't. We were very close when I was in high school. I never needed to act out, at least not with her. It was only the two of us, and . . ." I swallowed down a lump in my throat.

"Then you're a lucky young lady. I'll bet she's proud of what you've done with the store."

She didn't know about Mom. Why would she? Mom had left town almost thirty years ago, and had been neither Jo's nor Maude's age. I simply nodded. Talking about one death in a day was enough. I wasn't going to get into the story of my fabulous, healthy, strong mother abruptly dying of an aneurysm at age fifty-three a short thirteen months ago. I pulled out the tiny pink moccasins and handed them to Jo.

"I found these, too." I watched her. If they'd gone into the wall at the same time, they couldn't be Maude's. She wouldn't have been born then.

Jo's quick intake of breath was audible. "Good heavens," she whispered, staring at them. As she'd done with the high heel, she turned them, ran her finger down a seam, stroked the side. She looked up at me with full eyes.

"Yours, I gather." I kept my voice soft, too.

"In a way." She clasped them to her chest with both hands. "Those were different times, Robbie, the sixties."

So that must have been when the windows went in, in the sixties.

"You must know that things got wild at the end of the decade—free love, flower power, all that—but earlier, when I was a teen, we were very repressed," she said, shaking her head. "Very." She fell silent, lowering the moccasins to her lap and gazing at them.

I sipped my coffee. Was she going to go on or should I leave?

"There was a boy I adored," she finally continued, keeping her focus on the baby shoes. "I ended up pregnant. My parents made me give the baby up for adoption."

Pink baby shoes. What was that Hemingway's microstory? *For sale. Baby shoes. Never worn.* "I'm so sorry. That must have been really hard for you." I reached out and touched her arm.

"Worst thing I ever did. I was sure it was going to be a daughter, and I'd bought these pink shoes for her."

"I can't even imagine, Jo."

"I was right. It was a girl I gave birth to. A perfect tiny girl. I had to give my little Grace away when she was three days old."

"There was no way to keep her?"

"I was seventeen. I hadn't even finished high school. The boy's parents sent him away to military school when they found out. My parents made me go live with an aunt I hated, out in Iowa."

"Have you tried to find your daughter?" I'd had a college friend who'd located her birth mother.

"No. I don't want to disturb her life if she's happy. And no one has contacted me." She squared her shoulders. "That's why I stuffed these mocs down the wall, too. Later, after I was married, we found out after several years of trying that my husband couldn't have children, as I told you. But we very much wanted to have a family. So the supreme irony was that I had to adopt a baby girl myself. Or maybe it was supreme justice."

Chapter 17

Those moccasins had held a lot more emotion and history than I'd expected. Jo and I sat chatting for several more minutes, but she seemed to want to immerse herself in her memories alone, so I left the three shoes with her and made my way out.

I pulled my red wool scarf closer around my neck. The wind was damp, already starting to bring the sharp smell of snow. I hurried in the direction of the South Lick Public Library only a few blocks away. I'd read about a book celebrating the hundredth anniversary of the invention of the crossword puzzle. The book had been out for a few years already, since the original "word-cross" was invented in 1913, but I'd never gotten around to reading it.

One of the many Carnegie-built libraries across the Midwest, the building was constructed of brick and limestone, and featured wide welcoming steps up to a door with an arched fanlight. It had been modernized with an addition and a ramp in the back, but the front looked like it must have when it was new along with the new century.

I pulled open the heavy antique door of the two-story building. Georgia LaRue stood behind the long hundred-year-old wooden counter, her fingers on a keyboard, her eyes on a monitor. The library aide had been a fan of Pans 'N Pancakes since I'd opened, and she'd helped bring customers back when business slumped after the first murder.

She smiled. "Hey, Robbie. It must be Monday." Her well-padded figure was clad in a red sweater decorated with a sequined design.

"Everybody needs a day or two off, right?" I liked having mine on days when most people were hard at work. Places like stores and even the library tended to be emptier and easier to navigate than if my downtime had been on a weekend like everybody else's.

A balding man sat in an easy chair under the windows reading a newspaper, and I spied a woman at one of the computer stations in the next room, but otherwise the library seemed unoccupied.

"What all are you looking for today, hon?" Georgia asked.

"I want to read *The Curious History of the Crossword.* Came out a few years ago."

"Let me check." She tapped the keyboard, her long turquoise nails clicking as she did. She jotted down the number 793.732, handed me the slip of paper, then pointed. "Should oughta be in the fourth unit down in the East Room." She set her forearms on the counter and leaned toward me, glancing left and right before speaking in a low voice. "Heared you found Stilton's body."

"I did." Maybe I should have stayed home today, after all.

"That's quite the family. Chuck, rest his soul, was a real . . . um . . . jerk. You should have seen him in here, lording it over everybody because he was a professor."

"He seems to have acted that way to everybody."

"Maude wasn't much better," Georgia went on. "She cheated me last year when we was building an addition for my husband. When his dementia really set in."

"Really?"

"Absolutely. She give me a quote to design the addition and then charged me twice that. Said it was 'incidentals.'" Georgia surrounded the last word with finger quotes. "I was so dang upset about my hubby losing his mind that I hadn't gotten the first quote in writing. I had no real recourse." She tucked a strand of bottle-blond hair behind her ear.

"I'm surprised Maude can stay in business if she pulls stuff like that." I loosened my scarf and unbuttoned my coat. The library didn't stint on heat. "Was her design at least a good one?"

"In fact, it was. Wide doors and flat thresholds, lever handles instead of doorknobs, everything easy for wheelchair access. Orville had been in a nursing home last fall but the care was terrible, so I moved him back home and hired caregivers." Her eyes sagged. "We still get royalties from his books and his inventions and such. He was a brilliant professor, but nobody's home upstairs anymore."

"I'm so sorry, Georgia." I gave her a sympathetic look. "I'm going to go get that book. Be back in a minute." I found the history book, and picked up another one on the history of the jigsaw puzzle. I stroked the spines of the books in the 793 section,

which all seemed to be about games and puzzles.
A lot of people my age mostly read on their tablets,
but I liked the heft of a real book in my hands, another way I was an anachronism in my generation.
The smell of the paper, the crack of the binding,
even the cover art—all of it appealed to me. If I
traveled a lot, I would load up a bunch of books on
an electronic device as I had when I went to Italy.
But you couldn't beat the physical book, and at the
library the price was right, too.

When I approached the counter again, Maude
Stilton stood in front of it, dressed in black pants,
black wool coat, black scarf. Her hair hung limp on
her collar, and neither she nor Georgia looked at
all happy.

What was Maude doing in the library two days
after her husband was murdered?

"Telling me you want to extend your sympathies."
Maude's words slid out sharp and tense. "I don't
believe it for a minute. Nobody in this entire town
is sorry my Charlie is dead. I'm sick to death of
hearing it." She wagged her head back and forth
and did a simpering imitation of condolences, the
corners of her mouth turned down. "'I'm sorry for
your loss. May he rest in peace.' Blah, blah, blah.
It's all BS."

"You're going through a terrible time," Georgia
said. "I meant what I said. You have my sympathies."

Maude snorted.

I eased forward. "You might not want to hear it,
Maude, but I'm also sorry for your loss." I didn't
have a bone to pick with Charles. Unlike the rest of
the universe, apparently.

Maude looked at me out of a ravaged face. Her

dark eye makeup was smudged and it looked like her hand had slipped when she'd applied lipstick. "Thank you, Robbie. I appreciate that."

"Is there anything I can do for you or your family?" I asked.

"No. I can't even remember why I came here." She narrowed her eyes at Georgia. "But now that I am, I might as well be honest. For all I know, you killed him yourself, to get back at me about that job. The one where you lied and said I cheated you."

Georgia sucked in a gasp and backed up a step. "Maude, that's absurd, and you know it. I would never kill anyone."

"Maybe," Maude said, her eyes blazing into Georgia's face. "I'm going to let the police decide that. They've come up empty-handed so far." She turned and stalked out the door.

Chapter 18

I leaned on my snow shovel and took a breather. I'd been shoveling debris out the window since one-thirty and it had to be almost two-thirty. The sturdy plastic snow shovel was perfect for the job since it was wide and flat, and didn't add much extra weight to the load. Moving plaster and lath was dusty heavy work, and cold, too, since the window was wide open. I wore several layers of old sweat-shirts, a knit cap, and work gloves. My body was warm from the work, but my nose never seemed to warm up. And despite my mask, I needed to keep clearing my throat of filtered plaster dust.

I'd come home after that scene at the library, puttered in my apartment, and eaten lunch before heading upstairs. Poor Georgia. Not only had she essentially lost her husband, but Maude had ac-cused her of murder. That didn't make sense. It must have been Maude's grief speaking. Jo had said Charles was psychologically abusive to Maude and their son. I reflected on how you never knew what really went on inside a relationship. Maybe Charles expressed his love for Maude in a way that those outside the marriage couldn't see. Still, I hoped Octavia wouldn't take Maude's suggestion seriously. Getting hauled in for questioning wasn't a bit of fun. I knew. I'd been there.

That made me think of Lou. I'd give her a call again tonight, maybe even head into Bloomington and take her out for a beer. I looked out the open window. It hadn't started snowing yet. *Snowing.* Never mind driving my van into the university town. The old girl did not like navigating the hilly route on slippery roads.

I wandered over to the artifact table and turned the pages of the newspaper, marveling at how big it was, and with such small print. I leaned over to read. The edition was from June 10 and one of the headlines was about Charles Dickens having died. I flipped through a few pages until I spied an article about underground tunnels. I needed to get back to work again before I lost my warmth, but I left it open to that page so I'd remember to come back and read it.

I set to shoveling again. As usually happened, the repetitive motion of physical work, whether removing rubble or preparing biscuit dough, freed up my mind to work through problems. I was still stunned by Jo's revelations.

She'd been pregnant out of wedlock in a time when that was unacceptable. She'd stuffed her mother's favorite shoe inside the wall out of anger at being forced to live with an unpleasant aunt and give up her baby. She'd lost a daughter, for whom she'd bought tiny pink moccasins. And then, when her husband was found to be infertile, Jo had adopted someone else's little girl. What a strange continuation of a cycle.

Jo obviously hadn't liked Charles at all. How could one man have so many enemies? Having observed Charles in action at several department dinners, I guess I shouldn't have been surprised, but which of his enemies had chosen Friday night or early Saturday to finally end Charles's life? I wanted to figure out the identities of others he'd antagonized. Partly because I hated the thought of Lou being under suspicion, but also because the puzzle aspect of an investigation fascinated me, drew me in, even though I knew Detective Octavia didn't appreciate my help.

Part of that puzzle had to be the question of Friday night. How could I find out if Maude had reported Charles missing? If she hadn't, why not? Maybe he had a mistress somewhere or had said he was going to a friend's house for a party. But no, after the dinner he'd said he was walking home.

My thoughts were as jumbled as the pile of plaster.

One last shovelful into the container and I was done with the pile of rubble. I slid the window shut and latched it, then pushed the bits left on the floor into a small pile out of the way. There wasn't much point sweeping up until I was completely finished with the demolition phase. The thought of heading downstairs to shower, grab a beer, and read my library book was alluring. But so was the prospect of having a nice welcoming guest suite for when Babbo and Maria came to visit in a few months.

I slid on a clean face mask, grabbed the pry bar, and started on a new section of wall. Abe and I hadn't finished the back, so I kept going toward the corner where it joined the east wall. Maybe I'd find more treasures in there.

I hummed as I worked, but it turned into a string of swear words when one section of lath was particularly stubborn. It refused to come out. I hammered the pry bar, and worked it into the wall until the slats crashed out all at once. The momentum carried me backwards and made me drop the hammer. It hit my shin bone and a speck of dust got into my eye. Trying to blink away the dust, I swore again. This was no business for the weak and dainty. Although neither word had ever been used to describe me.

An hour later I pried out one of the last sections before the corner join. With it came another really old newspaper, another treasure. I set down the pry bar and gingerly brushed the dust off the paper, then carried it to one of the western-facing windows. The sky was overcast with the impending storm, but enough natural light came through to read by since it was still a couple of hours before sundown.

It was the *Brown County Democrat*, the same local paper that was still being published, but the date was 1913. In fact, a picture of the ribbon-cutting ceremony for the new library graced the front page. Everyone wore hats, men and women, and the women's skirts hovered right above their ankles. One man in a top hat held a giant pair of scissors and beamed for the camera, about to snip the ribbon held by two young ladies in white.

This was so cool. I should donate it to the library. Maybe it had gone into the walls when the upstairs was first being finished. I knew my building had been constructed in 1870, but that didn't mean it was completed on the inside at that time, although I thought the store was in operation earlier than this date. Maybe they'd used the upstairs for storage and hadn't needed to finish the walls until later.

I knelt on the floor and spread the paper out in front of me. Carefully turning the pages, I examined the ads that lined the edges. Finally on page seventeen I saw an advertisement for the South Lick General Store, with an address of 19 Main Street. My very store. *Sweet.* I carried the paper to the artifact table.

After I pried out the last bits of plaster and lath where I'd been working, I spent another half hour shoveling out the newly created rubble. By the time I'd latched the window again, flakes were beginning to float down from the sky and the light was disappearing. I'd put in a decent afternoon's work and this was a good stopping point. I examined the east wall, next up on my round-the-building plan.

"That's funny," I said aloud. There seemed to be a rectangular shape set into the wallpaper, almost like a cabinet door. I'd never noticed it before. The bottom of the shape sat a couple of feet up from the floor, but the shape, about two feet by three feet, didn't have a handle to pull it open. I tried to wedge my fingers in with no success. It was likely an old window an owner along the way had closed in and papered over.

I was itching to find out what was in there but I was tired, and it was my day off. On the other hand, I didn't have any plans for tonight. I picked up the crowbar. And heard the restaurant phone ring downstairs. I glanced at the stairs, at the crowbar, at the stairs. The stairs won.

Chapter 19

I puttered in the restaurant a few hours later. After the call, which had turned out to be a wrong number, I abandoned work for the day. I showered off the plaster dust and spent twenty minutes playing with Birdy. The Monday *New York Times* puzzle had been way too easy, as it always was. And even though I finally sat down with a glass of wine and the puzzle history book, I didn't find myself settling into it, and took my wine into the store instead, pausing for a minute before I switched on the lights to get lost in the sight of the snow falling light and fluffy like freshly grated *parmigiano*

Thinking of Italian cheese reminded me of when I'd visited my father in Pisa. He'd made a delicious but really simple thick soup called Sullo Scio. I had all the ingredients already. I was hungry and I wanted to shake up the Pans 'N Pancakes lunch menu a bit to keep my customers coming back until spring rolled around. If I could do a good job of reproducing his dish, I'd serve it starting on Wednesday and see what South Lick thought about a taste of north-central Italy. I brought out garlic from the walk-in, snipped rosemary from my topiary plant in the front window, and opened a can of Roma tomatoes in basil.

As I peeled and minced garlic, I thought of the 1913 newspaper ad for the South Lick General Store. Maybe I should copy what people did on Facebook and throw a Throwback Thursday party in the store, except instead of photos from a few years or decades ago I could stage the store from a hundred years earlier. People could come dressed in fashions from that era, and I could figure out period-appropriate party food to serve. The store was certainly thriving back then, based on that ad in the newspaper.

The store decor hadn't changed that much, if you didn't look closely at my iPad with its Square reader next to the cash register. The electric outlets and the modern dishwasher under the counter were tucked into unobtrusive spots. I'd left the stamped tin ceilings and the antique shelving, and had restored the graceful wood trim after I'd redone the outer walls. Everybody got more than a little stir crazy in March. The weather hadn't really warmed up, but most of the snow and ice had gone, leaving mud in its wake. A throwback party might be just the ticket.

After I minced the rosemary, I warmed olive oil and butter in a saucepan and gently sautéed the garlic for less than a minute. Then I rough-chopped the tomatoes in the can, and added them with their juice to the pan, followed by the rosemary, and threw in a can of drained chickpeas, too. Babbo hadn't used them in his version, but we'd eaten chick peas in other dishes typical of the Pisa area, and the little leguminous nuggets would add protein. I added a quart of chicken stock and brought it all to a boil. After locating a package of tagliatelle, I broke the long flat ribbons of the pasta into smaller pieces before adding it. Of course, if the soup came out not only edible but delectable, I'd have to multiply the recipe. Since I was pretty much a pro at doing that even with baking, quadrupling a soup would be a snap. I inhaled. The smell would convert the most ardent of soup haters.

I left the mix to simmer and went to look at the snow again. My California upbringing had not included the simple mesmerizing joy of watching white stuff fall from the sky. Whether a steady straight-down storm like this one or a howling blizzard, I never tired of gazing at it. And I'd seen all forms in my four years in Indiana. I put on the outside lights so the flakes glistened in the illumination like fairies dancing. A gust of wind made them twirl and swirl before returning to their steady descent.

A noise made me cock my head. It wasn't the purr of the pot simmering on the industrial cooktop. It wasn't Birdy, whom I'd left snoozing on the couch in my apartment. It wasn't a car driving by—the road was justifiably deserted. What was that sound? It was distant, muffled, and seemed like it was coming from the upstairs corner of the ceiling—where the stairs led to the second floor. I frowned at that corner. Nobody could be up there. The only access was from right here in the restaurant, and all the doors and windows were locked tight. The building inspector had said, when I pulled the permit for the upstairs renovation, that I needed to add another egress if I was going to house the public up there. I'd promised to add an outdoor set of steps, but I planned to do that later in the spring when the weather was nice.

I switched off the outside lights and wove through my cookware shelves to the stairs. I ran up, my feet clattering on the old wood, and pulled open the door at the top. After I switched on the lights, I looked around but all seemed as I'd left it this afternoon. The building included an attic space above the second-floor ceiling. The noise could be from squirrels, or even mice coming in from the cold. I decided not to worry about it and headed back downstairs.

What I needed to do was call Lou, and it was the perfect time. After I stirred the soup, I took my wine to the easy chair next to my desk in the corner of the store and pressed her number.

After I greeted her, I said, "How's my favorite suspect doing?"

She groaned. "Now that those heels are off I'm feeling a lot better. There's more than one downside to not being prepared for class."

"Were the students suitably impressed?"

"Of course." Lou laughed. "But you should have heard the grief I got in the department office. Zen wondered if I was going to a job interview."

"How's she doing?"

"She didn't really say. I told you, she keeps her feelings and private life very private."

"Heard anything else from the police?"

"I don't think so. I really just walked in and haven't looked at my messages," she said. "I try to stay away from my phone on teaching days. Can you hang on a second and I'll check?"

"Sure."

"I'll call you back if we get disconnected."

I stroked the old brocade upholstery on the arm of the chair as I waited. When the sound on the phone changed, I looked at it. Sure enough, the call was no longer connected. I checked the soup, which was almost ready, and cleaned up the cutting board, washing and carefully drying my favorite Wusthof knife. I sampled a piece of pasta. It was just before al dente, so I turned off the heat and covered the pot. The pasta would continue to cook.

Whatever Lou was doing was taking a while, but if I dished up the soup, she'd call at that exact moment. There must be a law of probability about that, something like Murphy's Law. Except this one would be: *If an interruption is expected, it is most likely to occur as soon as you have served yourself a portion of delicious hot Italian soup and you are very, very hungry.*

I didn't test *Jordan's Law*, instead straightening a vintage cake pan here, lining up nested aluminum measuring cups there. I hurried over to the phone when it finally rang.

"Robbie, I'm in big trouble," Lou said in a voice so low I could hardly hear her.

"Why? What happened?"

"My lawyer, the one my dad arranged, said the police want me back in there. That they have an eyewitness who puts me at the scene of the crime at around the time Charles died."

My heart sank like a lead plumb-bob. "That's absurd. Whoever it is, is lying. Right?"

She didn't speak.

"Lou, talk to me. You're going to be fine. You did not kill Charles."

"But I was out there, Robbie. On the lake that morning. By myself. I did a loop on the lake. But I didn't see Charles! I wasn't even on that section. I went down from the parking lot."

"Somebody is clearly lying. Your lawyer will protect you, won't he?"

"She. It's a woman. I hope so. But she said I have to go back in. They wanted me tonight, but she convinced them to wait until tomorrow because of the snow."

"Lou, I'm so sorry. You know I'm here if you need me."

In a voice weak and distant, she said she needed to go, then disconnected. She didn't believe me about being fine. I wasn't sure I believed me. Simply because a jerk of an ice fisherman saw her on the ice didn't mean she was a murderer. Lou's lawyer was going to have to convince Octavia of that. The lawyer had better be good. Octavia could be a formidable opponent.

Chapter 20

I couldn't sleep in the next morning. I'd gotten so used to having only one day off I became restless on the second day. I'd rather have been up and laying bacon on the grill with a house full of hungry locals seated in my restaurant. I reminded myself that I would switch back to the former schedule in April or whenever the weather warmed up. In the meantime, I had a two-day weekend like most normal people, except mine was on Monday and Tuesday instead of Saturday and Sunday.

I'd eaten the soup after the call with Lou last evening, and it had been good, although I would have enjoyed it more if I hadn't heard her unsettling news. The soup was definitely tasty enough to serve tomorrow.

After my quick morning routine—sit-ups, dressing, coffee brewing, cat feeding, toast eating—I took my second cup of coffee into the store to make sure I ordered whatever I didn't have on hand so I could serve hearty portions of Sullo Scio the rest of the

week. My supplier listed giant cans of chick peas
and plum tomatoes, and I ordered up a few gallons
of stock, too. Rosemary, garlic, and olive oil I was all
set with. I inventoried the walk-in and ordered
more breakfast supplies like orange juice, sausages,
and syrup. I added onions, lettuce, and tomatoes
for the burger crowd at lunch, and threw in a few
pounds of mushrooms so I could add a mushroom
burger special.

The snow had stopped overnight and the world
was a beautiful pristine sight when I pulled open the
front door of the store. Of course, the view across
the street was a slice of heaven in any season. Today
the woods were coated with a couple of inches of
new white, as were the hills rising up behind them.
I waved as a town snowplow crunched by pushing
the snow off the road into an ever rising berm on the
far side. I'd have to check, but I thought we might
be getting a record snowfall this winter, or certainly
more than in recent years. Being this far south and
with climate change, some winters it didn't snow
at all.

I locked up again and sat down to catch up on the
Internet for a few minutes. It was still only seven
o'clock, but Abe had sent me a text saying he missed
me and what about dinner tonight. I responded yes,
but that it would have to be an early one, and asked
if he was cooking. Nothing from Lou, but I shot her
a quick text saying I was thinking about her and to
contact me with news.

Speaking of news, I checked the online *Brown
County Democrat.* The only bit related to the murder
was that the lake was open to the public again. I

was surprised there wasn't a notice of a funeral or memorial service or even an obituary for Charles. Maybe the authorities hadn't released his body yet.

A few minutes later, I tied a clean kerchief over my hair and headed upstairs to work. I needed to shovel out my steps and walkways, but that could wait until it warmed up outdoors. I was still enough of a Californian that I'd just as soon avoid cold hands and feet if I could.

First order of business up there was that shape in the wall. I grabbed the pry bar and worked the flat end into the vertical line on the left side of the rectangle. Whatever was underneath budged, but not by much. I worked my way all the way around the top and down the right side. It finally gave way as it swung open like a miniature door, with hinges inside on the left side.

What had I found? A hidden cupboard? I peered into the dark cavity. "Yo," I called out. The sound wasn't dead, as it would have been in an enclosed space. Instead it kept going. So maybe this was a laundry chute, or a dumbwaiter shaft. *Cool.* I hurried over to my tools tarp and grabbed the big flashlight. I shone it into the darkness. And stared.

On the wall opposite, fastened into the wall only a couple of feet from my face, hung a metal ladder with thick rungs like iron dowels. I trained the light on the ladder and followed it down until I couldn't see anymore. *What in the world?* I stepped back with narrowed eyes. To the right of the opening was the door leading to the stairs I'd trod coming up. They led onto a landing, and then the stairs went down along the right outside wall of the building to the store area. I'd never thought about the space from the top of the stairs to the back corner. Of course there would be an unused area there, since the interior wall up there didn't butt back out toward the outside. *Huh.*

Looking into the secret passageway again—that was what I was already calling it—I felt a bit like Nancy Drew, or Encyclopedia Brown. I pointed the light up and saw Spanish mosslike cobwebs festooning the corners and a century of dust on the studs holding up the eaves. Then I looked at the ladder again. Why weren't the rungs dusty? Glancing at the door, I spied a handle I hadn't seen when the door had swung open without warning. The handle, a smooth metal thing like a drawer pull, was screwed into the door. But it wasn't dirty, either.

My heart rate sped up to an alarmingly fast thudding. A person had been on that ladder in recent years. I hoped it was last year when I bought the building. But the building inspector hadn't found this door, this passageway. Jo hadn't told me about it. I certainly hadn't been up or down the ladder. Who had? And when? And where did the passageway end up, anyway?

Last night I'd heard a noise coming from up here. My scalp prickled. Icy fingers of dread crept over me. I stepped away from the door and felt for my phone in my pocket, then cursed. I must have left it downstairs. My puzzle mind wanted to climb down the ladder and at least find out where it ended up. My inner child's mind said no way was I going into a scary dark cramped space and my claustrophobic's mind agreed wholeheartedly.

My logic mind, the one fully aware that a murderer was freely walking around somewhere, told me that under no conditions was I exploring that dark cavity alone.

I was happy to dismiss the first mind and pay attention to the rest.

Chapter 21

Downstairs twenty minutes later, I jabbed the END button on my phone in frustration, paced to the front door of the store, and stared at the snow. Which apparently wasn't too deep for people to get to work. I'd been unsuccessful at finding a single soul able to come over on a Tuesday morning and go exploring with me. I trudged back up the stairs to the second floor and stared at the passageway. Nancy Drew would have climbed right down there, the heck with being alone, hang the danger. But I wasn't a fictional teenage sleuth. I was a twenty-seven-year-old adult in possession of an appropriate portion of common sense. And, in my past, a really bad experience with cramped spaces.

I laughed and shook my head. It was likely only a utility shaft. Or a second egress. Maybe whoever built the store was terrified of fires and wanted to make sure he provided another way out. I still wasn't exploring it by myself. I had demolition tasks to do and they were going to get done. Instead of tearing out the wall around the shaft, though, I moved to the front wall. I wanted to be able to close that little door again. I also realized I hadn't thought through the process of tearing out the wall next to where the stairs went down. When I started ripping it out, plenty of dust and debris would fall into the stairwell and then filter into the store. I needed to save that task for the minute I closed the store next Sunday. I could hang a tarp to keep some of the dust out, and then I'd have a full two days to clean up before reopening again on Wednesday.

Have pry bar, will demolish. I worked steadily on the front wall for two hours, standing on the six-foot ladder for the top sections, and kneeling for the lowest. I studiously ignored the door in the wall. I really didn't expect anyone to come creeping up through the passageway when my back was turned and hurl a knife into my back. Still, I'd closed the door and hauled my table saw over in front of it. Just in case.

I was taking a break and stretching my back when I saw a South Lick police cruiser pull up in front of the store. *Uh-oh*. I ripped off my gloves, dropped the tool, and clattered down the stairs. I opened the door to see Buck shuffling up the steps through the snow.

"Sorry, I haven't shoveled yet," I said.

"Not a problem, Robbie." He removed his uniform hat and peered down at me. "What in heck you been up to, all covered with dust like a creature from the chalk mines?"

"I'm working on the upstairs. Thought you knew that. I plan to open a few bed and breakfast rooms up there. You know I'm closed on Tuesdays this winter, right?" Maybe he had hopes of breakfast. Maybe his visit wasn't murder related.

He bobbed his head with a dejected look on his face. "I know, and I'd be a lying son of a cooncat if I pretended I wadn't disappointed." He brightened. "Don't suppose you need a coffee break right about now?"

I shook my head with a laugh. "Come on in. Sure, I can use both coffee and a break. Actually, I could use your help with a small project." I could bargain with the best of them.

Ten minutes later, after I'd washed my face and hands and brewed a pot, I was on my way back to Buck when I glanced out the front window. A big black SUV rolled by on the street in front almost like it was going to turn into a parking spot, too. I hoped people knew what CLOSED meant.

Once the vehicle got by the store, it sped up and disappeared.

I sat at the table and poured our mugs of coffee. "So what brought you by, other than wanting a cup of coffee?"

"Little bit of this, little bit of that."

"What's new in the murder investigation?" *Couldn't hurt to ask.*

He sipped his coffee then wrapped his fingers around his mug, fingers so long they looked like they could have gone around twice. "Welp, you know I ain't sposta talk with you about none of that."

"My friend Lou said someone accused her of being on the lake that morning right where we found the body. She was around there but says she didn't go anywhere near that spot. Who's been telling lies like that?"

"Hmm." He tapped the table. "Far's I know, they ain't arrested her or nothing. She and her fancy lawyer did show up this morning, but they left near as soon as they got there."

"Good." *Great, really.* I hoped Lou wasn't too shaken by this whole experience. I knew all too well how disturbing it was to be suspected of a crime.

"I will tell you one small little thing," Buck said. "Stilton didn't die of no drowning. Autopsy showed there wadn't no water in his lungs. He was dead before he was stuffed down that hole like an old piece of garbage." Buck's nostrils flared and I saw a rare swerve away from the sharp but easygoing, slow-talking officer I'd gotten to know over the course of the fall and winter.

"You're in this business to see justice done," I murmured.

"You're darn tooting I am, Robbie. Murder ain't right, no matter which way you skin the hog."

I wrinkled my nose at the image of a hog being skinned. Then again, I freely ate ham and bacon, and served up plenty of it to my customers, too. It shouldn't bother me. Then I thought about what he'd said. "So if he was dead before he went into the hole, the second set of footprints must be from the person who took him out there."

"Kinda looks that way, don't it?"

"You didn't come by only for coffee today," I said. "Did you?"

He leaned back in his chair and stretched out his

legs. "How well do you know Ms. LaRue, over to the library? She eats here pretty regular, don't she?"

This can't be good. Why is he asking about her? "I don't hang out with her personally, if that's what you're asking. But, yes, she's been a faithful customer, even when other locals were staying away. And I think she's honest and trustworthy." I lifted my chin. If this was the result of Maude slinging lies about Georgia, I'd go to bat for a woman I belatedly realized I would call my friend. Maybe I should see if she wanted to hang out sometime.

"Now don't go getting your knickers in a twist. Seems she and Ms. Stilton had a kind of disagreement over a work project. Ms. Stilton is suffering something horrid from her husband's violent death. Yesterday she come in and suggested Ms. LaRue might have been the one to do the deed, so to speak."

"That's as ridiculous as saying Lou Perlman killed Charles." I frowned at him. Georgia had been furious at Maude, for sure. How well did I really know either woman? Not well, at all. I'd learned over the last half year that the person you least imagined to be a killer could, in fact, be pushed over that line to take another person's life. I sure hoped it wasn't Georgia, but I had to admit I wasn't a hundred percent positive.

"We got to check out every possible suspect." He drained his coffee. "Or rather, Octavia does. We're just the helpers, so to speak. You said you was wanting some help. What would that be, now?"

"This is going to sound foolish, but I found a secret passageway. And I didn't want to investigate it on my own. Would you mind walking through it with me?"

His eyes bugged out and his mouth dropped open. Picturing the look on his face was going to entertain me for years to come.

Chapter 22

I pointed the flashlight down the three-foot square shaft.

Buck exclaimed, "Whadd'ya got here, girl?" He turned to look at me and then back at the metal ladder.

"I don't know, but I'll show you the reason I didn't want to go down there alone." One of the reasons, that is. I showed him the cobwebs and dirt above, then I trained the light on the ladder. "No dust. No dirt. Not on the door handle, either. And why isn't there a handle on the outside? Why didn't anyone notice it or discover it when I bought the building?" I told him about the inspector missing it, and Jo not mentioning it.

"So you're thinking somebody's been coming up here recently. Spying on you or something?" Buck asked, scratching his sandy-colored hair.

"Could be. Could be a person down on their luck who knew about the passageway and hoped to steal something of value or stay out of the weather. Or even teenagers with too much time on their hands.

I have no idea. I also don't know where it ends up.
Do you have time to check it out with me?"

"Whyn't you let me go on down first?"

My inner Nancy Drew argued with this, and my
inner scared little kid embraced the idea. I finally
said, "That's fine. Let's go. You take this light. I have
another one." He was a heck of a lot taller than me,
and stronger, too, when it came right down to it. If
there was a door on the other end that was stuck,
he might be able to free it up without my help.
There sure wasn't enough room for two of us to
occupy the passageway at the same time.

Buck jammed his hat back onto his head. He was
too tall to scooch into the opening, so he sat on the
edge and lowered his legs in, leaning his torso out
until he'd moved his feet down enough rungs to let
the rest of him follow. I dashed over to my tarp of
tools and scrabbled around in it. I thought I owned
another flashlight but couldn't find it. I heard him
sneeze, but the sound was hollow, like he was in
a cave.

"Bless you," I called down the shaft. "I'm on my
way. One second." I grabbed my work light, a strong
bulb in a cage with a hook on it, and stretched out
the extension cord, which just reached the top rung
of the ladder. After I flipped on the light, I hung it
from the top rung and took a deep calming breath
before I climbed in. I could do this thing. After all,
I was twenty-seven, not seven. I made sure one hand
was always hanging on tight to a rung and started to
descend.

"Almost down," Buck called.

"I'm on my way." My body half blocked the light
from above. The dark walls around me had been

there for almost a hundred and fifty years. The sharp ends of nails stuck in toward me. I needed to be careful not to snag the back of my shirt or my elbows on them. My pulse throbbed in my neck, and I had to keep swallowing down the excitement. Or the fear. As I kept climbing, the light grew dimmer. I stopped and peered at the walls. What must be the base of the first floor was at my eye level. I knew there wasn't a door leading to the shaft from the first floor, or if there was, it'd been blocked up decades ago. The shaft most likely ended in the cellar—that damp, dark cellar I basically didn't use for anything except to house the furnace. I'd never seen a door in that area of the cellar wall, but I hadn't looked for one, either. As I recalled, old boards were stored down there leaning against the wall. A doorway could be hidden behind them.

"I'm at the end." Buck's voice wafted up. "Now I got to figure out how to get out of this dang trap."

A few more rungs and my feet were right above his head. I twisted my head down and to the side to see him with his back to the ladder, inspecting the wall with the flashlight. "There's no door?" I asked, hearing my voice rise almost to a screech.

"Might could be. Lemme see." He felt around on the wall. "Yup, here's a door. I'd kick it in, but I ain't got room to get no purchase on it."

He definitely didn't have room to get his knee high enough to put any force behind a kick. I watched as he put his shoulder to it. The door gave way and he stumbled through. I clambered down as fast as I could go without falling. I could barely see a thing except a moving flicker of light through the opening. I stepped carefully toward it and over a threshold. "Wow."

Buck was ahead of me, bent over and creeping along a passageway not much taller than I was. It wasn't the cellar, or rather not a part of it I'd ever seen. Old wide boards stretched overhead and the walls were of a rough-hewn wood with lots of splinters and cobwebs. Four-inch-diameter logs, several still covered with bark, all with knobby knots extruding, served as posts every couple of feet. Underfoot was tamped down dirt. Damp dirt, too, since Buck's feet weren't raising any dust. My nose detected mildew and a faint odor of something else, maybe old manure.

"You coming?" he called.

"Right behind you." I definitely didn't want to be left behind. Underground in the dark in what was essentially a tunnel? No way. I was lucky to be keeping my panicked claustrophobia at bay as it was. While I walked, I tried to keep my bearings on where we were. We'd come down the east side of the house and then turned toward the right at the bottom of the shaft, so we must be going toward the back of the property. We might not be in the cellar, but the passageway was equally cold and damp. And was a lot more enclosed. "I wonder what this tunnel was made for," I said, almost more to myself than to Buck.

What if the passageway was part of the Underground Railroad? I'd read about an Indiana Quaker named Levi Coffin who had helped hundreds of slaves escape northward. We weren't that far from the Ohio River to the south or Cincinnati to the east, both of which had been escape portals where slaves had passed through. I felt a chill, but it was from excitement rather than from the temperature.

Buck slowed up and started to turn toward me, straightening as he did. Bad move. He scraped his head on a beam overhead. "Dang, that hurt."

"Keep your head down, Buck. Let's get through this thing."

"Expect you're right." He hunched down again and forged ahead. "This is turning out to be more of a project than I'd reckoned on, Robbie. I'm going to have some explainin' to do when I get back to the station."

"Sorry about that."

When he stopped again, I peered past him. He was pointing the flashlight at another ladder exactly like the first one.

The only way to go was up.

Chapter 23

"I spose we're heading up?" Buck asked, twisting to look at me.

"Might as well." I followed him up the ladder, but it didn't seem as long a trek as the one down had been.

At the top, he stopped and played the light on the walls. "I don't see no door at all."

"Shine the light above you," I urged him. My skin was crawling from being in the enclosed space. There must be a way out. There had to be.

He peered at the top of the shaft. And pushed. Hinges complained, but a trap door opened. I'd never been so glad to see natural light. Which promptly disappeared again when the door fell shut.

"Dang it," Buck said. "Something's blocking it up there." He climbed up another rung, braced himself against the wall of the shaft, and pushed with both hands until the door went vertical. "Lemme get out and I'll fix it all the way open for you." He held the door open with one hand.

After he got his long legs up and out, I heard the scrape of wood dragging on wood. The door clunked wide open, falling all the way back.

I stared up. Above me loomed the high inside rafters of my own barn. I climbed out then dusted off my hands. We stood in the back corner where Jo had a left a pile of old furniture that I'd never gotten around to either fixing or taking to the dump. Broken ladder-back chairs had been dumped on their sides near a tall dresser that was missing a drawer.

"That there desk was half blocking the trap door." Buck pointed to a wooden desk decades overdue for a refinishing.

I squatted and peered at the floor. The rough, wide pine flooring showed the marks of the desk having been dragged across it. If a person had been down that tunnel and back recently, there should be other marks. I looked around, then pointed to several other sets of narrow tracks like the desk legs would have made. "Look, Buck. Somebody else pushed that desk before you did."

He bent over to look. Straightening, he pushed his hat back on his head. "You're right. And that means whoever it was pushed the desk back over the trap door when they came out so it wouldn't be obvious." He brought his face close to the desk's top. "Probably can't get no prints from this, but we can try if you want."

"I guess." I kept examining the floor, but any discrete footprints that might have been there had been scuffled into a mix, just like when I stirred baking powder and salt into flour. I hugged myself against the cold air in the drafty old barn. Motes floated like lazy snowflakes in the light from the high windows above the wide sliding door. My rattletrap Dodge minivan occupied the space in front of the door, and I'd fixed up one section beyond that to hold extra lumber and other building supplies that weren't hurt by freezing. I'd roughly renovated a room in the far corner with minimal heat, shelves, and a workbench as my workshop. I stored tools and paint in that space. In the year since I'd bought the property, I'd never cleaned out the corner where we stood.

"Tell you what, though. I'm putting a lock on the barn. I never thought I needed to before now, but if somebody thinks they can waltz through a hidden tunnel into my store, well . . ." I shook my head.

"Sounds like a plan. Listen, I got to be getting back to work."

"Of course. Thank you so much for coming through with me. Don't worry about fingerprints. I mean, I have no proof that anybody trespassed, really. Except I did hear a noise upstairs last night."

"You did? Why didn't you say so?" He frowned.

"I didn't see anybody. I thought maybe it was a squirrel in the attic or something."

"Huh. Welp, I'll get an officer over to check for prints when we find a free minute. And I'll be by tomorrow for breakfast." He ambled to the door and slid it open enough to pass through. "Thanks for the coffee."

"Pleasure's mine. Take care." I joined him at the door and waved, watching him shuffle through the snow and then disappear around the front. I took a step to follow him and froze. I turned slowly and stared into the barn. I'd relocked the front door of the store before Buck and I had gone upstairs. I knew my apartment door was locked. I hadn't brought my keys. Or my phone. *What an idiot.* I swore.

"Buck!" I called out as I ran around the front of the store, but the taillights of his cruiser were already heading down the road toward the center of town.

I'd been meaning to hide an extra key outside but had never gotten around to it. I was going to have to go back through the passageway. Down the ladder in one shaft and back up the ladder in the other. And in between I needed to traverse the dark mysterious tunnel, a space terrifying to a claustrophobe like me.

I stomped my foot and slapped my leg a couple of times. "Robbie Jordan, you're twenty-seven," I said into the chilly barn air. "You're healthy and smart, and you have a flashlight. Get over it, already."

Sliding the barn door shut with rather more force than necessary, I made my way back to the open trap door and grabbed the flashlight from where Buck had laid it on the floor.

I took in a fortifying breath. I could do this. And whether or not I could, I had to.

Chapter 24

Okay. I'd made it down the ladder.

I turned and stared into the tunnel, taking in a nice, deep calming breath. Gripping the flashlight and thanking my fairy godmother that I'd put fresh batteries in it last week, I let out the breath and started walking. I would not break into a panicked run. I would not. The last thing I needed was to trip and injure myself.

"One foot in front of the other, Jordan," I told myself. "You got this thing." In fact, holding the light made me feel a lot better. And it was kind of interesting checking out the construction.

Winters must have been a lot more severe back in 1870, so maybe this tunnel was a way to get from the house to the barn without going outside. Seemed like it would have been a lot simpler to build a connecting structure above ground, though. I mused again that it might have been part of the Underground Railroad. I shook my head. There was no longer a need for the Underground Railroad in 1870. Unless the barn predated the store.

A smaller house could have stood where the store was. Another piece of information to check into at the library or town hall.

At least thinking about the reason for the tunnel had taken my mind off the fact that I was in a small tight space twelve feet underground. I came to the place where the passageway took a turn. I was about to walk past when the light caught a bit of color.

What was that? I stopped and shone the flashlight on the rough boards.

About three feet off the ground a small scrap of red cloth had snagged on a thick splinter sticking out from one of the log posts. I was about to reach for it when I pulled back my hand. The scrap could be from clothing my intruder had worn. I peered closely at it. It was almost certainly from whoever had been sneaking along the tunnel. The cloth was too bright a color to be a hundred years old. I wanted to pull it out, but I knew I needed to leave it there for Buck or another officer to retrieve. If there was one thing I'd learned from associating with the police in recent months, it was that they needed to deal with evidence in the proper way.

I reached for my phone to snap a picture of the scrap. *Oops. No phone.* It was back in the restaurant. I needed to get through the tunnel so I could call them. But suppose the intruder came back and saw—No, that wasn't going to happen because I was going to lock that barn up tighter than a C-clamp holding a glued join.

I glanced behind me. The barn wasn't locked yet. Whoever the intruder was could be coming after me. I swallowed and hurried on, my heart thudding as loud and fast as a jackhammer. I'd never been so happy to see the ladder that led up to the second floor. I closed the door tight behind me before I started up. It was awkward climbing with the flashlight in my hand. I couldn't get a good grip on the rung, so I tucked the light into my back pocket. That made it shine up and behind me, which wasn't particularly useful. I was almost to the ground floor level when my foot slipped on a rung and bumped back down to the previous rung. At the same time, my hand lost the grip on the rung above. The flashlight fell out of my pocket and slid all the way to the bottom. My chin crashed on the metal ladder, but I managed to hang on with my other hand and keep myself from following the light. I looked up to the opening to the second floor. The work light I'd left shining down welcomed me, a beacon in a dark storm. Dark passageway, mental storm.

I forced myself to calm down again before carefully climbing up to safety, one rung at a time. I eased out of the shaft and through the small door. The wide open and well-lit demolition site was a beauty to behold. *Whew.*

My first order of business was blocking the entrance. I shut the door tight, dragged the heavy table saw over again, and jammed it against the door. It didn't have a lockable latch but I could remedy that later. I ran down the stairs and into my apartment.

I rummaged in my junk drawer until I found a nice heavy padlock. I slid the key onto my usual key ring before heading from my apartment out the back door. I locked up behind me, pocketed the keys, and headed to the barn. Some barns featured a separate people-sized door, but mine wasn't one of them. I pulled the hinged hasp away from the thick metal staple on the barn frame, opened the wide sliding door, and stepped inside.

I didn't want to unlock and lock the barn every time I came home. Before securing the barn door, I backed the van out and left it in the driveway, pushed the desk back over the trap door—just in case. I headed into my tool room and found another hasp and loop that could serve as a lock for the second-floor access to the tunnel. I knew from inspecting the property last year there were no loose boards in the barn walls to be easily pried loose, and the only windows were ten feet up and no more than two feet tall. A pretty tight fit for a person. If an intruder was so brazen as to haul a ladder to one of them and squeeze through, it was a long drop down inside.

It would be a pain unlocking the barn door every time I needed to get to my tools and paint, but for now the inconvenience was one I didn't mind enduring.

I slid the wide door shut, its antique wheels complaining in their tracks overhead. The snick of the padlock closing was a more comforting sound than I ever would have imagined.

Chapter 25

Back in my apartment, I jabbed END on my cell. I'd left Buck a message about the scrap of cloth I'd seen on the splinter of wood, since he didn't pick up. I doubted the whole tunnel discovery was connected to the murder, so I didn't want to bother Octavia. It wasn't really police business. At least I hoped it wasn't, but I wanted to let Buck know. Just in case.

I stuck the phone in my back pocket. Since finding the hidden passageway, I definitely didn't want to be without my cell.

I grabbed a quick sandwich and a glass of milk. When I returned to the demolition project, I realized I didn't have another padlock to go with the hasp and staple for the second-floor passageway door. But with the outer doors locked tight, including the barn's, and the heavy table saw against the entry door on the second floor, I should be safe. Mostly.

After I'd been prying lath off the front wall for

an hour, I thought about that sound I'd heard while I was making the soup. That it was possibly caused by an intruder raised the hairs on my arms and the back of my neck. I stopped and dropped my tool. Why would someone want to poke around on my second floor, anyway? It was awfully brazen to do it while I was in the building.

Was all this connected to the murder? The timing seemed way too coincidental. The sooner I figured out who the intruder was, and if it was the same person who killed Charles, the sooner I could focus on my work. My gaze fell on the newspapers I'd discovered.

I hurried over to the artifact table. Where was that article about underground tunnels? I found it and scanned the text. It turned out to be an instructional piece on shoring up passageways that had been built, as I thought, to connect houses and barns, including those that had also been used to hide slaves on their way north. *Great.* I had a hundred-and-fifty-year-old tunnel that might collapse. Unless a previous owner had shored it up. I was pretty sure Jo hadn't. If she hadn't mentioned the tunnel at the time of sale, I doubted she even knew about it.

The other newspaper was the one I wanted to donate to the library—the one from a hundred years ago, the one with the library inauguration. And I wanted to talk with Georgia, anyway.

I showered off the plaster dust and dressed, then took twenty minutes to shovel off the porch and front stairs. The snow was light and the work was a breeze compared to shoveling rubble. I walked the few blocks to the library carrying the newspaper, which I'd carefully inserted into a flat paper bag. Georgia wasn't at the front counter. *Damn. Double damn.*

A young man in a bow tie and a pink Oxford shirt tucked into tight jeans glanced up and raised his eyebrows with his lips slightly pursed. "Can I help you, ma'am?"

Ma'am? He was at most five years younger than me. Or maybe ten. Well, probably not ten or he'd still be in high school.

"Where's Georgia?" I asked, glancing around. I didn't add, *Where the heck did they get you?*

"She's on her lunch break, ma'am. Can I help you with anything in her absence?"

"Do you know where she usually goes for lunch?"

"Over to that pancake place, I think. You know, the one where the body was found." His lips were now totally pursed, plus a bit of a curl on the left side.

Yeah, my pancake-and-dead-body restaurant, which he'd apparently never frequented or he'd know who I was. *Wonderful.*

The big clock on the wall read one-fifteen.

"Never mind, I'll see if I can find her around town. Thanks, anyway."

"You're welcome, ma'am. Good luck."

I turned away without responding and a moment later wandered the downtown streets looking for Georgia. For all I knew she'd gone home for lunch to visit with Orville. Or maybe she was taking some respite time for herself. With a husband with Alzheimer's, she could well use a break. Although the sun shone, it didn't warm the air much, but it was helping the snow melt, at least along the shoveled sidewalks.

I approached the Jupiter Spring gazebo. Its columns, set in limestone blocks, held up an octagonal covered structure that supported a domed top. Ornate metal grillwork included the word *Jupiter*. The town had recently cleaned and repainted the whole thing, giving it a flavor of how it looked when it was built at the turn of the last century.

I squinted at the figure seated on a bench outside the gazebo with her back to me. "Okay if I join you?" I asked when I got close.

Georgia glanced up with a start. "Sure, Robbie. Plant yourself." She scooted over to make room. "What are you doing out and about?"

"Looking for you. I found this old newspaper in the wall of my upstairs yesterday. I thought the library might like to have it." I sat and extracted the paper from the bag.

She took the paper and peered at the date. "Nineteen thirteen? Nice find. You know I'm only a library aide, but I think the reference department would be happy to have the paper."

"And see." I pointed. "It has an article about the founding of the library."

Georgia scanned the front page and smiled. "Don't you just love the clothes back then? I'd much rather wear a shirtwaist and a long skirt. And the hats are so gorgeous."

"I agree." About the hats, anyway. "Why aren't you a regular librarian? I don't think I've ever asked you."

"It's called education. I went to a community

college for a couple years, but I don't have a degree in library science." She lifted a shoulder and dropped it. "It's okay. I love the work, and I get benefits, which Orville and I need."

I focused in front of us at the spot where the spring had been. The middle of the circle featured a metal sculpture with silvery cables rising up and spilling over instead of actual water. I pulled my scarf closer around my neck and turned on the bench to face Georgia. "I keep thinking about the murder."

She winced and averted her eyes.

"I wanted to ask if you knew about any other people, locals, who had a beef with Charles. I can't picture any of the so-called persons of interest actually killing him—my friend Lou, her department chair Zen Brown, Maude, Ron. None of those makes any sense. And definitely not you."

"You know, Chuck was very charming in public. From a distance. I think a lot of folks liked him, thought he was smart and a nice guy, but if you had any close dealings with him, whoa. Watch out. He'd stab you in the back."

"That sounds bad."

"I'd seen him in action." She glanced at me. "Not a pretty picture. Actually I think he was worse to women. Back when my Orville still was in possession of his mind, he told me he saw Chuck chewing out a lady electrician who'd done work for him, saying she charged too much. This is a well-respected lady in town, mind you. Electricians get a pretty penny for their services because they deserve it. Orville said Chuck couldn't get away with treating a man that way or he might get slugged in the face."

"Interesting." It was true. Most women I knew might argue at the time or silently stew later about such an interaction, but they wouldn't confront a man physically. "So have the police been to see you recently?"

She nodded slowly, looking at the sculpture in front of us. "Sounds like you know they had."

"Buck stopped by the store this morning and mentioned what Maude said yesterday."

"That woman," Georgia said, facing me, eyes flashing. "She has the nerve. Listen, you know her. Think you could convince her to go back to the police and tell them she didn't mean it, that she was just upset?"

"I don't really know her that well, Georgia."

She slapped her hands on her thighs. "I don't know what else to do."

"I'll guess I'll try." I thought about the rest of my afternoon. "I should have time to take some food by for her and Ron later. I'll see if she'll back off from thinking you killed her husband. The police don't believe her, do they? That you would kill Charles to get back at her?"

"They're not telling me what they believe or don't believe." Georgia rubbed her forehead with a gloved hand. "They asked me to go down to the station after work last night, and made me meet with the lady detective. Wanda was there, too." Georgia watched me. "I told them I didn't kill Chuck Stilton. But I was home alone during the period when they say he died. Orville was home with me, of course, but he doesn't have a clue what's happening, and there weren't any caregivers at the house Friday night. Saturday morning after the caregiver showed up I went out for a walk alone. I didn't see nobody, so it's my word against Maude's."

"It's a pretty outrageous claim from her," I said. "They can't have any evidence against you."

"Of course not. It's an outright lie. But I'll tell you, I'm not surprised. The woman has zero scruples about anything. She and Chuck were pretty well matched." Georgia peered into the gazebo as if it was an oracle holding answers. "If I was going to kill someone? It would be Maude herself."

Chapter 26

By three o'clock I was back in the store. I'd meant to buy a padlock for upstairs, but Georgia's final comment had been so unsettling I totally forgot. At least the padlock on the barn door was still locked and secure, and I knew I'd blocked the upstairs access.

My supplier had just dropped off the delivery. I put it way and went to work peeling garlic for tomorrow's soup. I threw a collection of arias on the speakers at a pretty good volume and sang along, pretending I knew Italian as I worked. I was heading out to Abe's house at six for dinner and wanted to get the soup done before I left. I was making extra to drop off a container for Maude and Ron on my way as a semblance of a condolence gesture. And maybe have a word with her about Georgia while I was there, not that I thought it would do much good.

I minced the garlic and set it aside, then chopped the rosemary. *Poor Georgia.* The police interest in her couldn't progress any further unless the real killer faked evidence, but I knew well the icky feeling of being suspected, even falsely, of a crime like murder. I still didn't know much about the crime itself. What would evidence even be? Buck had said Charles was dead before he was put into the lake, but he hadn't said how he died. Bashed over the head? Poisoned? Stabbed or shot? I doubted I could get Buck to tell me. Octavia was going to have to find the murder weapon, or traces of blood in somebody's car—actual evidence. I narrowed my eyes. Was there blood on the ice near where I'd found him? No, I was sure I hadn't seen any.

I set the garlic to warm in olive oil and butter in the big soup pot, then added a huge can of Roma tomatoes with basil, another mega can of chick peas, the rosemary, and a bunch of stock. I put the lid on the pot and stretched my arms to the ceiling, feeling a few construction muscles I'd forgotten I had. Cooking breakfast and lunch used an entirely different set of body parts than ripping out walls and shoveling debris.

A new sound crept into the music. I finally realized the antique wall phone was ringing. The bell gave off a harmonious analog sound, the sort of thing cell phone ring tones try to duplicate digitally but never quite get right.

I wiped my hands on my apron and hurried to answer it. "Pans 'N Pancakes, Robbie Jordan speaking."

"Robbie, it's—"

"Hang on a sec," I yelled. I couldn't hear over the aria and dashed over to turn down the music. When I got back to the phone, I said, "What was that again?"

"It's Zen Brown. I'm on the front porch. Can I come in?"

I heard the knock on the glass in the front door and saw her face peering in. I laughed. "Be right there." I hung up and unlocked the door.

"Thanks. I kept knocking, but you couldn't hear me, so I found the store number online." Zen's hair, which had been gelled and spiked when I'd seen her before, lay flat on her head. While she hadn't worn glasses on Friday or Sunday, today she sported a pair with rectangular black frames.

"Do you want to come in?" I asked. "I'm closed today, but . . ." I took a closer look at her tense face. "Just come in."

"I don't want to bother you."

"It's okay. I'm making soup and it's basically done." I stepped back until she was inside, then I closed and locked the door. "Let's sit down. Glass of wine or coffee?"

Her shoulders dropped like she'd been hunching them and finally relaxed. "I'd love a glass of wine, thanks. There's a matter I want to talk to you about." She sank into a chair at the nearest table.

"I'll get the wine from my apartment. Be right back." A minute later I poured Pinot Noir into two restaurant mugs and pushed one toward her. "*Salute.*" I held mine up before taking a sip.

"That's right. Lou told me you went to Italy recently," Zen said after she sipped from her mug. "You found your birth father didn't you?"

"Yes. I mean, I wasn't adopted, but I'd never known about my father until a few months ago."

She tilted her head to the side. "How'd that go? Meeting him in person."

Why is she asking me about my personal life? "It was pretty nice. He and I connected really well, and I have the cutest little half nephew who is three. His Italian is already better than mine."

"Interesting." She lowered her head and stared into her mug like it was another universe.

"I met my half brother and half sister, too," I went on. "She didn't seem particularly happy to have me there. I tried to be nice but never got through her shell."

"What's her name?"

"Graciela," I said.

"Pretty name."

"I know. We share hair and skin color from our father, but she's slimmer and taller than me, and three years younger. Maybe she's simply used to being the only daughter. Even though she's an adult, she wasn't a bit friendly to me." I was rambling. Zen surely hadn't come to ask about my family.

"That's too bad."

"At least Alessandro—my half brother—seemed to like me. I'd never been out of the States before, and the trip kind of gave me a travel bug."

"Really?" Zen glanced up.

"Really. I'm dying to see other places now," I said. "Not that I have the luxury of closing the store and traveling again any time soon, mind you."

"So you'd never been to Europe."

I shook my head. "It didn't happen. California was my world, with occasional trips to see my aunt out here."

"I'm such an academic, I travel all over the world for conferences and such." Zen stared into her mug again. She raised her head and shook it. "I stopped by to chat with you about this murder business."

I'd been curious about the reason for her visit. "Kind of a scary time, isn't it?"

"Yeah. I hope I'm not imposing. I hardly even know you. Lou told me you'd solved a couple crimes in the past."

"I wouldn't go that far." I swirled a finger around the top of my mug. "But I did find a body in my store a few months back. Not the greatest of experiences."

"I just came from the police station. A Detective Slade asked to interview me, and this was the first opening I had in my schedule. She wasn't too happy about that, believe me."

"I can imagine. I've worked with her in the past. She's tough, but in my experience I'd say she's fair. On Sunday, Buck said they'd had trouble reaching you."

She rolled her eyes. "I have an IU e-mail account and office phone, which are listed on the department Web site. Because I took a couple days of personal time and turned off my cell, it's like a national emergency with these people."

"If Octavia was willing to wait until today, that must mean they don't suspect you of killing Charles." I watched her. "Right?"

"Of course they're not going to tell me what they think and don't think, but the detective certainly asked a lot of questions about my dealings with Stilton. What his performance reviews were like, how long I'd known him, what other conflicts we'd had. The works. I just left there and my appointment began at one o'clock."

My wall clock obligingly chimed once for three-thirty. "She was probably also asking about where you were Friday night and early Saturday, right?"

Zen didn't answer for a moment, then said, "And what if I don't want to tell them?" She didn't meet my eyes.

"Zen, you have to. They need independent verification that you weren't, couldn't have been, on the lake that morning helping Charles go for one last swim in a million gallons of ice water. You might want to get a lawyer."

Zen swore with some emphasis.

"You don't want to be arrested for his murder, do you?" I asked in a soft voice.

Her eyes wide, she finally looked at me. "Of course not."

"Then you have to tell them where you were."

"You don't understand." She drained the last swallow of her wine and stood. "I can't."

Chapter 27

I rang the doorbell at the Stilton house several minutes after five, my container of soup in a handled bag, along with a sack of biscuits that were still warm. It wasn't much, but if Maude was feeling like no one in town cared about Charles' death, it might help soothe her. The house, in a new development south of town, didn't match its more conventionally built neighbors. It featured sleek windows and unusual convergences of roof lines. The walkway hadn't been shoveled and I'd struggled over frozen bumps and icy patches.

A big black SUV with snow tires sat in the driveway, one of many such vehicles I saw these days. I flashed on the SUV that had slowed in front of my store and then driven off, but this kind of car was everywhere in the county.

Nobody answered the door. I saw lights on indoors, so I gingerly rang again, and a minute later the door finally pulled open.

Ron stood facing me, earbuds trailing down to a phone in his other hand. He wore a T-shirt and his feet were bare under a pair of jeans that hadn't visited a washing machine in quite a long time. "Hey, Ms. Jordan."

"Ron"—I waited until he pulled out one earbud—"I brought you and your mom some food. Is she in?"

He turned his head and yelled, "Ma!" He faced me and said, "One sec," then ambled off down a set of stairs.

Okay. The kid obviously didn't have many manners beyond not calling me by my first name. He seemed to be over his sadness of yesterday, at least for now. It was cold, but I was dressed for it in a warm sweater and my tall black boots, plus a wool coat, hat, and gloves.

Maude finally appeared in the doorway, holding a glass containing an amber-colored liquid in one hand. Her eyebrows went way up. "Robbie, what are you doing here?"

"Ron didn't tell you I was here?" I extended the bag. "I brought fresh homemade soup for you both. And a batch of cheesy biscuits to go with it."

She tilted her head to the side and smiled, just a little. "Well, aren't you sweet, then. Come on the heck in."

"Thanks. I can't stay long, but wanted to offer my condolences again."

Maude nodded without speaking as she led the way into the living room. I shut the door and followed. The room could have been in *Better Homes and Gardens*. If someone had tidied and cleaned it, that is. The tall windows in different geometric shapes let in slanting afternoon light that fell on cascading stacks of newspapers, used glasses next to crumpled napkins on the coffee table, an old sweatshirt thrown over the back of the couch, and visible dust on the end table nearest me. On the mantel stood a framed picture of a young woman in uniform in front of a large American flag.

Maude sank into a recliner. "Take a load off." She gestured toward the couch with her drink and then took a generous swig from it. Her voice wasn't slurred—yet—but she seemed a lot more relaxed than she'd been any time I'd seen her previously, and way more than she'd been at the library yesterday. Her clothing was more relaxed, too. She wore a long red sweater, leggings, and shearling slippers. "You drink whiskey?"

I perched on the couch after I set the bag on the coffee table's only bare spot. "No thanks. I'm off to a dinner."

"Heard you've been dating Abe O'Neill. Good man, that one."

"He sure is." Guess I shouldn't be surprised that my romantic life was common knowledge. I pointed to the picture on the mantel. "Is that you?"

Maude glanced at it. "Indeed it is. In my younger days, obviously. Decided to get my act together and serve my country at the same time." She shrugged. "Did both, but I got out after one tour. No interest in being career military."

"So how are you holding up?" I asked.

"Like crap, frankly. Whole town stares at me when I go out. Police aren't worth jack. All my worthless son does is stay in the basement playing ridiculous games. I can't focus on my work, and I have a big project I'm supposed to be designing. Things could be a lot better." She drained her glass. "You're actually the only person who has stopped by."

"I'm so sorry to hear that." I was shocked to hear her refer to her own son as worthless. He'd just lost his father. And to say that to me, whom she barely knew. Then again, I had just shared a bunch of personal details with Zen. I was equally shocked that a near stranger like me was the only person to show Maude sympathy. "I know the police, at least Buck and Octavia, are working hard to figure out who committed the crime. It can't be easy for them."

She blinked at me. "What do you know?"

"I know they've been interviewing people. I've heard that a number of people, um, didn't get along very well with Charles." I wasn't going to mention Lou or Zen by name.

"I didn't get along with him, either. That doesn't mean I killed him." Maude snorted. "That lady detective hauled me in there for an 'interview,' too." She surrounded *interview* with finger quotes. "Like I would murder my own husband, my only son's father."

"Will you be holding a service for Charles any time soon?"

She frowned. "I don't know when they're going to release his body. Who would come to his funeral, anyway? Nobody liked him. My own mother didn't like him."

Ouch. "Does he have family in the state?" I didn't know anything about Charles or where he was from, except I thought I'd heard he grew up in South Lick.

"He and his brother weren't on speaking terms. Parents are gone. Me and Ronnie were pretty much it for him. And those IU folks. But they didn't like him, either."

"How about your family?" Jo had said they'd adopted Maude, but maybe there were other siblings I didn't know about, or other relatives.

"No siblings. A few cousins out in Connecticut apparently are too busy to come and pay their respects. No, all I have is Mom." She pressed her lips together.

"Well, do let me know if you arrange a service. I'll make a point of being there." I suspected the town would turn out *en masse*, in fact. Not out of caring for Charles particularly, but because of the notoriety of his being murdered. "This house is lovely," I went on. "Did you design it?"

She sat up straighter. "I surely did. Charlie and I figured out what we wanted, and then I implemented it."

I must have looked surprised when she said *Charlie*.

"People in town called him Chuck, but he hated that nickname." Her voice took on a sad tone. "We finished the house right before the baby was born. Those were happier days." She stared out the front windows.

I thought back to what Jo had said, that Charles gave Maude a hard time, and Ron, too. Of course, the early days of a relationship are often happier ones, especially if you close your eyes to warning signals, like I had with my ex-husband before he became *ex*.

It was time for the hard part. I didn't want to confront her about Georgia, except that I'd promised I would. "Maude, about Georgia LaRue. I heard what you said to her at the library. You don't really think she killed Charles, do you?"

Maude's mood changed from nostalgic to stormy in a flash quicker than lightning. She stared at me with narrowed eyes. "She sure could have killed him. Drugged him and stuffed him down that ice hole. I told the police as much. She accused me of lying and cheating, and she wants revenge because I refused to go along with her fake story. She's the liar and the cheat. If you ask me, she's a murderer, too."

Chapter 28

Abe's kitchen smelled tantalizing, almost like Thanksgiving, when I walked in. I was a few minutes late, but I hadn't wanted to cut Maude short. After she'd accused Georgia again, Maude had brightened and seemed to want to tell me about her latest design project, so I let her, even though listening to the things she'd said about Georgia had left an acrid taste in my mouth.

I sniffed. Sautéed onions, for sure. Roasting meat, maybe. And a touch of cinnamon? The bad taste was going away fast. Abe came back in from hanging up my coat.

"What's cooking? It smells fabulous in here." My lunchtime sandwich was a faint memory, and I was glad I hadn't accepted a drink from Maude. With no food in me, it would have put me over the tipsy edge. "Didn't you work today?"

"Early shift. Five to three. Been cooking ever since I got home." He leaned over and hit a key on a tablet propped up on the counter.

"Watching a movie while you cook?" I asked.

"An episode of *Race to Escape*. Ever seen it?"

"No. What is it?"

"It's a new type of game show. Two teams are in identical locked rooms and they have to figure out how to get out in an hour. It's really smart. They have to solve all kinds of puzzles and work together. We should watch together sometime."

"That's my kind of game show. Solve the puzzle to get out of the room."

He smiled, deepening the dimple that left me weak in the knees, and pulled me in for a long hot kiss. "Hungry?" he said when we detached.

"Of course. In more ways than one." I pulled back a bit. "But I have to be up bright and early tomorrow." My stomach gurgled out loud.

He laughed his delightful rolling laugh. "I get the message. I have another fiver tomorrow morning, too. Let's eat."

A couple of minutes later we sat across from each other at a small antique table in his combo dining-living room. His cottage was laid out almost exactly like Jo Shultz's, both inside and out, with the same open pass-through from living room to dining room, and the same wide covered porch and roof line. Abe had added a dormer on the back and a basketball hoop on the driveway for his son.

Green candles softened the light and a steaming bowl of food in front of me sat on a vintage tablecloth decorated with what looked like Jell-O molds and flowers.

I leaned over my bowl, wafting the flavors upward with my fingers. "Mmm." I spied meat, carrots, fat green olives, a slice of lemon, and other delectables, all in a rich brown sauce.

"Lamb tagine." Abe lifted his glass of red and extended it toward me. "Cheers."

"Cheers. And *buon appetito*." I clinked then took a sip. "I thought I smelled something like cinnamon in the kitchen."

"Good nose. Plus saffron, cardamom, and ginger, and a bunch of other spices, too."

"On couscous, which I love." I tasted a bite. "This is really nice. You learned to cook from your father, didn't you tell me?"

"Exactly. Mom preferred tofu and tempeh. Yuck. And I was always hungry because I was such an active kid, so I asked Dad to teach me how to cook meat, stews, things that stick with you." Abe savored a bite, too. "Robbie, next Sunday I want to take you to meet the folks. They've been asking about you. Can you come down to their house for dinner after the restaurant closes? I'll drive us." He reached his right hand across the table to my left.

Meet the parents. I swallowed hard. Was I ready? "Of course, Abe. I've heard so much about them. Will Sean be there, too?"

"Yep. He's going to spend the whole weekend with them." He sipped his wine. "They'll be glad you can make it. And I'll make sure there's no tofu in sight. Now tell me about your day. Did you finish tearing out the front wall?"

I finished chewing a bite and swallowed. "I had quite the day." I told him about finding the tunnel and exploring it with Buck, about the dust-free ladder, about the noise I'd heard. "I hated going through the passageway, especially when I had to come back through alone." An involuntary shudder rippled through me.

"I'd think it would be fun. I've always loved caves and tunnels."

I stared at him. "Not me. Something terrible happened to me in high school." My stare dropped to my plate, remembering.

He reached across and touched my hand. "Want to tell me about it?"

I looked up. "I guess. I was fascinated by caves when I was a kid. My friend and I found some to explore in the hills. The summer I was fourteen I went by myself, and the passage kept getting narrower and narrower. Because I was fourteen, I forgot to bring extra batteries for my head lamp. When it gave out, it was so, so dark in there. I just froze for a while. I had to force myself to scooch out backwards and then feel for the entrance until there was light from the outside again."

"You were brave."

"Stupid, more like it. I could have gotten lost in a side tunnel and died. Ever since, well, I don't do well in dark tight places." I shook off the memory of my last cave.

"I'll just have to go spelunking alone, I guess." Abe grinned, then sobered. "But it's worrisome that somebody might know about that passageway from your barn to the store."

"It was definitely spooky thinking an intruder might have snuck into my space. Now there's a good padlock on the barn door, and I left my heavy table saw pushed up against the entrance on the second floor."

"Who would want to get into your store uninvited? A robber, maybe, who hoped to find where you keep your money at night?"

"No idea. I have a good safe in my apartment, and I try to get the money out and to the bank regularly." I sipped my wine.

"You know, I've heard about other tunnels to barns. I'll try to remember where."

"For tending animals in the winter, I'd assume. But why not build an extension to the house that reaches the barn, instead?"

"Not sure." He shook his head. "That's definitely what they do in New England. I saw all kinds of linked structures when I drove around Vermont the one time I went there. It must be colder there than here."

"Seems like an aboveground structure would be a lot easier to build than a tunnel. I also talked with Georgia from the library, and Lou and Charles's department head today, Zen Brown. They both were questioned by Octavia about the murder. I don't think she has a clue about who killed Charles. Buck told me Charles didn't drown. He was dead before he entered the water."

"Interesting. No water in the lungs, I guess."

"How'd you know about that?" I asked.

"I trained as a paramedic at one point. Thought I wanted to join the fire department. Decided not to, but I stay certified in CPR. Comes in handy when you work with loads of electricity like I do."

I shuddered. "You take all kinds of precautions about not getting shocked, I hope?"

"Of course." Abe peered at me. "Hey, don't worry. I like this life of mine way too much to get careless. Especially the part that includes you." His look was warm verging on hot.

"I'm glad to hear that." I frowned then.

"What's wrong?"

"I took soup and biscuits over to Maude and Ron Stilton on my way here tonight."

"How'd that go?"

"Her house, while nicely designed, is kind of a wreck inside. She must really be grieving for Charles and she seems so all alone except for her son and her mother. Why doesn't she have friends around here?"

"From what I know of her, she can be prickly." Abe said. "Could be it's hard for her to get close to folks."

"That's sad."

"Are they holding a service for Charles?"

"Not yet. She said she wasn't sure anyone would come." I grimaced. "Maude was heavy into the whiskey at five o'clock. But I should talk. I've certainly been known to have an afternoon whiskey, myself."

"Right, but you taste a small glass to relax and then you leave it. I've never seen you crocked."

"True." I told him about Georgia asking if I could help with getting Maude to reverse her accusation. "It didn't go so well. Maude said she thinks Georgia's lying about the project and that she killed Charles as a form of revenge."

Abe exclaimed, "Good thing the police are on the case."

"Agreed. While I'm curious, I've done what Georgia asked me to, and it's not my business, really. Not my puzzle."

"I like your attitude. Now eat your dinner and let's not talk about death. Deal?"

I smiled. "Deal."

Chapter 29

"Robbie, where are you? I've asked you three times if we should make more grits." Danna gave me an exasperated look.

My cheeks warmed, but not from the heat rising from the grill. I'd been thinking about my evening with Abe. He'd asked me to stay, but I'd reluctantly gone home after dinner. I knew I'd be worthless this morning if I slept over, no matter how attractive the proposition and propositioner were.

As I looked over the crowd an hour after sunrise on a cloudy, windy day, I knew I'd made the right decision. Danna and I had been working for an hour before the sky started to lighten, and it looked like it was going to be another busy day at Pans 'N Pancakes. We'd made grits as a special again, this time baked with sausage, cheese, and eggs. The dish was moving well. I ordered stone ground grits from the Original Grit Girl. She used only unbleached corn and the flavor was outstanding.

"Making more is a good idea," I finally said to

Danna. "But when will we get time to cook the grits? Anybody's guess. We should have made double earlier."

"I know."

A couple of minutes later I had a brief respite between tables ordering and the food being ready, and reflected yet again on how lucky I was to have Danna as my assistant. Co-chef, really. I hurried to put a covered pot of water on a burner. Once it boiled, she could stir the grits from time to time when she wasn't flipping pancakes or omelets or turning bacon and sausage.

Phil came whistling in carrying brownies for the next couple of days. When he saw how busy we were, he stashed them in the cooler. "Sorry I can't stay to help. The paycheck calls. Come by the farm one of these days and catch up, okay?" He grinned at me.

"Absolutely." I waved before he went out the way he came in. He was staying at Adele's farm while she and Samuel did their service work in India. Sheep needed tending twice a day, and it gave Phil a break from the apartment he shared with a few other guys.

Danna and I bustled about for the next half an hour until the clock chimed eight, doing what we did best—a kind of orchestrated cooking/serving/ cleanup dance. I glanced up the next time the cowbell jangled to see Ron Stilton shuffle in with two other boys his age. They seemed to be in a heated discussion, but looked at me long enough to see me wave them to a table.

I carried over menus and a pot of coffee. "Hey, guys. Coffee?"

A pasty-faced dude to Ron's left looked up with bleary eyes. "Yes, please, ma'am," he said, his soft round face looking like he still didn't need to shave.

At least one of them had manners, even if they did include calling me *ma'am.* Ron held up his mug without speaking. Couldn't he at least ask nicely if he wanted coffee?

The third guy, a skinny redhead with bad acne, shook his head but kept his eyes on the phone in his hands. "Large OJ for me, please."

"Looks like you guys were up all night," I said lightly. They smelled ripe, too, the scent of greasy hair and shirts worn too many days in a row wafting up as they pulled off hats and jackets.

The polite one nodded. "That's right, ma'am."

Somehow from him the *ma'am* didn't bother me. Ron fixed his eyes on his own phone.

All righty, then. "The Specials board is over there." I pointed, poured two coffees, and headed to pour the orange juice. I passed Danna. Ron was such a contrast to her. Both were nineteen, both locals. The similarity stopped there.

She rolled her eyes. "Gamers." She stirred the grits with a bit of extra force.

They must have been playing games all night. Maude had mentioned that was all Ron did. I went back to take the gamers' orders.

After Ron asked for the grits bake, he finally glanced up at me. "Hey, that soup you brought was sick. Thanks. Mom liked it, too."

"You're welcome," I said. "So I hear you're into ice fishing. How's it been this winter?"

The redhead snorted but didn't say anything.

"Not bad. I like to get out on the lake and clear my head once in a while."

"Never catch much, though, do you?" the pasty-faced one said.

"Caught a murderer. That's better than any stinking fish." Ron sat back looking satisfied.

"What?" I stared at him. "What do you mean?"

"I saw that girl out there, that student of my dad's. She must have already done him by time I saw her. She was coming right from the spot where they found him. Where you found him, right?" He blinked at me.

"I found your father's body, yes."

Ron had to be lying. Lou had said she was nowhere near where we found Charles.

Ron tapped the table with one dirty-nailed finger. "It's only a matter of time before they arrest her."

"Hmm." *As if.* I clamped my jaw shut and nearly bit my tongue trying to keep from saying more.

"Stilton here's always trying to get us to go ice fishing with him," the redhead said. "But if people are getting knocked off on the ice, you're not going to catch me out there. No disrespect to your dad, dude," he added quickly.

"Hey, he didn't respect me," Ron said with a bit more bravado than I would have expected. "Doesn't worry me none."

What had happened to his grief of two days ago? Maybe he thought he needed to put on a guy act in front of his friends, display a measure of teenage machismo.

I cleared my throat. "I'll get those orders in." I turned toward the grill. When I heard a snicker, I looked back over my shoulder, but it wasn't aimed at me. The three were all looking at one of the phones, pointing and sharing something funny.

Chapter 30

As often happened, Danna and I had a lull in business at around eleven. We took the chance to use the facilities, sit down, and eat. I made us a big omelet and carried it on two plates with biscuits and bacon to the table where she sat.

After I'd eaten a few bites, I put my fork down. "What's up with Ron and his friends?"

"That's all they do, play video games. It's way disgusting. They don't even wash half the time."

"I picked up a hint of that," I said.

"They're losers. They were like that in high school, and they have parents who support them in their dweebhood. Not my idea of a good time, or dudes worth knowing."

"Ron said he saw Lou on the ice that morning coming from the spot where I found Charles. That's got to be a lie. She said she was out on the ice alone but wasn't anywhere near that part of the lake."

"Just ignore him. Probably wants attention."

The bell jangled and we both turned our heads to see Buck amble in with a newspaper tucked under his arm. Danna started to stand, but I waved her down.

"I'll get it. Have a seat, Buck. Breakfast or lunch?" I asked, standing.

"Breakfast, please," he said, looking hopeful as he sat. He spread out the *Brown County Democrat* on the table.

I ladled out an order of pancake batter, added four slices of bacon, and set up a plate of biscuits. "Over easy?" I called to him.

When he gave me a thumbs up, I carefully cracked two eggs on the grill.

"So how's it going, ladies?" he asked.

"Not bad," Danna said. "Gainfully employed doing what I love. Could be worse. I could be a worthless gamer dude." She raised one eyebrow, the light glinting off the tiny gold ring piercing it.

Buck nodded knowingly. "The Stilton boy and his friends been in?"

I flipped Buck's pancakes and called over, "How'd you know?"

"Town this size, how could I not know? They're pretty harmless, anyway, far's I can tell."

I took him the coffeepot and poured, then hurried back to slide the cakes, eggs, and bacon onto a plate. I ladled meat gravy on the biscuits and served up a portion of grits, then carried it all to the table.

Buck beamed at the mountain of food. "I don't rightly know what we did without you, Robbie, before you gone and open'd up your store. This here's perfection."

Danna laughed and stood. "I bet you ate a lot more donuts back then." She headed for the sink.

A dribble of gravy hit Buck's uniform sweater. He

dabbed at it with a napkin but kept on shoveling in his breakfast. As he chewed, he pointed at the paper. "Interestin'." He swallowed. "Some reporter is dredging up a few old stories. Like this here one. Girl killed herself couple three decades ago. Reporter says it might coulda been murder, not suicide."

"Really? Do they say why they think that?"

"Nope. Article's pretty short on specifics, as a matter of fact."

"Do you remember that death?" I asked.

He squinted through one eye for a moment. "Nah. I was over in Bloomington in college then. Didn't know the girl, anyhoo."

"I wanted to tell you something I learned about the current death." I told him what Ron said about Lou. "He's lying, Buck. Lou said she wasn't anywhere near that section of the lake."

"His word against hers." He lifted a shoulder and dropped it.

"But that's outrageous! He's a kid without a job, apparently. Lou is on her way to earning a doctorate."

"And since when did gettin' some learning govern whether folks 're capable of murder?"

I opened my mouth, shut it, and stood. "I need to start lunch prep."

"Hey now, don't be gettin' your feelings hurt, Robbie. Like as not Ms. Perlman is perfectly innocent. But speaking of not innocent, I got your message. I come by to eat but also to fetch that scrap of material from the tunnel. You got time to show me where it was?"

I glanced at the clock. "I guess, if we move fast.

Let me put the soup on to start heating first. Okay with you, Danna? I need to show Buck something in the . . . in the barn." I hadn't told her about the tunnel and didn't want to get into it right now. I grabbed my gloves and slid into a coat.

"Go for it. If anybody comes in, I'll just pretend I'm the head chef." She grinned and twirled, then bowed, one hand in front of her waist, the other in back. "*Chef de Cuisine*, at your service."

Chapter 31

Buck and I were halfway to the barn when his phone buzzed. He paused and answered it, then disconnected. "Sorry, Robbie, I gotta go. I'll try to get back this afternoon to get that scrap of fabric. It don't seem that urgent."

Maybe it's not urgent to you, I thought. "All right. It's not going anywhere." I watched as he ambled a bit faster than usual down the drive toward the street. Something else was apparently more urgent. *What?*

I turned to go into the service door on the side of the store building when I stopped short and whipped my head toward the barn door. Something didn't look right. I strode toward it. And swore.

The quarter-inch-thick metal shackle of the padlock had been sawed through near where it entered the body of the lock. Its hook hung from the staple on the door frame as if taunting me, while the hasp lay open and empty on the door. The ice in my bones didn't come from the chilly wind, nor did the goose bumps on my scalp. I reached out to touch the lock with my gloved hand, but pulled my hand back before I did. This was more than sneaky teenagers exploring a tunnel or even an intruder predating my purchasing the store. That shackle was thick. It must have taken a special saw to cut it. And not a little planning.

Someone wanted very much to get into my building. What was so important in my building that somebody would do this? They had to know I would see that the barn had been broken into.

"Get a grip, Jordan," I told myself. "Call it in." I patted my pockets. No phone. I'd thought I was coming out here with Buck, and my phone sat on the desk in the restaurant.

I slid the door open a couple of feet and peered into the shadowy space. With the gunmetal sky outside, little light made its way in through the high windows, but I thought everything looked like I'd left it. Except . . . on the rough wooden floor a couple of yards in sat a piece of paper folded in half and propped up like a tent, as if whoever left it wanted it noticed.

That paper definitely hadn't been there when I'd locked up yesterday. I pushed the door wide open, glanced behind me to make sure no one was lurking there, and stepped in far enough to snatch the paper, then hurried back out before opening it.

In typed capital letters it read: BETTER LAY OFF ASKING QUESTIONS ABOUT THE MURDER. YOU WOULDN'T WANT TO BE NEXT.

I brought my other hand to my mouth with a sudden intake of breath. Charles's killer was my tunnel intruder. Or someone close to that person. I needed to get Buck, and quick. Better yet, Detective Octavia Slade. I stared at the note, reading it over and over. The words filled the page, in what had to be nearly a sixty-point font.

A sound rustled in the woods to the side of the barn. I stood frozen in place. Who was there? The person who'd left the threat? The murderer? My heart started a stampede-paced beat. I didn't know whether to dash for the store or chase down the noisemaker. I glanced back at the store. It seemed a hundred miles away. If whoever had left the note was still around, running across open space would be a very bad idea. Even standing there I had a target painted on my chest.

A squirrel jumped onto a branch of a black walnut tree with a rustle. It scampered to the tree trunk. I patted my chest. Not an intruder. Not a murderer waiting with a gun. Just a squirrel. But maybe my threatener had gone back through the tunnel and was waiting at the top of the ladder.

I slid the barn door shut. Not that it would keep anyone out, of course, but it would prevent snow from getting in, if we got more. I'd been so busy I hadn't checked the forecast. Speaking of snow, I looked more carefully at the area in front of the door. It was the end of a gravel drive that curved around the store from the street and led to where I stood, making the entrance to the barn hidden from the street. I didn't see any evidence of a vehicle. No wheel ruts or tire tracks in the snow. Unfortunately, Buck and I had walked there, and I'd made tracks again, so I doubted the police were going to be able to figure out from footprint impressions who'd cut my lock.

I was leaving that up to the authorities. I took the note and hurried to the store. I glanced behind me before I pulled open the service door, feeling like I was in a horror movie with a killer stalking me on my own property.

Chapter 32

Before I took off my gloves inside, I stashed the note in a gallon plastic bag, my hands shaking as I sealed it, then slid it into my desk drawer. I stood there for a moment in the warmth of the store, with its smells of grilled meat and rosemary, trying to get my emotions under control about the cut lock and the note. This space, my restaurant, was supposed to be a refuge, a welcoming public place, but it was at odds with the threat I'd found.

Once again, there was a way for a person with bad intentions to get into my personal space as well as my public space without me knowing it. This was very bad news. I thought hard about when the lock could have been cut and the note deposited. I hadn't checked the barn door when I returned from seeing Georgia, when I'd left for Abe's, or when I'd come home last night. It could have been cut any time I was out of the house yesterday. Or overnight. Or even this morning. I'd trusted a small device to make me safe. Big mistake.

Danna shot a whistle in my direction as the

cowbell jangled. It was noon, and the restaurant was filling up for lunch, with more customers waiting at the door. Murder was certainly good for business, but I'd much rather have brought these people in for reasons other than that. I shook off those thoughts. I had more pressing issues. I needed to call in the note. I had to help Danna. Both at the same time, which was a physical impossibility.

I glanced at her and back at my phone on the desk. "One second," I called to her. I got a dirty look in return, but turned my back and pressed Octavia's number.

"Yes?" was her curt greeting.

"I'd locked my barn last night but a minute ago I found that the padlock is cut. And I discovered a threatening note inside the barn." I rushed on even though I could hear my nervousness. "The note told me to back off asking questions about the murder. Said I could be next." I kept my voice down and my back turned to the increasing noise level behind me.

I could almost hear Octavia perk up. "Secure the note. Stay indoors. Is your restaurant open?"

"Of course. And it's busy."

"Don't go anywhere. We'll be over as soon as we can."

"Can you hurry? There's an underground tunnel that leads to my second floor. Ask Buck about it. Somebody could be upstairs right now."

"We'll get there as soon as we can."

"Okay." I frowned. "But maybe come in quietly? I don't want to alarm my customers." I disconnected then hurried over to wash my hands and apron up. I looked at Danna. "I'm sorry, Danna. Tell you later."

She gave me a *really?* look. "These two orders are ready for the small table in the corner." All business, she pointed at two loaded burger plates. "Then you need to write the soup on the Specials menu."

"Got it. Do we still have grits?"

"Not much, but some."

I delivered the burger plates to two women about my age wearing work clothes. Construction work, not bank work. Both wore ruddy faces like they worked outdoors.

"Thanks," the one with dark hair in a ponytail said. "Any news on the murder front? I heard you found the body." She cocked her head, eyes bright. Obviously I was as eager for news as the next person, but I was getting tired of people assuming I knew all. Or could talk about it if I did.

I opened my mouth, then shut it. What was the use? I shook my head and headed to the Specials board. I printed SULLO SCIO under the grits item, then added TUSCAN CHICKPEA SOUP by way of explanation. If I'd used vegetable stock I could have added VEGETARIAN, but I'd made it with chicken stock, which tasted a lot better in my opinion.

As I headed for the next party waiting to order, the message on the note blared in my brain. *You could be next.*

Chapter 33

Instead of slipping in without calling notice to themselves, the police arrived twenty minutes later with sirens blaring. I gaped as chaos unfolded. Buck and Wanda rushed in, leaving the cowbell on the door clanging the news of their entrance. They drew their weapons and clattered up the stairs to the second floor. From the front window, I saw state police pour out of two cruisers and run for the barn. The buzz of conversation and clinking silverware quieted in the restaurant as people stared. One trim-looking man with a military-style haircut leapt to his feet, but the woman he was with convinced him to sit again.

Danna stood up straight from the grill and faced me, alarm on her face, a spatula in one hand. She lifted both hands in a *what's going on?* gesture. I'd never gotten a chance to fill her in on the tunnel, the note, or my fears.

Octavia walked in the front door and beckoned to me. I held up my hand. "One second." I turned to the full restaurant, plus the three ladies perusing the cookware section and the four gentlemen standing in a clump waiting for an open table. "Folks, you can relax," I said in a voice that would reach everyone. "The authorities are just acting out of an abundance of caution." I hoped that was the right phrase. "They're checking on a tip we received. You're all fine and safe. Isn't that right, Detective Slade?" I smiled at her, but flared my nostrils and tried to shoot a few daggers from my eyes.

"Exactly right, Ms. Jordan. Ladies and gentlemen, please continue with your meals."

Whew. For a minute I'd thought she was going to ask me to clear the place—which would have definitely been bad for business.

I faced her. "What's up with the sirens and everything?" I kept my voice low, but my tone was challenging.

"Sorry, Robbie," she said softly. "Things got out of control. It's been quiet in here since you called? No noises from upstairs? You stayed down here inside?"

"No noises. We've been super busy and still are. So yes, I've been in here."

"I'm heading to the barn. I'll text you when we need you."

"Wait. I'll give you the note."

She nodded and followed me to the desk, where I'd stashed the plastic bag.

I handed it to her. "I had gloves on when I touched it."

"Good."

"You can go out by the service door." I pointed to the door in the left side of the building beyond the kitchen area and watched her slide out the door.

The *food's ready* bell sounded. Danna looked even more annoyed than before.

I hurried to her side. "I'm really sorry," I murmured. "Found the padlock cut on the barn door and a threatening note inside."

Her eyes went wide.

"Yeah, exactly. Thus the flurry of cops. And I still need to run upstairs and make sure nobody came through the tunnel."

"The tunnel?" Her voice ended on a screechy note.

"Ms. Jordan," a customer called from across the room, waving his hand.

At the same time, Danna swore softly. "Too much going on." She flipped a scorched turkey patty into the trash and started over.

"I'll tell you everything as soon as I can. I promise." I rushed over to one of the many impatient diners.

It was ten minutes before everyone was placated, served, given their checks, or had their orders taken. I caught Danna's eye before heading up the stairs. She nodded in a *go ahead* kind of way.

I knocked on the closed door before opening it. "It's Robbie," I called into the space. I definitely didn't want to startle Buck and Wanda if they still had their guns out.

Buck motioned me in from where he stood in front of my table saw. Wanda peered out a back window toward the barn.

"Had it been moved?" I asked.

"Nope. Not as far's I can tell, anyhoo." He pointed to the saw, then the door. "No scratches or nothing."

My relief was more welcome than a cool shower on a sticky Midwestern August day.

Chapter 34

Fifteen minutes later, I watched from the barn door with my arms folded across my chest as Octavia directed two state police officers—one to take photographs, the other to dust for fingerprints on all kinds of surfaces. One of her people had slipped the padlock into a paper bag. Danna was once again holding down the fort inside.

The wind from the morning had blown the clouds through and the barn was a lot better lit, even without the officers' portable lights. Above their heads motes danced as if ignoring the much more serious work going on below. The police had checked the snow out front before entering the barn, and my assessment had been pretty much on target—nothing usable out there in terms of identifying the intruder from footprints.

Octavia joined me. She wore her usual sensible blazer. A hot pink blouse glowed like a bougainvillea under her jacket. I'd never seen her wear a bright color before. Bougainvilleas ranked a close second to my favorite California flower, the gardenia.

"We're about ready to investigate the tunnel," she said. "Why don't you show us the entrance and then go back inside the restaurant. How did you find the second egress?"

"I'm tearing out walls up there and I came across the opening. It was hidden by the wallpaper."

She cocked her head, the streaks of silver in her dark cap of hair glinting with sunlight streaming in the open door. "And why are you tearing out walls?"

"I'm renovating so I can add bed-and-breakfast rooms. Since it's winter, I have time to fix up the upstairs."

"I didn't realize you were a carpenter, too. Interesting." Her dark eyes assessed me from behind black-rimmed glasses.

"Do you think someone is actually in the tunnel?" Boy, was I glad I'd been able to offload my worry about the note writer and lock cutter to the professionals.

"Our officers will find out soon enough."

"Did Buck tell you about the scrap of fabric?"

"No, what's that?"

"I had to go back through the tunnel after I showed it to him yesterday because I'd left my keys inside the store. On my way, I noticed a bit of torn fabric on a big splinter in the tunnel wall. I left it in place. Maybe it was torn off the coat of whoever went along there."

"We'll check it out. What color was it? And where in the tunnel did you find the fabric?"

"It's red." I thought back. "I saw it where the tunnel takes a turn. I think there's only one turn. Do you want me to go with the guys?" Not that I wanted to. That was the last place I wanted to be.

Especially if they thought my intruder might be in there. I shivered, despite having thrown on a down jacket before I went outside.

"No, they'll find it, I'm sure." She stepped back, indicating I should enter the barn. "Please."

I headed over to the area where the old furniture was piled. "I pushed this desk back over the trap door." Octavia and I watched as a state police officer pulled the desk away, opened the door, took more pictures, and climbed in. Another officer followed him.

"There's only one way to go, I'm pretty sure," I called down after the second one. "And there's another ladder at the other end, which goes up."

"Got it," drifted up the passageway.

"I'll talk to you in the store after we're done. You don't have anywhere you need to go this afternoon?" Octavia asked.

"Nope. I'll be there." I headed back to the restaurant. Let them find the stalker. It wasn't my puzzle.

"Oh, Robbie?" she called after me. "Might want to get a locksmith over here and put a decent lock on this door."

I waved my assent.

Chapter 35

The restaurant was still full and buzzing with speculation when Octavia pushed in through the service door on the left side of the building. "Show me the way upstairs, please," she said in a brisk tone.

I pointed to the other side of the store. "I'll take you." To Danna, hard at work flipping burgers, I added, "Be right back." I was telling her that a lot lately. I led Octavia to the stairs. Heads turned at nearly every table as I started up.

I could hear footsteps above our heads. Either Wanda, not a woman you'd call light of foot, was pacing, or the officers had made it all the way through.

"Robbie, hang on. I need you to go back down to the restaurant," Octavia said. "Might not be a good place for you up there."

I turned sideways and looked down at her. "Why not?"

"Never know what they might have found in the tunnel." She beckoned to me.

I wrinkled my nose as I descended. I didn't want

to think about what the officers could have come across. I was curious but also reluctant to be presented with any more surprises.

I stood back so she could go up. "The door's unlocked at the top of the stairs." I heard the latch click shut behind her. Did she think they were going to find my murderous intruder cowering at the bottom of a ladder? Or a body in the tunnel? Maybe the murderer had struck again, and cut the padlock to stash the victim in between the barn and the store.

I squared my shoulders at that awful thought. A body in the tunnel? I'd never been one with a vivid imagination. My brain was more of an engineer's, not an artist's. But lately thoughts like that sprang into my mind. I hadn't heard of another death, though. If there'd been one, I'm sure the breakfast or lunch crowd would have informed me about it.

It was time to get back to the work of a chef and business owner, not indulge in wild and scary flights of fancy. I bustled over to a table that needed clearing.

"Miss, what in heck is going on here?" a silver-haired man asked from the next table over. He sat with three other gentlemen, all appearing to be of retirement age, all waiting expectantly for my answer.

"The authorities are just checking something out. It's nothing to worry about." I tried to smile reassuringly. "Can I get anyone some more coffee?"

Footsteps and muffled voices continued above us as I hurried about taking orders, delivering food, clearing tables. I was clearly going to have to do something about sound transmission before I closed in the new rooms up there. I groaned. That meant prying up the floorboards and adding rock wool insulation, maybe even resilient channel, between the floors to deaden the sound, since I hadn't torn out the ceilings of the store and restaurant and insulated from below. The original antique stamped tin added a fabulous look that I loved and that many customers remarked on. Floor work would have to go on my upstairs to-do list.

I picked up three full plates after Danna rang the bell. She glanced with raised eyebrows toward the ceiling.

"I promise I'll tell you after we close," I murmured and hurried off with the food to a table of impatient customers.

Twenty minutes later Octavia clattered down the stairs.

"Here's the detective now," Danna said.

Octavia beckoned to me. "Can you come upstairs, please?"

I stood. "Sure. I assume they got through the tunnel all right?"

"Yes. But there was no scrap of cloth."

Chapter 36

What? I stared at her. "How could they not find it?

She shook her head. "We're going to need you to go through with us and show where you saw it."

"Right now?" I glanced at the clock. "I really can't. Can't you see how crowded it is?" Not to mention that the tunnel was the very last place I wanted to go, ever again. That creepy trapped feeling was closing up my throat again. I tried to swallow it down. "I close at two-thirty. I'll go through then."

She stared at me, then nodded. "All right. But two-thirty sharp."

"Sure." I turned back to my curious customers and the even more curious Danna.

Forty-five minutes later, I followed the last diner to the door, thanked her, and flipped the sign to CLOSED. When I turned, Octavia stood at the bottom of the stairs.

"Ready?" she asked. "Let's get going."

"One second." I took in a deep breath and exhaled the tension and irrational fear, like a meditation teacher had taught me during college. I repeated the breath, doing my best to take in the calm and well-being of the world and let out all that was negative.

"What are you doing?" Octavia asked.

"I have a claustrophobia issue. I'm just trying to stay calm."

Octavia rolled her eyes.

"Back in a few," I called to Danna, who had her arms immersed in the deep sink.

"Got it, my *Capitan*." She gave a mock salute with a hand that dripped sudsy water.

I headed toward Octavia. She trotted up the stairs with me following at a normal human pace. What was the big hurry?

Once on the second floor, I joined the small cluster of officers. Wanda stood, as she often did, with feet slightly apart and arms hanging out from her sides as if she were a muscle-bound male cop instead of a well-padded female officer. Heck, if I were the only all X-chromosomed officer in a department, I might stand like the guys, too.

"Hey, Wanda," I said. "How's it going?"

"Hey yourself, Robbie."

It'd taken Wanda months to understand she could call me Robbie instead of Ms. Jordan. She was older than me, but not by much, and we'd all eaten dinner together at Buck's house more than once in the past. On police business, she seemed to like to keep it official until recently.

I joined the two state police officers conferring with Octavia at the entrance to the tunnel. "You really didn't see the red fabric at the bend in the tunnel?"

"No, ma'am." One officer shook his head.

"Any other surprises down there? No dead bodies, I hope." I started to laugh, but when I saw Octavia's face, I covered it up with a cough. Like that would convince her.

"No surprises, ma'am," the officer said.

"Officer Paul will escort you through the tunnel, Robbie." Octavia motioned sideways toward the small open door as if she were escorting me to my seat at the symphony. "He has a light."

I scooted into the hole after the younger of the state police officers. Stepping onto the ground at the bottom of the ladder, I did another breathe-in-and-out routine of the damp musty air until I was calm enough to follow him. Paul was already a yard ahead.

"Hang on there, Paul. I'm a few steps behind you and can't see too well back here."

His light paused and waited. "Name's John, ma'am."

Huh? "I thought Octavia said your name was Paul."

He chuckled. "I'm the guy with two first names. John Paul. Like a pope."

I laughed, too. "Now I get it." I would never remember which was first and which last, unless I treated his name as if it was a word to remember for a crossword. Like pope names. Not that I expected to be spending much time with him in the future.

"Tell me where do you think you saw that piece of fabric?"

"I didn't *think* I saw it. I actually saw it. Where the tunnel bends. Up a bit farther." We made our way through the low, dark, dank passageway. Even though it was my third time through, the tunnel seemed lower, darker, and danker than before. What had the officers found that they didn't want to tell me?

His flashlight rounded the corner and stopped. "Here?" he asked.

"Yes. Can I use that?" After he handed me the light, I ran it up and down the wall on my left until I found what I was looking for. "See, there's the big splinter thing." I trained the light on the jagged spike of wood, which pointed back the way we'd come. Sure enough, the scrap was gone. I leaned way in. "I think there is a thread left on it. Can you see? It's a red thread." I handed him the light. *Whew.* At least I hadn't imagined it.

"Good eye, ma'am."

I smiled to myself in the darkness.

"Mind holding the light for me?" He handed me the flashlight, pulled out a small camera, and took pictures of the splinter.

"The splinter thing is horizontal and pointing toward the front entrance," I said. "That would mean whoever snagged their clothing was leaving."

"Nice deduction, Sherlock." His voice was respectful and verged on admiring, despite the words themselves sounding a bit sarcastic. He placed his hands, gloved in blue latex, on the base of the splinter and pulled against the grain. The wood broke off with a satisfying crack. He yanked a bag out of his back pocket and slid in the overgrown splinter.

"The fact that the cloth is gone must mean whoever cut the padlock came through here, found the scrap of material, and removed it." I looked at him, but since I didn't want to shine the flashlight in his face, I couldn't see his expression.

"Sounds like a plausible scenario."

"Did you find anything else when you guys came through here?" I asked. Maybe this friendly young guy would tell me what Detective Follow-the-Rules Slade wouldn't.

"Sorry, ma'am. Not at liberty to say."

Chapter 37

After Paul—no, John—after Pope Guy and I had come up from the tunnel, Octavia had asked me to wait for her downstairs. I counted the till and carried the majority of it back to the safe in my office. While Danna cleaned pots, humming to whatever flowed from her phone to her earbuds, I wiped down all the tables and set them up for the morning. Then I put away the clean pots as Danna vacuumed under the tables.

I waved at her until she switched off the machine and drew out her ear buds. "I think we're good here, Danna, when you're done with that. But before you go, any ideas about specials for tomorrow?"

"I don't know, but that Italian soup was really popular. There's only a couple bowls left."

"Did you get any?"

She shook her head.

"Take it home, then. No suggestions for breakfast specials or lunch?"

She wrinkled her nose. "How about apple fritters? Or maybe turnovers?"

"Both pretty labor intensive. We do have the deep fryer, though. And I'll bet people will love fritters," I said. "Sure, why not? How about for lunch?"

"We haven't offered salmon burgers for a while."

"Have to special order that. I'll put salmon on the order for the weekend. Good thought."

"So what are the detective and the other officers doing upstairs?" she asked, lowering her voice.

"I haven't gotten a chance to tell you." When I'd come in from finding the cut padlock, Danna had already been running herself ragged with a lunch party of eight, a book club celebrating the sixtieth birthday of one of their members. We'd been on the go ever since. "Sit down and I'll fill you in." I gestured to the easy chair near my desk and grabbed the office chair for myself.

I told her all about finding the tunnel, and then the cut padlock and note this morning when I'd gone out with Buck.

"That's creepy. And scary." She gazed at me. "You seem pretty calm."

"I'm not that calm." I held out my still shaky hand, then folded my hands in my lap. "The police wanted to explore the tunnel, especially now that I found that note. The last time I went through I saw a scrap of cloth on a rough edge of wood, and they're going to collect that, too."

Danna tucked her long legs up under her. "It's like a Nancy Drew book, isn't it? *The Secret of the Hidden Tunnel*," she said in a deep dramatic voice.

"I've thought the same thing more than once. So you read those books, too?"

She laughed. "Mom owns a collection of vintage ones, from like the fifties. Way cool."

"Agree. When I was ten I found a few from the forties. Too bad this isn't a nice two-hundred page book where the girl sleuth makes everything come out all right in the end. I keep thinking about who wrote that threat, and why. Have I been asking too many questions about the murder? I don't think I have."

"Who have you talked to about Mr. Stilton's death?"

I reached behind me and grabbed a pad of paper and a pencil off the desk. "Lou, of course. And Zen Brown. But neither of those were in public." I jotted their names down, anyway. "I visited Jo Schultz at her house. I stopped in to see Georgia at the library and Maude showed up. Then last night I took soup over to Maude and Ron." I wrote down *Jo, Georgia, Maude, and Ron.*

Danna pulled her mouth to the side. "I can't see any of those people killing Professor Stilton."

"You never know, Danna. I've been talking to Abe, too, but he sure didn't write that note. If he did, we're in big trouble."

"I'll say. And there's been talk here in the restaurant, too," Danna said.

"Can't stop that." I tapped the pencil on the paper. "Maybe a local here in town killed Charles. Nobody has much good to say about the poor man. Or maybe there's a professor or a student at the university who hated him. I should touch base with Lou and Zen again, anyway. I'll ask them, even though Octavia should have done that already."

Chapter 38

It was four before Octavia came back into the restaurant to interview me. I didn't mind. I had bookkeeping to catch up on, orders to put in for later in the week, prep to do for tomorrow. I'd called a couple of locksmiths in the afternoon, but nobody had picked up, and Abe hadn't either. All I could do was leave messages about needing a good lock on an outbuilding. My barn was still unsecured, but the biscuit dough was in the cooler, I'd wrapped fifty sets of silverware in blue napkins, and I'd prepped the dry ingredients for fritters by the time Octavia returned.

We sat across from each other at one of the tables. One of the festive strings of tiny white lights I'd left up after the holidays created an incongruous illusion sitting on Octavia's head like a crown, even though it was several yards behind her on the wall.

"Get you a cup of coffee?" I offered.

"No, thanks." Her cell rang and she excused

herself, turning away after checking the display to answer it. Her voice was softer than the tone she usually used. She must be talking with Jim.

I heard her say something about "later" and "me, too."

When she disconnected and turned back to me, pink tinged her cheeks. I was surprised by how this conversation didn't bother me. *Good.* I must be over Jim deserting me for her.

She drew out a small notebook and a pen, but before she could speak, I said, "How was the murder investigation going before this popped up?"

"To be frank, more slowly than I'd like."

Wow. She was finally sharing something about the case. I hadn't expected her to answer me. "Any real suspects? I mean, besides Lou Perlman, who never would have killed Charles." I knew the question was a long shot, but what the heck.

She cleared her throat. "Let's get started."

A long shot going nowhere, apparently.

"First, thank you for finding that thread," she said. "I hope it proves useful. Any idea where the cloth came from?"

"No, not at all."

"Have you been away from the property since you put the padlock on the barn door?" She observed me, her pen poised above the paper.

"I secured the door yesterday morning. Before noon, I think. But yes, I was out yesterday afternoon, then back, then out again last evening."

"Give me as close to the exact times and locations as you can."

"Let's say I was out from one to three—"

"Where?"

"I went to the library and then walked around town for a while."

Octavia cocked her head as if she didn't quite believe me, but she didn't comment on what I'd said. I didn't think she needed to know about my conversation with Georgia. Or maybe I should tell her.

"Please go on." She made a rolling motion with her hand.

"Then at about five I took soup and biscuits to Maude and Ron."

"Stilton?" Octavia's eyebrows went up. "You're personal friends of theirs?"

"Not really. I simply thought it would be a nice gesture. As it turns out, Maude really appreciated it. She said no one else in town had even stopped by." Which was pretty sad for a person who grew up in South Lick. Right in my building, in fact.

"What time did you get home?" Octavia asked.

"I went from the Stiltons' to Abe O'Neill's house for dinner. I got home around ten."

"Long dinner," she murmured as she jotted down the information.

I kept my mouth shut. I didn't give a flying flamingo what she thought about the length of my dinner.

"You didn't check the padlock when you got home?" she asked.

"No. It was late and I was tired. I usually park in the barn, but last night I left the van in the driveway. I didn't see that the padlock had been cut, if it even was by then. Maybe they did it during the night."

She sighed. "I'm going to need to have my guys check out where everyone of interest was during each of those times."

Cool. She was talking about the case again.

Octavia checked her notebook. "One to three, five to ten, and overnight, of course. Is that right?"

"Yes. Does everybody include Georgia LaRue?"

"I can't tell you that, Robbie. You must realize the way we do investigations by now—we don't leak information to civilians. Especially not to people involved in the case, which you are."

"Just in case, I'll save you some time. When I was at the library and walking around town yesterday, I spoke with Georgia at the gazebo for half an hour. She was on lunch break and we walked back to the library together. She couldn't have gotten over here, left a screwy note, and cut a padlock during that time."

"All right, duly noted." Octavia looked straight at me. "And no one that you know of was here when you were out?"

"Nobody I invited."

Chapter 39

I parked a few blocks away from the sprawling Indiana University campus right before five and began my trek to Lou's building. I hadn't talked with her in a couple of days. Besides wanting to know how she was doing, I thought I could pick her brain about who else on campus was at odds with Charles. Being warned off the case by the note in my barn had produced entirely the opposite effect. I was determined to figure out the puzzle of who killed Charles—so I could feel safe again.

After I'd called and asked if we could meet, Lou told me to come onto campus and join the departmental Hump Day Happy Hour and then we could go out for a bite to eat. She'd said they gathered for a happy hour on the weeks they didn't have the Friday night dinner. I'd switched on all the outdoor lights before I left and kept the inside of the store lit up, as well as my apartment. I'd also made sure the door to the passageway on the second floor was blocked by all kinds of heavy stuff. What else could

I do? I didn't have a remote camera, although that might be a good thing to set up.

Since I didn't want to arrive at the happy hour too early, I wandered up a slope past Maxwell Hall with its Romanesque peaked turrets, around the little gazebo-type structure that was the Rose Well House at the edge of Dunn Woods, and wove between Kirkwood and Lindley Halls. It was the oldest part of the campus, with buildings named for the founders. Mostly built of rusticated limestone, or so Lou had told me, they featured tall windows and lots of steeply peaked roofs. Maybe *rusticated* meant bumpy, because the stones were irregular, not smooth blocks.

As I walked, I thought about what Buck had said while he read the paper. A suicide from thirty years ago that might be a murder? That was interesting. Maybe they'd done a DNA analysis, the kind of thing that wasn't available back then. I'd have to check online when I got home, see if I could learn anything more about it.

I skirted the chemistry building before arriving at Ballantine Hall. Not a picturesque, graceful, nineteenth-century trustee of the campus, it was a huge unattractive set of stone building blocks that looked like something out of the former Soviet Union. The shadows stretched long, and the breeze was brisk, especially in the wind tunnel next to the ten-story building. I found my way up to the seventh floor and to an open door down the hall from which laughter and conversation spilled out. I wasn't quite sure why I'd agreed to Lou's plan. Did I really want to schmooze with a bunch of sociology scholars I'd never met, or that I'd only seen at the Friday dinners? I peered in. Maybe Lou would already be ready to leave. I wasn't exactly an introvert and I usually enjoyed parties, but it'd been a long day.

"Robbie, there you are," she called out from across the all-purpose room, which looked like it might usually host seminars or other meetings since it held long tables and regular chairs, not desks. "Come on in." Her voice carried above the hum.

Heads turned and the conversation quieted.

Great. I pasted on a smile and gave a little wave. Lou pushed toward me through clusters of several dozen men and women from age twenty to seventy. Most held either a bottle of beer or a plastic cup of wine, although I saw a half-empty gallon of cider on a table by the door. Dress was academic casual— sweaters, tweed jackets, a couple red-and-white IU sweatshirts, the occasional skirt and leather boots, plenty of denim.

I was glad I'd changed into my own version—a fuchsia tunic-length sweater with skinny jeans and my low boots. A table near the door was piled high with coats, so I added my own to the collection.

After Lou hugged me, she said, "Wine?" and gestured toward the boxes of red and white next to the cider.

"Sure, why not? Red, I think."

She handed me a cup of red. "And eats, too." Another table held a platter of cheese interspersed with veggie nibbles. A basket of crackers and stacks of small plates and napkins sat nearby. Suddenly famished, I loaded up a plate with cheese and crackers.

"You know Tom." Lou gestured toward her friend. "Let me introduce you to a couple more people."

Five of us had been chatting for several minutes,

me mostly eating instead of talking, when the name *Charles* floated out of a conversation nearby. I glanced at Lou, whose shoulders sagged. The fellow grad students we'd been talking with reacted, too. One shook her head as if in sorrow, and another pursed his lips.

"It's a real shame," Tom said. "Stilton was brilliant."

Lou opened her mouth and then shut it again. I didn't blame her. Brilliance didn't excuse bad behavior, and speaking ill of the dead was in equally poor taste.

I spied Zen across the room talking to an older man. "Excuse me," I said to Lou. "I want to say hi to Zen." I set down my plate on a chair under the window and approached Zen.

"Robbie," she said in a surprised tone. "What are you doing here?"

"Lou and I are going out for dinner, and she told me to come by here first. Hope you don't mind."

Zen laughed. "It's good to have fresh blood around here. Especially a non-academic."

After the guy she'd been talking to excused himself, I said, "How are you?"

She stopped smiling. "You mean, are the police still harassing me about the murder? Sort of. It's a real pain."

"That isn't quite what I meant. But what do you mean, *harassing?*"

"Trying to get me to say where I was that night and morning." She turned to look out the window next to her.

I looked, too, at the campus spread out in front of us. With no leaves on the trees the view from the seventh floor went on and on with points of lights in all directions piercing the dusk. I turned back to her. "Is there anybody else on campus who would have gone so far as to kill Charles?" I kept my voice low enough so no one around us would hear, but the background buzz took care of that, anyway.

Her gaze traveled around the room. "Nobody and everybody. The guy was a jerk. Sure, if you dug deep, a shrink would probably say he was unhappy with his own academic standing. Who knows, maybe with his physical stature, too. No matter the reason, he took it out on others. But kill him for it?" She focused on me. "Would you kill someone simply because they were unpleasant and mean?"

"Of course not."

"Me neither. Same goes for most human beings, right?"

"I believe so." I took a sip of wine.

A woman in a jacket so professorial it even bore leather elbow patches beckoned to Zen.

"My two cents?" Zen stared at me. "I think the police should quit trying to involve Lou and me. They need to look closer to home."

Chapter 40

"Ready to get out of here?" Lou asked a few minutes later.

I'd given up on socializing and was examining the view, which really was stunning. "Sure." We headed to the coats table.

Zen was slipping hers on when we got there. "I'll walk out with you guys." She zipped up a red hip-length coat in a puffy down and pulled on a red-and-white fleece hat.

We filed into the elevator a moment later, with me following Zen. I laughed. "Nice repair job." I pointed to the back of her coat sleeve, across which was plastered a piece of gray duct tape.

Zen shook her head. "Got too close to the wood-stove. Fabric like this just melts." The floors dinged by until we landed at G with a bump.

Had the fabric melted? The thread I'd found was red and pretty close to the shade of her jacket. Surely, she wasn't my intruder, the author of my threatening note. Or was she? I wanted to shake off the dark cloud that seemed to surround my view of the petite marathoner, but it wasn't that easy.

We made our way out of the building and back into the wind tunnel, which felt even colder after being in the overheated building. Lou unlocked her around-town bicycle from the rack. I tugged on my fleece beret, but kept my eyes on Zen as she talked with Lou. If it was her, why would she have talked about Charles's killer like she had? That answer was easy—to throw me off the track.

Lou laughed. "I thought that meeting would never end."

Zen glanced at me. "We were both in an interminable School of Social Sciences meeting yesterday. Went from noon to almost six."

From noon to six. That cleared Zen for the earlier hours in the day, but what about the evening? She still could have come by, cut the padlock, and left the note.

"Good thing those meetings are only once a year," Lou said.

Zen nodded. "I'm heading home. See you." She turned and walked with a brisk step, disappearing around the side of the building.

I watched her go. *Huh.*

"Earth to Robbie?" Lou said, jostling my arm. "Where should we go? Bears, Nick's, somewhere else?"

"Sorry." I smiled at her. "I read about a brewpub called Function Brewing. It's up on Sixth. Want to try that?"

"Let's do it."

We walked briskly back the way I'd come onto campus. Lou, rolling her bike beside her, told me about working with Zen as her adviser. "She's pretty cool. I think it's going to go so much better than trying to work with Charles. Not that that's a possibility anymore, anyway."

"I'll bet she'll be a lot better than Charles." If she wasn't arrested for murder, I didn't add.

A clutch of students walked toward us, mostly clad in pajama bottoms, red IU hoodies, and Uggs, all but one staring at her phone. At the last moment they veered around us to the right. Cell phone radar, maybe?

"So who was Maxwell, anyway?" I asked as we passed that building on our right.

"Father of the university, they say. He got the state legislature to approve buying land to start a state seminary back before the Civil War. The seminary turned into the university."

"Nice. I wonder if any of his ancestors still come here to study. Maybe they get a free apartment in Maxwell Hall."

"Ha. I doubt it," Lou said. "I heard there was a Maxwell grad student in linguistics, but that was a while ago. So what did you and Zen talk about?"

"She says the police are still harassing her about the murder. She stopped by the store yesterday and said she can't tell them where she was that night and the next morning. What's up with that?"

"Maybe she was with a lover. Maybe a female lover. And doesn't want her cover blown."

"I suppose," I said as we waited to cross busy Indiana Avenue. "Is Octavia still calling you?"

"She didn't yesterday. I guess that's an improvement. Anyway, now she has to go through my lawyer."

"I also asked Zen who else on campus, even in your department, might have killed Charles. Or at least disliked him enough to think of killing him."

"Like all of us? Robbie, you can't follow up on everybody who disliked Charles. That's what the cops are for. Right?"

"I know. But get this." I told her about discovering the tunnel, and then finding the cut padlock and the note. "It's pretty creepy. I found a scrap of cloth in the passageway, too."

She stopped short in front of Nick's English Pub and turned toward me. "That's scary."

"Dude." A burly male student and his friends nearly bumped into us as they stepped, reeking of beer, out of the pub. "Gotta share the sidewalk, y'know."

"Sorry." I pulled Lou to the curb and out of their way. "Yes, it's totally scary. But it made me even more determined to figure this thing out." We started walking again.

"I get that. But you have to be careful. Like, really careful. Did you get a new lock yet?"

"No. I was supposed to, but I couldn't get hold of any locksmiths. Octavia said they'd send officers around to patrol every hour."

"Yeah. And the bad guy comes on the half hour. That's stupid. You should spend the night with me."

"Thanks, but I can't. I have to cook in the morning." I supposed I could call Abe. No, that would be way too wimpy. "I'll be fine. Listen, I'll park my van in front of the barn door, and I'll leave all the outside lights on until daybreak."

"You know what you should do?" Lou flashed a wicked grin. "Stretch razor wire across the drive. At knee level and at throat level." She made a slicing noise across her throat. "They'll never know what hit them."

Chapter 41

Man, was I glad I'd left all the lights on, inside and out. When I drove up after eight, it was way dark. I did what I'd promised Lou I would—I pulled up in front of the barn door and parallel parked, getting the passenger side as close to the door as I could. I'd stuck another padlock on there before I left, but it wasn't any bigger than the previous one. Whoever wanted to get in would, if they were determined to. At least parking so close would make it somewhat harder. I definitely needed a decent lock, though. So far, not a single locksmith had returned my calls.

I locked the van and turned toward my apartment, sizing up the dozen yards to the back door. A cold breeze picked up and rattled the branches of the oaks, the walnuts, and the maples, setting the few remaining leaves to chattering. I cocked my head. That was only wind in leaves, wasn't it? Was there another sound? My skin prickled, my feet instantly rooted in cement. My back was to the van, the big, heavy, metal van, but crossing the open space to my apartment would expose me.

I breathed in and out, telling myself I lived in a normally safe town. That my intruder so far had managed to stay hidden and must want to remain that way. That the police were driving by regularly tonight. That the noise this morning had been only a squirrel. That—.

"Ahem." Behind me someone cleared their throat.

I screeched as I whirled.

"Relax, Robbie." Wanda held up both hands. "Just checking out the back of the property." The flashlight she held aimed a narrow beacon at the sky.

"Geez, Wanda. You scared me. I didn't see your cruiser."

"Detective Slade said to keep an eye on y'all. So that's what I'm doing. Cruiser's around the other side."

I waited a moment until my heart stopped exploding out of my neck. "Thanks, then. You surprised me."

She snorted. "I guess. Hey, nice move parking the van like that. Gonna make it a lot harder for the bad guy to get near the barn door."

"I hope I got close enough so whoever it is would have to be really skinny to fit in there."

"Or they'd have to climb up on top of the van and hang down over." She snickered.

A giggle bubbled out of me, one of those post-adrenaline-rush kind of laughs. The image of a murderer going through contortions to get to the padlock and leaving his—or her—rear end in the air was vastly entertaining. Plus I'd never heard Wanda laugh before.

She'd put on a real tough cop act last fall, and I didn't really blame her for flashing a dose of bravado. But for the moment, we were just two adult girls dissolving into unstoppable laughter.

"He might slip and get stuck upside down," I said between chortles.

"Like a yoga pose, right? Downward facing thief?" She covered her mouth, but another snort came out and we were off again.

"Whew." I wiped my eyes when the laughing seemed to ebb. "Thank you for watching out for me tonight. Trying to get a locksmith today was a total fail."

She played the light over the door to my apartment at the back of the building. "Here, let me make sure you get in okay." She was all business again.

Or all caring. Maybe that was what being a public safety officer was all about. Caring enough about the public to keep them safe, or try to, anyway.

We walked together across to the small patio outside my door. The porch light lit up the now-withered orangey-red bittersweet berries I'd stuck in pot of evergreen boughs before Christmas. The pot sat under the porch roof and I'd kept the snow brushed off the arrangement because it looked so cheery.

I unlocked the door and turned. "I'm good now. Thanks again, Wanda." Should I ask her to come upstairs and make sure door to the passageway hadn't been disturbed? No. I'd be fine. I could check on my own.

"All in the line of duty."

"You stay warm tonight." I waved as she headed around toward the front. I shut the door and flipped the dead bolt, its clunk warming my itty-bitty heart. After the vandalism last November, I'd made sure I was safe in the store and my apartment. They boasted decent locks. I hadn't thought I'd need to secure the barn, too, never suspecting the two buildings were connected.

Birdy ran to my ankles, mewed, and ran back into the kitchen. Ah, yes, dinner time for kitty cats. I switched on the lamp and dished up his treat, then hurried upstairs. It all looked secure and undisturbed, but I left a light on upstairs to make it look occupied. Just in case.

After I made it back down and sat at the kitchen table, Birdy jumped into my lap, chirping as I stroked him. The glowing wood of the table Mom had made was a comforting sight and the kitchen smelled faintly of coffee, cinnamon, and the remnants of Birdy's chicken-in-gravy Fancy Feast.

I stroked the table with my other hand. "Mom, I'll bet you never ran into a murderer when you lived here." She'd grown up in South Lick, but had adopted Santa Barbara as her new hometown when she was in her early twenties—and pregnant with me. "What would you do, faced with a threatening note?"

The ringing of my phone interrupted my communing with Mom's spirit, even though it wasn't really that. Merely my wishing she were still alive to share parts of my life.

"Sorry I missed your call earlier, Robbie," Abe began.

"That's okay."

"You wanted a locksmith? I thought you got all new locks last fall."

"I did. This is for the barn. Remember I told you about the tunnel? Well, somebody cut the padlock I'd put on the barn door, and they left a note in the barn threatening me."

"No! Really?"

"Apparently it was from Charles's killer." I relayed the wording of the threat. "It was pretty freaky. Octavia and her team came over in the afternoon and checked stuff out."

"Good."

I told him about having seen the scrap of cloth and then it being gone later. "But we found a thread still down there, so they took it as evidence. Took the whole piece of wood it was stuck on."

"Robbie, that means the killer has been in your tunnel, in your store, your building. That it wasn't a random burglar. Are you all right?"

I could hear his concern. "I'm fine." I tried to keep my tone reassuring.

"I wish I could come over, but Sean is here for the night."

"That's right, you have him every Wednesday. Don't worry about me. The police are patrolling, and I just ran into Wanda checking out the perimeter on foot."

"But the barn is unlocked. Whoever it was could get back in. Get to you."

I described how I'd left the van. "I'll be okay." At least I hoped so.

His voice turned husky. "I don't know what I'd do if something happened to you."

"Same here, Abe." I laughed. "I mean, I feel the same way about you. But don't worry."

"I'll try not to. And this might help." He gave me the names and numbers of two locksmiths in the area, which I jotted down.

"I have a proposition for you," he said, his voice smiling.

"Sounds racy." I smiled back, even though it was only at the phone.

"Friday happens to be my birthday."

"Oh! How did I not know that?" Maybe I'd never asked him.

"My parents have a getaway cabin in the woods and it's really special to me. I want to celebrate there. With you. Only for one night. We'll get you home in time for the morning rush, don't worry. How about it?"

A secluded getaway with Abe? No brainer, even though it would guarantee I'd be dragging on Saturday. Thank goodness it was the off week for the department dinner. And I could try out that new, very short, very lacy red silk number I'd ordered. The type of birthday present I knew he'd appreciate. "Tell me what time. I'll be ready."

Chapter 42

I left messages with both locksmiths before I went to bed. Disturbing dreams haunted my sleep, though—windows breaking, something being dragged, dark figures lurking outside.

Before starting work the next morning, I checked the barn door, but nothing looked disturbed. As I worked on breakfast, I alternated between replaying that feeling of dread when I'd heard the rustling in the dark and new giggles bubbling up at the thought of a bad guy getting stuck upside down between the van and the barn.

It was barely past six and I was already dragging. I hoped I didn't break anything.

Danna pushed through the door promptly at six-thirty. Some mornings she stumbled in yawning as if she'd been up until the wee hours. Today, she almost bounced over to where we kept the clean aprons. She pulled one over her dreads tied back with a dark red scarf, and tied the apron around a black striped bowling shirt that resembled referee garb.

"Got a good night's sleep?" I asked.

"You bet. So we're doing fritters today. What else?" She whistled as she washed her hands. "How about a couple dozen quick bacon-cheddar scones?"

"Sure, if you can pull them off. I already have bacon started on low and we have plenty of cheese." Where was she getting the energy? I personally was not feeling so bouncy.

"We got any chives?" she asked.

"Only outside under the snow."

"No probs. We can do without."

After we worked in silence for a few minutes, she glanced over at me. "Any more scary notes?"

"No, thank goodness."

"I got your back, Robbie, you know?"

Danna was a good person to have on my side. She was fit from playing on a volleyball team, and she was a lot taller than me.

"I know, and I appreciate that. I didn't have a particularly restful night, though, so I'm glad you're perky today. One of us has to be." I finished mixing up the first batch of pancake batter, then added the wet ingredients to the fritter batter. "That threatening note makes me want to get this case solved."

"For sure."

"You said you went to school with Ron. Is there one of his friends you might be able to talk to? I'm curious about where Ron was the night his dad was killed."

"Ew. You think he might have murdered his own father? Like in Oedipus?" She looked horrified.

"I doubt it, but you never know. His mom said he was ice fishing that morning. So he was on the lake.

If she was telling the truth." I laid a row of sausages at the edge of the grill to warm.

"Why wouldn't she?" Danna tilted her head.

"Ron's her only child." I glanced at the clock. It was almost seven, time to unlock the door and turn the sign to OPEN. "What if he did it and she's covering up for him?"

"Gah. But, yeah, one of his friends is kind of more normal than the others. Me and Jacob used to be in drama together. I'll let you know what he says." She laughed. "If I offer to bring him scones and fritters, he'll be all over it."

"Would that be the sort of soft-looking guy Ron came in with yesterday?"

"Exactly. He's not big on exercise, if you know what I mean. Except with his thumbs." She shook her head. "I don't get gamers at all. I know a few girls who are into it, but mostly it's guys. Sit around all day twiddling your thumbs killing people on screen or trying to scale a tower or whatever? Not for me."

"Thanks for agreeing to talk to him, but be careful, right? Talk to him in a public place. I'd hate for you to be in danger." I switched on the deep fryer and pictured the unlocked barn again. "I need to get a new lock for the barn today. I put in calls to a couple locksmiths last night, but the ones I called yesterday never got back to me, so I'm not hopeful."

"Mom's cousin over in Nashville is a locksmith. I'll text her and get his number after I get these in the oven." Danna rolled out the scone dough, deftly sliced it into triangles, and slid them onto a baking sheet. "She'll make sure he helps you out."

"Great. It'll be a huge relief to get the barn secured. How's your mom, anyway?" I hadn't seen the mayor in a few weeks.

"She's had super bad allergies this winter, so she's always sneezing and wheezing. And there's a new guy she's hanging with." Danna snorted. "He's too smooth for me, like bordering on smarmy. But hey, I don't have to date him, right?"

Chapter 43

Murderer or no murderer, threatening note or no threatening note, the fine residents of South Lick still wanted breakfast. Once again the place was hopping. *Good.* Maybe I'd make it through until spring after all. If there weren't any more intruders. Any more violent deaths.

Octavia pushed through the door at around eight-thirty. I gave her a wave from the cash register, then finished my transaction with a woman paying for her takeout order of biscuits and coffee. Octavia stood in the waiting area working on her phone.

"There's a small table over by the wall," I said, approaching her. "Did you want to eat?"

She glanced up. "Thanks," she said, but she seemed distracted. Little lines formed above her top lip and her mouth pulled a bit to the side, like she was chewing on the inside of her cheek.

I followed her to the table, giving it one more swipe with a cloth before setting down a clean place-mat. "Coffee?" I handed her a menu.

"Please."

When I brought back the pot, I asked, "Know what you want?"

"To find the bad guy." She grimaced as her shoulders sagged, not her usual posture, and dark smudges under her eyes made it look like she hadn't been getting much rest lately. "Sorry. You meant breakfast."

"Case isn't going so well, I gather."

"No, it isn't. Too many persons of interest, not enough evidence, too many lies. Or at least one big lie."

"You mean from the murderer?"

"Exactly. Hey, everything all quiet overnight?" she asked. "I know Wanda and a few others kept a pretty close watch on the place."

"I know. Yes, nothing went on. And I, um, sort of blocked the barn door with my van. Still haven't gotten a locksmith to call me back."

"I'll see if we have any names on file. Sorry, should have thought of that yesterday." Octavia surveyed the room. "You haven't seen Ron Stilton in here lately, have you?"

"He was in for breakfast yesterday with a few friends."

"I can't seem to locate him. If he happens to come in again, will you text me or Buck? Or call the station."

"Is he a suspect?"

She looked over her black-rimmed glasses at me.

"Okay, I know. You can't talk about it." I really should tell her what Georgia said. "So, speaking of persons of interest, I was out Tuesday afternoon, like I told you. I went to see Georgia La Rue."

"So you said. And?" Octavia's dark brows came together.

"I just wanted to say that I'm sure she wouldn't kill Charles. Has Maude told you she thinks Georgia did?" I stared at Octavia, but she didn't respond. "Anyway, Georgia told me she was home that night and morning when Charles was killed. The problem is her husband can't vouch for her. He has dementia." I was rambling.

"Robbie, we already know all this. Do you have anything new to offer?" She tapped her sensibly trimmed fingernail on the table.

What had Georgia said? *If I was going to kill someone, it would be Maude herself.* "No, nothing new."

After Octavia ordered a vegetable omelet with dry wheat toast, I took the order slip over to Danna. "She's looking for Ron," I murmured.

"The detective is?" Danna whispered, her focus shifting in Octavia's direction.

"None other. But she won't tell me a thing."

"Of course not. Ron had better watch out. I get the impression that detective gets what she wants."

"You can say that again."

Chapter 44

The rush had kept up right through lunch. I'd been too busy to think, almost. And because I hadn't expected such a crowd, we kept running out of menu items—turkey burgers, coleslaw, our special local root beer—even though I'd just placed an order a couple of days ago. Or maybe it was because I'd been too distracted with everything else to remember to keep up with supplies. It was not like me. The murder and the invasion of my property was throwing me off more than I'd realized.

I rolled my eyes at Danna after one more disgruntled customer complained that the item she wanted wasn't available.

"I'm going to have to do some serious ordering this afternoon." I checked the wall clock. One-thirty and at last several tables were empty. "Why don't you take a break? Looks like things are easing up."

She tore off her apron with a look of relief and made a beeline to the restroom. We'd barely had time to do even that since seven this morning. I flipped a couple of hamburgers and dished up a cup of chicken soup. The next time the cowbell jangled, I looked over to see Georgia stomp in. When she spied me, she hurried over to the kitchen area.

"Georgia, how—" I stopped speaking when her condition registered. Her hair, usually neat, was all flyaway and her eyes looked like she'd been crying. "What's wrong?"

"Can you help me? They said they have to talk to Orville. To my demented husband! It's absurd. He looks like the lights are on but there's nobody home upstairs."

"You told them of his condition, I assume. Can they even do that, ask to interview him?"

"I have no idea. They said maybe he'd have a glimmer of memory about that night."

"The night Charles was killed." Even if Orville was able to say Georgia was home, I wondered if it would hold up in court. And what if he said she was away, but it was a delusion?

She nodded with a frantic movement. "They came over to the library, interrupted my shift." She turned away and paced a few steps, then turned back. "I don't know what to do."

I sniffed. "Hang on a second." The burgers were nearly overcooked. I slid them onto their plates, told Georgia to sit down, and delivered the order. I gave another party their check and cleared a vacated table. It was more like five minutes before I got back to Georgia.

She'd sat, but one knee was jiggling up and down like she was keeping time to really fast music.

"Try to calm down," I said, sitting across from her. "First, do you have a lawyer?"

"That's what Donnie said, too. That I needed a lawyer."

"He's right. You do."

"But that's expensive. Orville's care already costs so much. Anyway, I didn't do anything wrong, and Orville sure as heck didn't. What can the police do to us?" She shook her head. "The one thing they can do is upset Orville by asking him questions. He doesn't do very well with a change in his routine."

I thought for a moment. A customer caught my eye and waved. I held up my index finger, signaling *just a minute*, and stood as I said, "Let me ask my friend at the university. Maybe there's a pro-bono law firm that could help you. Like legal aid or something." Or I could ask Jim. He was a real-estate lawyer but probably knew somebody who offered those services.

"Maybe." She stood, too. "I'm sorry to bother you, Robbie. I can see you're busy."

I'd never heard that note of resignation in her voice before. "It's okay. The rush seems to finally be over."

"You're so smart, I thought of you first. Some of the people in this town"—she raised her eyebrows—"well, they're not exactly rocket scientists."

"Neither am I." I patted her arm. "If I get the name of anyone, I'll let you know. When did the detective say she wanted to question him?"

Georgia checked her watch. "At three. I'd better get home. I told the library I wasn't coming back today and they weren't happy about it. If I lose that job, I don't know what I'll do."

"You won't. I'll call Lou right now."

"Thanks, Robbie. You're a peach."

I watched her pull open the heavy antique door before heading to my customer. That was nice, if she thought I was a peach. But I'd be a piece of rotten fruit if I didn't figure out the killer soon. All these innocent people—Lou, Georgia, Zen—being harassed, and I'd been threatened.

Where was the guilty one?

Chapter 45

When my phone rang an hour after we closed, I assumed it was Lou returning my call, but it was Zen on the line.

I greeted her. "What's up?"

"I think I told you I'm in training for a marathon, but now I've decided to do a triathlon, too, which means riding a bike. Not my strong suit. Would you have time to stop by and take a look at my bike?"

I laughed. "And biking is mine, but running sure isn't."

"It's a long course triathlon, which means a half-marathon distance run and a one-point-two-mile swim. Those I'm fine with. The fifty-six mile cycling route? Yikes."

"That's a lot."

"I wanted to really push myself."

"I guess." More pushing than I was interested in, but, hey, to each her own.

She groaned. "Might have been a mistake. Anyway, I want to see if you think the cycle I have would be good for the job or if I need to get another one."

"Happy to. I've done my ordering and there's a locksmith working on the barn right now. I think he won't be here much longer, though."

One of Abe's locksmiths had finally gotten back to me and had showed up exactly when he said he would.

"How about at four-thirty?" So much for spending the afternoon in demolition mode, which I needed to get back to. If talking to Zen about bikes could lead to a casual inquiry about her alibi, it would be worth postponing renovation work.

"Four-thirty it is. It shouldn't take you more than fifteen minutes to get here." She gave me directions before she hung up.

At four forty-five, with a shiny new key on my key ring, I pulled up to her brown split-level house at the end of a long driveway. I could barely see the neighboring houses through the woods on either side. She must really like her privacy.

I experienced a quick pang of anxiety. Octavia thought Zen was a person of interest in the murder. What if she'd in fact killed Charles? I'd seen that patch on her red jacket. Could she be my intruder? I didn't think so, but I'd sure been wrong before. And here I was walking into her house isolated from neighbors, nobody knowing where I was.

I pulled out my phone and sent a quick text to Lou. FYI, at Zen's house for a little while. Wanted somebody to know.

I slid the phone back into my bag. As I approached the house, Zen pulled open the front door. She wore black yoga pants and a light blue sweater.

"Sorry I'm late. The locksmith took longer than

I thought." I got one of those flashes of déjà vu, but I'd never been there before. What was it? Something seemed oddly familiar.

"No problem. Come in."

As I followed her down the hall, I thought maybe what seemed familiar was the layout of the house, which was kind of like my aunt's. I sniffed. Or maybe it was the scent of baking, which was how Adele's kitchen often smelled.

The hall ended in a big combo family room and kitchen. A round table was covered with papers and a laptop computer. The back wall was a stunning bank of windows running from knee level to the ceiling. Outside the woods huddled before us, with black-capped chickadees flitting in to extract seeds from a hanging roofed feeder and then getting edged out by brilliant red cardinals.

Zen led me to a bike leaning against the side wall.

"A Quintana Roo." I ran my hand over the frame. "Excellent starter bike. Which model is it?"

"Dulce."

I touched the two-pronged fork holding the front wheel. "Carbon fork?"

"They said the whole frame is carbon," Zen said. "Whatever that means."

I lifted the bike up a few inches with one hand and set it back down. "It means it's nice and light. You'll do fine with this."

"I hope so. I couldn't believe bikes are so expensive. I saw ones for three times as much, but . . ." She lifted a shoulder and dropped it as her voice trailed off.

"This one's good. When's the race?"

"Not until May. But I need to get going on my training now."

"I'd be happy to go riding with you one day if that would help," I said. "Once the snow melts."

"Really?" She turned to me and her blue eyes popped. "That'd be great."

Her blue eyes. That was what looked familiar to me, not the layout of her house, not the scent of baking. And her height, her trim build, her self-confident manner. But who did she—? *Oh!* She reminded me of Jo Schultz. Funny. I shrugged mentally. Everybody had a virtual twin. In fact, I'd met a woman when I was in college who looked so much like me people were always getting us confused. And we weren't in any way related.

"Can I offer you a beer?" Zen asked. "Or a glass of wine, or something stronger?"

"Sure. Red wine if you have it."

"Have a seat, then."

I slid out of my coat and sat on the couch. The room was decorated simply, with bright throw pillows on the black couch and several striking vases painted in black and white geometric designs.

A minute later, she handed me a glass and set a basket of goldfish crackers on the coffee table. She sat with her own glass in a chair at an angle to the couch. Both pieces of furniture were positioned to have a good view of the great outdoors.

"Thanks." I grabbed a few crackers and munched them before tasting the wine. "You have a fabulous view here."

"I know. It's only a rental, but I wish I owned it. Have you heard any news about Charles's murder?"

I shook my head. "I don't think they've made any

progress at all, which is worrisome. It's been almost a week, as you know. I read somewhere that if they don't crack a case in the first forty-eight hours, they might never."

"That's awful." She looked out into the dappled late-afternoon light. "Imagine a person getting away with killing. Walking around, buying groceries, going to church. Or maybe plotting the next victim."

"Yeah, it's creepy. It might help if you told the detective where you were that night and morning. At least they could stop wasting time trying to figure it out on their own." I might be overstepping, but it was the truth.

She pulled her mouth to the side, gazing at me. After a few long moments she spoke. "It's like this. Part of it is that I'm trying to hold my own in a department that's half made up of older white guys. I'm gay, Robbie, and I'm afraid if I come out it's going to somehow get thrown back at me." She picked a piece of lint off the arm of the chair.

"I would have thought at a big university it wouldn't be a problem."

"It could be worse. But even more important is my family. Not my sister, but my parents. They're really, really conservative. If they find out I'll never hear the end of it. They'll want me to go to one of those places that claims to cure homosexuals. As if." Zen pressed her lips together.

"That's tough. I'm sorry you have to deal with that from your own parents."

"I know I'm a throwback—everybody's out these days—but that's how I feel."

"And you're afraid if you tell Octavia, it will get back to your family."

"Exactly. Probably shouldn't even have told you. That night and into the next morning I was with my girlfriend. Well, you met her in your restaurant the next day. Karinde."

"Would she vouch for you?" I sipped my wine.

"Maybe. Except she recently went off on a three-month silent retreat. I couldn't do it, but she likes to meditate and there's this place in Massachusetts, IMS, which sponsors long retreats. That was why I wanted to spend that time with her, phone off, before she left." Zen rubbed a silver ring on her right hand with her thumb.

This wasn't good. Saying you were with someone who couldn't confirm the story wasn't any different from saying you'd been alone. Was she telling the truth? My gut was telling me Zen hadn't killed Charles, but what did I know, really?

"You look like you're thinking hard over there," Zen said.

Oops. I cleared my throat. "I still think it would help if you told Octavia. And if you mention your concerns, I imagine she would honor them."

"At least if my parents were to find out, they won't have to worry about gayness in the gene pool. I have a sister who lives in Bloomington. That was one reason I wanted to come to IU, so I can hang with her and my nieces. I'm adopted and she isn't. She's not going to catch lesbianism from me." She laughed wryly.

Wait. Adopted. Gears clicked in my brain until they aligned and a window on the truth popped open. Jo Schultz had given up a baby for adoption.

And she was exactly who Zen reminded me of. "Did you ever try to find your birth mother?" I asked, trying to keep my voice casual.

"Yes. After I turned twenty-one. But I didn't have any luck, and I dropped it. Mine was a happy childhood, at least until high school when I realized I was gay. I'm lucky to still have both parents alive and well despite them being homophobic. They live up in Fort Wayne. I don't feel the need to trace my roots anymore."

Chapter 46

As I drove away from Zen's, I called Lou, who didn't pick up, and let her know I was leaving Zen's and I was fine. I was on my way to Adele's farm where Phil was dog- and house-sitting. He'd called and said his car wouldn't start but he had desserts to deliver. As I drove, I thought about the odds of Jo's birth daughter, if that was who Zen was, living so close to Jo. I wished I could tell her, but if Zen didn't want to trace her roots, that was her decision. And I wished I could talk it over with Adele.

I gave a couple little beeps of the van's horn to let Phil know I'd arrived, and a minute later I stood in the cheery warm kitchen. When Adele was home, it invariably smelled of fresh bread. Today the enticing aroma was of Phil's famous Kahlua brownies. Two wide trays of them sat wrapped and waiting on the kitchen counter next to a tray of peanut butter cookies. Adele's border collie Sloopy snoozed on his bed in the corner of the room.

"Thanks for coming out here, Robbie," Phil said.

"Not a problem. What's wrong with the car?"

"I don't know. I'm so not mechanically inclined. Triple A is coming out in an hour. I only hope it isn't expensive." He glanced at the trays. "But at least you'll have your desserts."

"Which my customers love, as you know."

"I know. Hey, sit down. Get you a beer?" He gestured at the table.

"Thanks, but I'll pass." Everybody was plying me with alcohol these days.

"I'm going to have one. Soda instead?"

"Just a glass of water."

He brought over a board with a small log of chèvre, plus a hunk of cheddar and a small brick of a rich yellowy-orange. "That one's double Gloucester. To die for." He added a plate of thin baguette slices before bringing over a bottle of beer. "Here's to spring!"

"To spring." I clinked my glass with his bottle and took a sip. "Can you get to work tomorrow if they have to tow your car?"

"A friend said she'd pick me up if I'm still stranded." He popped a slice of cheddar into his mouth. "My cousin is using Grandpa's car until he and Adele get back, and my folks are on a trip."

"Phil, you grew up around here. Do you know Jo Schultz?"

"The former owner of your store? I don't know her well, but she always seemed like a nice lady. Not sure how her grandson Ron turned out to be such a dweeb."

"What do you mean by *dweeb*?"

Phil twisted his mouth. "He's a slob and a gamer. It's like that's his whole life. Really? A person who doesn't work, doesn't want to travel, doesn't have ambitions? I don't get it."

"Pretty much what Danna said, too. The detective was in the store earlier asking about Ron. Maybe she thinks he's a suspect in the murder. Jo told me Charles was psychologically abusive to both Ron and his mother."

"That guy was abusive to everyone he met."

Seemed to be a universally held belief. He must have been a good father, at least for a while, or Ron wouldn't have been grieving for him that day outside Jo's house.

"Surely Charles had some redeeming traits?"

"If he did, I never saw them. Who else are they looking into for the killing, do you know?" Phil asked.

"I know that Octavia is investigating my friend Lou, which is ridiculous. And Georgia from the library, also unlikely, if you ask me."

"Ms. LaRue? She's cool. She helped me with a research paper when I was in high school."

"Octavia has also been questioning Zen Brown, who was Charles's department chair. In fact, I just came from Zen's house."

"Zen? So she's like a Buddhist?"

"No, her full name is Zenobia, but she tells people to call her Zen."

"Dude, that's a name on par with mine, like the opening to a bad joke. Philostrate and Zenobia walk into a bar . . ." He grinned, then knit his curly black eyebrows together. "But was that safe? To go hang out with a murder suspect?"

"Seemed safe enough. She wanted me to check out a bike she's using in a triathlon." I looked at him. He was one of my best friends. I could trust him. "The funny thing is, I think she's Jo Schultz's daughter."

He swallowed a swig of beer. "No, that's Maude. Ron's mom."

"Jo told me she'd given up a baby for adoption when she was a teenager. I realized she and Zen look a lot alike. Same eyes, same build. And Zen told me she was adopted."

Phil whistled. "Did you tell this Zen person what you thought?"

"No, and please don't tell anyone. Zen said she didn't feel the need to search for her birth mother at this stage of her life. Who am I to disturb that peace?"

Chapter 47

By the time I got home with the trays of desserts, I was full of delicious cheese and bread, which was perfect since the six-thirty on the van's dashboard clock read *dinnertime*. I aimed the headlights at the new lock on the barn and got out to check it. *Whew*. It was still locked tight and looked intact. Worth every pretty penny I'd paid the locksmith.

After I put away the desserts, the first thing I did was check upstairs. What a relief that all seemed secure. I fed Birdy and threw a load of restaurant laundry—cloth napkins, dish towels, aprons—into the washing machine in my back hall. I headed back into the restaurant, leaving the door from my apartment open. I smiled to myself as I got out ingredients for a double batch of biscuits. I could prep for the morning as well as for Saturday, since tomorrow night I'd be happily ensconced with Abe in a secluded cabin somewhere. What a sweet idea to invite me. My face heated up at the prospect of a night's worth of intimacy mixed in with the other sweet stuff.

Birdy ambled in behind me and hopped up on the desk chair to bathe. He ended up snoozing curled up with his feet in the air. I was cutting butter into flour when my cell buzzed from my back pocket. I wiped off my hands and extracted the phone.

Danna had texted. **Got info about Ron. Time to talk?**

Instead of texting back, I called her. "So you found out something?" I asked after we exchanged greetings.

"Yeah. I was right. When I took Jacob those pastries, he was so ready to talk. Get this. He said Ron is on probation."

"Really? For what?"

"Jacob wasn't quite sure, but he thinks it was for road rage. One condition is that Ron isn't supposed to play violent video games."

Aha. "And that's what he was doing Friday night, probably well into the morning."

"You got it." Danna sounded positively delighted. "Until like eleven Saturday morning, their little group was at Jacob's playing one of the worst games for knocking people off."

"Funny. Maude said he was out ice fishing."

"I don't know. I'd tend to believe Jacob. He's too much of a nerd to lie."

"I suppose Ron didn't tell the detective because he was violating his probation," I said.

"Exactly."

"I have to tell the police Ron was lying about seeing Lou on the lake that morning. Think Jacob would tell them the truth?"

"Unlike the other ones, he's a good student and

is actually taking his college classes seriously. So yeah, I'd say he would tell the truth if asked directly."

"Thanks for helping out, Danna. What's Jacob's last name?"

"Brunelle."

"I'll let Octavia know. See you in the morning?"

"Of course. Chill, Robbie."

"You, too." We disconnected and I stared at the phone for a minute. Call Octavia? Nah. She might think it was an emergency. I tapped out a text to her, instead. Learned Ron Stilton lied. He couldn't have seen Lou near ice fishing hole. Call me if you want more info.

A call came in, of course, right when my hands were all floured up and ready to do the quick knead of the biscuit dough. It wasn't yeasted and didn't need much kneading, only enough to pull the flour, butter, milk, and eggs together. I decided to finish the chore and didn't call back until the dough was wrapped and stored in the walk-in cooler. I washed and dried my hands and checked the display. Yep, Octavia. I pressed the phone icon without listening to the message.

When she picked up, she omitted a greeting and asked, "What do you have?".

"My assistant Danna talked to a gaming friend of Ron's."

"Name?"

"Jacob Brunelle. He says he was playing a violent game all night and into the morning with Ron. And that Ron didn't tell you because a condition of his probation is that he not play that type of game."

"Interesting. How does Danna knows these guys?"

"They all went to high school together." Should I tell her about Zen's alibi? I knew two secrets about her, or thought I did. Her possible relationship to Jo wasn't relevant. But her alibi for the night of the murder certainly was.

"Octavia, I talked with Zenobia Brown this afternoon."

The police detective swore under her breath. "Haven't I asked you to stay out of murder investigations?"

"Listen, we were talking bicycles, okay? Zen ended up telling me about the night Charles was killed."

"Oh?" Octavia was finally paying attention.

"Yes. She was with her lover, a woman named Karinde. Zen hasn't come out publicly and she's worried about her homophobic parents finding out. That's why she didn't tell you."

Octavia didn't speak for a moment, but I could hear tapping, like she was typing information. "Last name of this Karinde?"

"I didn't get that. Zen said she left for a three-month Buddhist retreat in Massachusetts and can't be reached."

"Ms. Brown should have told me. I assume they have telephones in New England."

I'd never heard Octavia so exasperated.

"I assume you're going to tell Zen I told you. She'll be upset, but I thought you should know."

"Thank you. I appreciate it." Octavia cleared her throat. "Everything okay there at your store? You got a lock on the barn, I heard."

"All seems secure. Thanks for asking." I thought about my conversation with Zen. "Um, Octavia?"

"Yes?"

"If it's possible to reassure Zen that you'll keep her . . . you know, preferences confidential, I think she'd be grateful."

"I'll see what I can do."

"So both Zen and Ron have alibis," I ventured. I doubted the detective would talk with me about the case any further, but it was worth a try.

"Possibly. Depends on if they check out."

"Any leads on the red thread from the tunnel?" I felt like I'd been seeing red everywhere since I found the scrap of cloth.

She didn't speak for a moment. "It's a common fabric. And a very common color, I'm afraid."

True. Especially near a university whose colors were red and white. "Georgia told me you were going to question her husband. How did that go?"

Octavia groaned. "Nice talking to you, Robbie. Thanks for the tips." She disconnected.

As I'd expected. My thoughts raced as I assembled the dry ingredients for the pancake batter. Zen was going to be really unhappy with me. But justice needed to come first.

I headed into the walk-in and pulled out cabbage and carrots to make a fresh batch of coleslaw, but my brain kept churning. If, in fact, Ron's and Zen's alibis checked out—and I didn't see why they wouldn't—they were out of the suspect pool. But Lou wasn't. She had been on the lake by her own admission. Georgia wasn't cleared, either. If anything, Ron and Zen having alibis made it look even worse for my friends.

Chapter 48

By eight o'clock I'd done all the prep I could and was back in my apartment. I ate a peanut butter sandwich, then made a cup of apple spice tea, adding a spoonful of honey and a couple glugs of bourbon. I puttered around my rooms, straightening a picture here, swiping dust off an end table there. I sat down to read the latest Louise Penny novel, but my mind was on real murder, not a fictional one in Canada.

Time to create a crossword. I'd crafted one in the fall and it'd helped my brain get organized. Working with a puzzle was the thing my mind did best. A minute later I was at my kitchen table with a couple sharp pencils, a pad of graph paper, and a ruler. On a separate sheet I wrote list headings labeled ACROSS and DOWN, and set to work. I penciled *ORVILLE* into the grid, wrote *Georgia's only chance at an alibi* in the DOWN list, and realized I'd never talked to her after the threatened questioning of her husband. Did I even have her phone number? And did I want to interrupt my puzzling? I pulled my phone out, deciding that talking to her was more important, and ran a search on her.

I didn't find her phone number, but I found her e-mail address on the Web site for the local chapter of an Alzheimer's support group. I thumbed a message asking her to call if she could, or at least let me know how the questioning went. Then I added GEORGIA to the grid, too, and penciled in RON as a connector even though I knew he'd been cleared.

Hating to do it, I connected LOU going across with one of the Ls in ORVILLE, and then used the E for ZEN.

An incoming text dinged on my phone. Speaking of Lou, there she was.

Got your message. Glad all was OK.

I thumbed back. Yep. Sorry for alarm.

No worries, she responded.

You're good?

Totally.

Hey, do you know of Legal Aid in B'ton or on campus? I tapped in. Friend here needs cheap law advice.

Will check into it.

Thx. CU.

Bye. I set my phone down. Nice of her to get back to me. I'd been fine at Zen's, of course, but it didn't hurt to be prudent.

I added REVENGE in the grid with an ACROSS clue of *Common motive* and then bisected it with ICE FISHING going down. *Ice fishing*. Why had Maude lied about Ron being out on the ice that morning? Surely someone would have seen him if he'd been

out there. Since he hadn't been home, maybe she
was afraid he'd killed his father, and made up the
ice fishing story to protect him.

MAUDE connected with the other *E* in REVENGE.
Was revenge even the motive? The killer could have
struck out of hurt, anger, or jealousy. Or the myriad
other human emotions that pushed people to
commit crimes. I jotted down several of those. I
guessed I'd have to add *Jo* to the puzzle, too, despite her diminutive size and advanced age. She
clearly hadn't liked Charles and knew how badly
he'd treated her daughter and grandson. I stuck
in *OCTAVIA* and connected her to *Jo*, then added
ADOPTION, too. It seemed to be integral to the lives
of three of the suspects—Jo, Zen, and Maude.

What about people's alibis? I added *ALIBI* hanging off *ADOPTION*. Ron and Zen were the only ones
who could prove where they were when Charles was
killed. Speaking of when he was killed, I still didn't
know exactly when it had been. If it had been in the
night, wouldn't Maude have reported him missing?
Unless, as I had mused earlier, she was used to him
not coming home. She'd admitted they didn't get
along well, something Jo certainly confirmed, so
maybe Maude didn't care if her husband stayed out
all night. Who could I ask about it?

As I thought about that, I added *CHARLES* off the
A of *ALIBI*. Seeing the *A* brought my thoughts to
Adele. That's who would know. It was eight-thirty.
What time did that make it in India?

I tapped out a quick e-mail to her and was aston-
ished to get a reply almost immediately. She wrote
that she was up early, and that everyone knew
Charles Stilton had had a series of women he'd

spent time with. Unfortunately, she didn't know of a particular one lately. *Wow*. What a resource she was. I thanked her and sent back a cyber hug to her and to Samuel.

I sat back and stared at my work. *Interesting*. Ron was the only male name in the pool of original suspects. Other men must have been in conflict with Charles—maybe the husband of one of those women Adele referred to. How to find them? Had I asked Lou about others in the sociology department? I thought I had and she'd responded along the lines of, "Who didn't Charles rub the wrong way?"

If I were to publish the crossword, of course, I'd have to make every word connect in two directions. The grid would need to be a standard square size. I'd add more words not part of the theme, or only tangentially, like the names of the lake and the town, and work on making the clues cryptic or indirect. Palindromes were fun to add, like *PUTUP* with a clue of *Advance in either direction*. Then I'd do the numbering, which could get tricky.

But this puzzle was only for me. And it was guaranteed to be incomplete, since I had no way of knowing who else Octavia and her team had talked to or were looking into. I laid down my pencil and finished my tea right before my phone buzzed with a call from Abe.

"Whatcha up to?" he asked after greeting me.

"I'm making up a crossword puzzle."

He laughed. "Just for kicks? I can't even solve puzzles and you can write them. You're amazing, Robbie."

"Actually I'm trying to sort out the facts of

Charles's murder. For me, seeing it all on a grid helps. Or I thought it would, anyway. I'm not coming up with any answers so far."

"Bring it with you tomorrow. Maybe two heads will be better than one."

"Good idea."

"I've been keeping an eye on the weather," Abe said. "It looked like we were going to get more snow, but now they're forecasting rising temperatures and rain. The driving will be a bit sloppy, but I think we'll be okay. My parents hire a guy to plow the road after every new snowfall."

"I'll bring my raincoat, then."

"Great. Pick you up at six-thirty?"

"I'll be on the front porch. Can I bring food or drink?"

"No, I've got it all planned. Just bring your gorgeous self."

I laughed. "I don't know about that, but I am looking forward to seeing you."

"Me, too, honey. Me, too."

Chapter 49

Danna and I were doing our usual busy dance the next morning, me waiting tables, her cooking for the moment. Buck was in early for breakfast, as were the usual regulars and a couple of parties I'd never seen before. It was Friday, so maybe folks were starting a weekend getaway early.

Buck sat at the table closest to the grill. "Where's me some breakfast?" he asked with a slow grin as I bustled by.

"Coming right up."

I delivered his order of grits, pancakes, sausages, and two eggs over easy, and stopped to chat for a moment. "Any news?"

With a baleful look, he shook his head real slow as always. "Afraid not. You okay over here?"

"Thankfully, yes. The new lock is holding and I haven't heard any strange noises." I hadn't checked the upstairs this morning. I'd do it later if we had our usual lull.

"That's good," he mumbled through a mouthful of eggs.

Zen burst through the door of the restaurant at several minutes before eight. I was on the grill by then, managing four orders of pancakes, three omelets, a row of plump sausages, and an oven full of the second batch of biscuits. She hurried to my side, fists on her waist, cheeks blazing with what looked more like anger than the effect of the cold outdoors.

"Please step back, Zen." I glanced at her. Was that smoke coming from her ears? I guess she heard from Octavia. "You can't be in the cook space. Board of Health says so." I saw Buck turn his head toward us with a calm but alert look on his face.

She obliged, but angled to the side so she could see me. "Why did you have to tell her?" she asked with a hiss.

"I'm sorry Zen, but a man was killed. Don't you think helping the detective learn the truth is more important than who you choose to spend time with in private?" The timer dinged and I pulled the pan of biscuits out, sliding them onto a rack.

Nostrils flaring, she folded her arms over her chest. "Once it's out, it's out. My reputation is shot and my parents will be here in person giving me hell. You have no idea how this kind of thing spreads."

"I suppose. I'm sorry I upset you." I wanted to shout, 'Don't you see clearing your name of murder is for your own good?' but I kept my mouth shut and flipped pancakes, instead.

She tapped her hand on her arm. "Karinde is going to be furious at having her retreat interrupted, too."

Again I felt like saying, 'Isn't she going to be there for three months? Will one phone call ruin it?' But I didn't. Maybe Zen was more afraid of angering her lover than of ruining her period of silence. As I recalled, they weren't getting along that well when they came for lunch last Sunday.

Zen looked at the big wall clock. "Crap. I've got to teach at eight-thirty."

I watched as she headed for the door. It swung open right before she got there, the cowbell announcing a new set of hungry customers. Jo Schultz walked in, followed by three other women. The four were a group of artists who occasionally came for breakfast. Jo nearly collided with Zen.

Zen reached out her arms. "Sorry. Are you all right?"

Jo nodded slowly. Zen pushed out through the door. Jo stood as if made of granite, her face toward Zen's exit as the cowbell jangled.

"There's a table free in the corner there, ladies," I called to them. Had Jo recognized herself in Zen?

One of Jo's companions elbowed her gently, and she followed them to the square table. I filled the waiting plates with orders and rang the little *Ready* bell.

When Danna bustled up, I said, "Swap?"

"Sure."

"The omelets are almost ready." I threw on a clean apron, grabbed an order pad and pen, and took the pancakes and sausages to their destination, the men's Bible study group that usually included Samuel. We chatted for a moment about Samuel and Adele's trip and when they'd be home, then I headed for Jo's table.

I greeted the foursome.

"It sure enough smells good in here," said a thin woman with a long brown braid hanging down her back. She sniffed. "Fresh baked something-or-other, meat, maple, coffee. I could live on the scents alone." She flashed a toothy smile.

"Thanks," I said. "We have two specials today. One is a French omelet with a mild local goat cheese, rosemary, mushrooms, and leeks, served with a croissant."

Danna's idea again, although we'd used frozen croissants. At least they were made by a local bakery.

"The other special is grits with cheese. Can I get you all coffee to start?"

Three of them ordered coffee, then shed their outerwear. Jo remained silent, staring at the exit. She still wore her red coat.

"I swear, Josephine, you look like you seen a ghost," said the woman next to her, a square-jawed older woman with cropped battleship-gray hair and paint under her fingernails.

Jo swallowed and rubbed her forehead, looking up at me. "I'll have coffee too, Robbie. Thanks." She glanced at the door again. "Do you know who that was? The person who just left, I mean."

"Her name is Zenobia Brown. She's a professor at IU. In fact, she was Charles's department chair."

Jo must have recognized a part of herself in Zen. She'd only seen her baby for a few days, she'd said, and that was over fifty years ago. But heck, if I'd noticed the similarity, Jo certainly could have.

Jo nodded slowly. "Is that so?"

"Yes. Let me get the coffee and I'll be back to take your orders." As I passed Buck's table, he held up his hand in a stopping gesture. "What was up with Ms. Brown?" he asked even as Danna slapped the bell.

"Can you hang on a sec? I have three things I have to do right this minute." When he bobbed his head down and up once, I rushed off. I managed to juggle three omelet plates and the coffeepot. I nearly tripped on an uneven part of the old wooden floor but caught myself. I dropped off the check for a man who'd eaten while playing chess against himself, then poured coffee for the artists.

"Do you know what you'd like to eat?" I held pen to order pad. I'd seen waitstaff who relied on memory, but I never wanted to chance that. Plus, if I wrote it down, all Danna needed to do was read it. We were definitely not part of the computerized order trend. I jotted down two French omelets with bacon and one oatmeal with fruit.

Jo hadn't spoken.

"Jo? What would you like for breakfast today?"

She drew her head up, eyes following, like it hurt. Her eyes were moist and the corners of her mouth turned down. "I'm not particularly hungry, as it turns out." She stood. "Girls, I'll see you next time. Robbie, do you have a minute to talk?"

I glanced around the restaurant and gave Buck, still watching, a *wait-a-minute* index finger. "Sure." I followed her out.

After the front door closed behind us, she turned to me. "That was my baby. This Zenobia is my daughter. She looks like me, walks like I used to. I know it, Robbie. I know it in my bones, in my heart."

What was I supposed to do? It wasn't a question of catching a murderer. Zen had confided in me about being adopted, about not feeling the need to continue searching for her birth mother, even though she'd tried to find her when she was younger. Jo had also shared with me her longing for her lost baby girl. I'd been so happy to find my own birth father last fall, so I knew the feeling.

I thought as fast and furious as I could. "That's amazing. After fifty-some years. Are you sure?"

"I think so." Tears trickled down her cheeks. "Her name is so beautiful, isn't it? Zenobia. Zen. I named her Grace, but Zenobia is much stronger. I like that." Jo's smile was wan, but it was still a smile. "Do you know how I can reach her?"

I made up my mind. "She's the chair of the sociology department at IU. I'm sure you can find her there." I swallowed. "She was upset with me about another matter just now. If you call her, would you mind not telling her right off the bat that I gave you her contact info?"

"Don't worry. I won't."

Chapter 50

I finally got back to Buck's table. "We're super busy so this is going to have to be quick." I lowered my voice so only he could hear. "In a nutshell, Zen Brown was upset because I told Octavia last night that Zen is gay. She was with a girlfriend the night and morning that Charles was killed. She told me that in confidence yesterday, but I thought Octavia needed to know that Zen has an alibi."

"You done the right thing, then. Good for you." His plate was wiped clean and he leaned back in his chair, cradling his coffee in both hands.

"Thanks. I think I just lost a new friend, though. Say, any result on that scrap of cloth?" Maybe he'd learned something since I'd talked to Octavia.

"Not so far."

Danna waved frantically from the grill.

"Gotta run. You have a good day, now." Another example of my starting to talk like a local, adding *now* at the end of that phrase. I smiled to myself as I hurried to the grill. Nothing wrong with fitting in.

By nine-thirty business was easing up when Maude

walked in with a gentleman I'd never seen before. She wore a black wool coat and carried an oversized black leather portfolio case. She paused inside the door. "Can we get a table for four, Robbie?" she called. "There's only two of us but I need to spread out a little."

I surveyed the restaurant. "Sure. Take that one." I pointed.

After they got settled, I carried the coffeepot and a couple of menus to them. "Did you want to order food? It's fine if you only want coffee." I wanted to encourage customers to come here with the intention of working, whether it was consulting with a client or writing solo. At least during the lull times, which it was.

Maude glanced at her companion, a handsome older guy with silver at his temples. "It's up to you."

"I'd like to eat first, if that's all right," he said, smiling at me and reminding me of Paul Newman, one of my mom's favorite actors. "I'm hungry, and I've been hearing about your place ever since I started making inquiries about buying land in Brown County."

"We can work afterwards, then." Maude looked up at me. "I'm putting together a design plan for his vacation home." She looked her usual well-put-together self, with her hair and makeup in order. She wore an elegant silver cashmere sweater over black wool pants, both of which looked like they'd come from a very expensive store.

"Great." I took their orders, and five minutes later delivered two eggs over easy with bacon plus biscuits and gravy for him and the special omelet for her. "How's it going, Maude?"

She frowned. "The police still refuse to release Charlie's body." She glanced at her companion. "I can't very well hold a funeral without him. I don't know what in blazes they think they're going to learn from the poor man's remains a week after his unfortunate demise."

"I'm sorry to hear that." *Huh.* A few days earlier she hadn't been planning a funeral, saying no one would come. Or no one cared. Something to that effect. Maybe this talk of services was only for show in front of her rich client.

"Enough talk of death," she said with a dismissive gesture. "Let's eat, shall we?"

I turned away to clear another table. I glanced up when the cowbell jangled and smiled. "Lou, nice to see you."

She hung up her jacket and walked over.

"No class this morning?" I asked.

"No. And I have good news." She looked better than she had in a week. Her eyes were bright and her face didn't have the worried, drawn look she'd worn all week. She'd sounded good in her text last night, too. If one could "sound" good in a brief thumbed message.

"Awesome. What is it?"

She leaned toward me. "One of the detective's guys found a neighbor of mine, the one right downstairs, who'd heard me in my apartment. Just like you said. The neighbor also said she can see from her window where I park my car and it didn't move until I went out to the lake."

"I'm glad the police are doing their legwork."

She frowned. "Took 'em long enough. But yeah, I'm glad, too."

"Does that mean you're in the clear?"

"Not completely. They know I was at the lake that morning, but the neighbor helped my case for the overnight period, anyway."

Surely the police must know roughly what time Charles had died. If it had been before ten when Lou went running, she was definitely cleared of suspicion. I glanced at Maude, but she was busy with her business dealings. I spoke in a low voice to Lou. "Did you hear about Maude's son?" I asked in a low voice. "He was never even on the lake that morning."

Her nostrils flared. "I did. I mean, fine that he has an alibi for the murder, but there should be consequences for him having lied about me. Why would he even say that?" She frowned.

"Good question. We might never know the answer."

Lou wrinkled her nose. "I struck out on that Legal Aid thing. Sorry. The one guy I thought would know is away for the semester."

"That's okay. Thanks for checking. I probably should have just Googled it." I smiled at her. "Hungry?"

"Absolutely. Getting that monkey off my back brought back my appetite." She inspected the Specials menu. "Wow, I'm having both of those."

I laughed and headed to the grill. At least I could remove Lou from the puzzle. Not that I'd ever really believed she belonged in it.

Chapter 51

All morning an internal buzz had been mounting about my date night with Abe. In between serving, sautéing, and smiling at customers I'd been imagining our evening. At ten forty-five only Maude and her client remained in the restaurant, still huddled over a table's worth of paper with computer drawings of home layouts. I'd just refilled their mugs with coffee when chagrin hit me like a two-by-four.

Danna passed me, heading for the restroom.

"I'm seeing Abe tonight for his birthday," I said. "Out at his family's cabin in the woods."

"And you're blushing about it." Danna grinned.

"Guilty as charged. But I don't have a present for him." I pulled a face. "I'm going to run out now and see what I can find. Okay?"

"Of course. Can you wait until I'm done?" She gestured toward the women's restroom door, on which Phil had painted SHE ALL before the store had opened last fall.

Ten minutes later under a steely sky blowing a damp wind through my hair, I realized I had no idea what to get Abe for his birthday. I was sure he wouldn't care if I showed up empty-handed, but I wanted to give him a gift. I headed downtown, not sure of my destination, and found myself passing the library.

Georgia. What had happened with the police interviewing Orville?

I ran up the stairs and pulled open the heavy door to see her in her usual spot at the desk. I waited until an older gentleman was done speaking with her, then approached. "Georgia, I tried to get a lawyer's name for you, but my friend couldn't find one. How did the interview go?"

She looked at me out of a strained face. "Exactly as I predicted. It was a rotten thing for them to do. Orville couldn't tell the detective anything, and now he's all messed up. Agitated, confused. He had a rough night."

"I'm really sorry." Poor Orville.

"That's the way it goes. Hey, at least I'm not in jail."

"They can't hold you if they don't have any evidence."

"Let's hope not." Georgia glanced at the clock. "I have to go set up the room for the genealogy group. Thanks for stopping in, Robbie."

Back outside, I still had the problem of the birthday present and even less time in which to solve it. "Think, Jordan, think," I said aloud. I snapped my fingers. Maybe Jo would sell me one of those gorgeous small wall hangings. She'd said she had some left over from a craft fair. I hurried the few blocks to her house. I knocked, rang the bell, and knocked again, but she didn't answer the door. I peered in the glass of the front door. No lights on inside, so she was either out or napping or whatever. I gave up and trudged down the front steps. Come to think of it, maybe she was talking to Zen.

Now what? I'd wasted my break time, and I didn't have a card for Abe, either.

Danna was going to need my help shortly. I aimed myself toward Pans 'N Pancakes, head down against the wind. Spirits down, too. I could make up a quick crossword puzzle for Abe, with things about him, his son, and us as clues. To do a good job, though, I'd need to spend a day or two on it. Time I didn't have. And he didn't do puzzles, anyway.

At a car's beep, I glanced up.

"Robbie, were you looking for me?" Jo said from the open window of a small Prius.

"I was." What a quiet car. I hadn't heard her drive up. "I wanted to buy one of your small weavings as a birthday gift."

"That's awfully nice of you." She smiled, her face displaying her normal good cheer.

"I'm sort of out of time, though. Have to get back for lunch prep."

"Did you need the weaving today?" she asked. When I nodded, she went on. "I know how busy you are. Why don't I bring a few by the store this afternoon and you can pick out the one you want. Say two o'clock?"

I stared at her. "Thank you. I would love that." What a great offer.

"Hop in and I'll run you back. Save you a bit of time."

It was only two blocks away, but I scooted around to the passenger door and got in.

As she hung a U-turn, she said in a soft voice, "I called Zenobia. She said she'll meet with me this evening."

"Really? That's wonderful." And it was. I'd been curious if Zen would refuse.

"Well, we'll see. I could be wrong about her. The whole thing is pretty nerve-racking, frankly."

I looked over at her. She looked straight ahead with a calm little smile playing with the corners of her mouth and didn't appear a bit nervous.

When we pulled up in front of my store, I climbed out. "Good luck with the meeting, Jo. I'll see you this afternoon."

Chapter 52

Our morning rush did not translate into a lunch rush. "This is one of the quietest middays I can remember," I said to Danna. At one o'clock we sat alone in the restaurant, each with a hamburger and a dish of coleslaw. We'd had a trickle of customers since eleven-thirty, but the last had left a couple of minutes ago.

"No kidding. Kind of nice not to have it be crazy all day, right?"

"For sure. Hey, did the delivery come while I was out?"

"It did and I put it all away. So what are you wearing tonight?" She raised one eyebrow and the tiny silver ring in it sparkled.

No way I was telling her about my new nightwear. "I haven't had time to think about it. Probably leggings and a long sweater. We're going to be in a cabin, you know."

"Yeah. A secluded cabin, I think you said?" She laughed and popped the last bite of burger into her mouth.

"Nothing wrong with that. I have a bottle of bubbly in the apartment I'm going to take along, too, since we'll be celebrating Abe's birthday." I drained my cup of water. "What about you, Danna? I've never heard you talk about a boyfriend. You must have guys asking you out."

She wrinkled her nose. "I don't know. The boys from here? Forget about it." She played with her fork, twirling it on the table. "There's one dude I play volleyball with who's pretty cool. Isaac grew up in Bloomington but now he works at the state park. Kind of like a ranger in training. And speaking of cabins, he lives in a totally basic one. Has a pump for water, heats with a woodstove, uses a composting toilet that doesn't smell at all. And he makes the most awesome metal sculptures."

"And?" I reached over and gently prodded her in the arm.

"And so far we're basically friends in a group, although we have hung out a couple times. Like, just us two."

Easy bet that was why she'd been late to work the other day. "I say go for it. What's awesome Isaac look like?"

She stood and picked up our plates. "He's cute. Has a big bushy beard, but he keeps his hair short. And he's taller than me. Can't say that about a lot of guys. Not that I care, of course, but I think they do. Who wants to get romantic with an Amazon?" She laughed again and headed for the sink.

We used the next hour, which stayed quiet except for one couple who came in to eat, to do all the rest of the prep for the next morning. I wouldn't have time tonight and I wanted to get in another few hours of demolition this afternoon. While Danna rolled silverware in napkins, I took a minute to run upstairs and make sure nothing was disturbed, which I should have done yesterday. I didn't see anything out of place and the saw still sat firmly against the door to the passageway. I let out a sigh of relief. Back downstairs I put a half dozen salmon fillets on to steam so we could offer salmon omelets in the morning and salmon burgers for lunch if we didn't use it all at breakfast.

Jo showed up right at two o'clock, a large cloth bag in hand.

I made sure one of our bigger tables was clean. "You can lay them out here. Thanks again for bringing these over."

She pulled out weaving after weaving and unfolded them from their tissue paper wrappings. They weren't any bigger than a sheet of printer paper but the colors were stunning. A few were mainly turquoise and purple, another was pastel blue and pink, while yet another was woven in a bold geometric black and white design.

I picked up one featuring browns and reds with a brilliant yellow thread winding through it. "This one is amazing. It looks like fall."

"I was trying to capture the sunlight weaving through the trees."

"I think Abe will like it. It looks sort of masculine, too, if that's not too sexist of me to say."

"Abe O'Neill?"

"Yes." My cheeks heated up again.

She peered at me. "You're dating him, I'd say. Good choice. Good man."

"I think so, too."

Danna, who'd joined us, leaned over the geometric design. "I love this one. You're selling them?"

"Yes," Jo said.

"Then I'll take the black and white one. Mom'll like it, too."

"How much do I owe you?" I asked.

"You both can have the special friends and family price," Jo said. "Twenty-five."

"Are you sure?" I asked. "I can pay the going rate."

"Me, too," Danna chimed in.

Jo batted away the suggestion and began to put the rest of the weavings back in the bag. Danna dug bills out of her pocket and handed them to Jo, then rolled her weaving up into a tube. "Awesome. Thanks." She stashed it in her bag and headed over to check the salmon.

Jo refolded the tissue paper around the one I'd selected and added a round sticker over the ends to hold them shut. I leaned over to see a logo of a loom with Jo's name woven into it.

"I like that," I said.

"I swapped a weaving for my artist friend's design services."

"My bag is back in my apartment. Wait one sec while I get your money."

Jo laid a hand on my arm. "Would you mind terribly much letting me see what you've done with the back?"

"Not at all. Come on." *Oops.* Had I made my bed this morning? Unlikely. *Oh well.*

"Be right back," I called to Danna.

Jo followed me into the apartment. It was a pretty short tour. We walked through the living room. After she poked her head into the bedroom, I showed her the bathroom and introduced her to Birdy in the kitchen.

I retrieved the cash from my wallet and handed it to her. "Thanks again."

She pocketed the money. "You've done a lovely job here. I never really used this space, you know, since we lived upstairs. But Maude used to have her friends over when they were in high school and they'd hang out down here." She cleared her throat, like she was clearing a memory. "Those days are past."

I was considering asking her if she wanted to see the upstairs when I heard Danna call to me from the front. "Time to get back to work, it sounds like," I said.

Jo's attention fell on the sheet of paper where I'd been fooling around with the Charles Murder puzzle. I'd jotted down clues, motives, opportunity, suspects. It included Jo's own daughter and grandson. And Jo herself. *Ouch.*

She looked me in the face. "You can cross Ron off that list. He's in big trouble with his probation officer, but he was playing those awful games that night."

"I heard. I'm sorry you saw my puzzle, Jo. It's the way I get my thoughts organized. The whole business must be painful for you."

In fact her eyes did look pained, like a shadow had passed over them. "That's life, isn't it? I don't believe Maude killed him, and I know I didn't. But does that detective believe us? That's anybody's guess."

Chapter 53

By three-thirty the restaurant was cleaned up and I'd closed the store. I slid the bottle of champagne into my apartment fridge and packed a small gym bag, including the wall hanging and the red silky item, plus toiletries and a clean set of work clothes for tomorrow. I threw on demolition clothes, grabbed my phone, and climbed the stairs. I could work for at least two hours before it was time to get ready. I definitely wanted to be freshly showered with clean hair for the evening, so I might as well get dirty first.

As I inserted the crowbar behind the plaster and lath on the front wall and pulled, I thought about my intruder—a person who had been desperate enough to come in at least once while I was in the building, judging from that sound I'd heard. Desperate enough to cut the padlock when I was out, too, not to mention leaving an anonymous threat. Had they hidden a clue to their identity after Charles's murder? But why would they? Maybe something else was hidden in these walls.

I didn't know what had gone on in Jo's family or in town in the years before I bought the building. It seemed like someone would have had plenty of opportunity over the years to break in. The upstairs was already empty when the store was for sale. That would mean someone had planned in advance to kill Charles. But why hide something in this particular building? Maybe it was a criminally minded friend of Maude's from her "rough patch" days or someone who didn't think anyone would ever look in the walls of a decrepit old building but knew about the passageway from an older relative.

I frowned. Nails screeched with a mighty complaint as I ripped down a satisfyingly large piece of wall all in one piece and tossed it behind me. I brainstormed with myself about what type of object someone would want to hide and keep hidden. Money stolen from a bank. Photographs that could get someone in trouble. Looted jewelry, even, or drugs. A book. A stolen library book. I snorted. This was getting ridiculous.

None of it made sense to me. I worked on prying a section near the floor but the nails wouldn't loosen. I put my whole body into it, legs apart, both arms on the bar. When the lath finally came away, I fell back onto my rear end and the crowbar flew out of my hands. The heavy metal grazed my right cheekbone on its way by.

I cried out, then sneezed hard from the plaster dust. I patted my cheek with the back of my work glove and checked the glove. At least the injury wasn't bleeding, but it smarted. *Great.* Show up for a romantic date with a big bruise on my cheek. I stood and checked my phone. Only four-thirty.

"Back to work, Jordan," I told myself. "Make use of the time you have." I knew I'd be too tired tomorrow afternoon to do anything except collapse. I didn't expect to get all that much sleep tonight.

I pried and pulled and pried and pulled, the pile of rubble behind me growing steadily. I welcomed the version of physical work after my days spent cooking and waiting tables. Demolition used my upper back and arm muscles, as well as my abs and quads when I did it right. It wasn't quite as good a feeling as a long bike ride, but it came in a close second.

When the light from outside grew dim, I flipped on the overheads and kept going. I was almost to the corner and really wanted to finish this wall. Then I would have only one more to go. I still needed to shovel the rubble out the window into the Dumpster. My cheekbone didn't hurt anymore, thank goodness. I worked around the window, with only three feet left to the corner. This section of the upstairs must have been Maude's room. It was wallpapered in a pink and blue striped paper like the kind a teenage girl might pick out.

Dragging the ladder over, I was about to put my foot on the first rung when I stopped. The wallpaper was less faded up to about four feet high, as if a small cabinet or dresser had stood there for many years. The way the light shone on it revealed a small square shape at about waist height that stuck out about half an inch. What was that? Another hidden door? If it was, it had been designed for dolls, not people. I pushed aside the ladder, grabbed a corner of wallpaper, and tore. To my surprise it wasn't glued to the middle of the wall and came right off.

The shape was a small door, as I had thought. It was about a foot square, with tiny hinges on the left side. A small hole in the opposite side showed where a knob must have been screwed in. I hurried over to my tools to get a screwdriver, but in my haste I tripped on a piece of board and went sprawling. I swore as my hands scraped along the floor in an attempt to rescue myself. It worked, in a way. I didn't hit my face again and managed not to fall on my knees. My phone fell out of my breast pocket where I'd slid it earlier. I picked it up and swore again. It was six-fifteen. *Yikes!* How had that happened? I glanced at the little door, dying to find out if anything was in there. I quickly grabbed a screwdriver, dashed over to the door, and pried it open. My hand went to my mouth. A book lay in a shallow cupboard. On top of it sat a doll. A doll with a grotesque grin and a long straight pin stuck into her neck.

Chapter 54

I clattered down the front steps of the restaurant, hair still wet, bag in hand, to Abe's old VW camper. I was ten minutes late, but I'd texted him that I would be. I wasn't sure I'd ever taken a faster shower. Good thing I'd prepacked my bag.

"I'm sorry I'm late," I said in a rush after I closed the passenger door. I leaned over to kiss him and tasted a mix of coffee and peppermint.

He laid his hand along my right cheek to pull me in for seconds and I winced.

"Did I hurt you?" He sounded bewildered.

"No, I hurt myself this afternoon. Had an unfortunate meet up with a flying crowbar."

He switched on the overhead light and peered at my face. "Ouch. You poor thing."

"I'll be fine." I smiled at him as I buckled myself in with the lap belt, all the vehicle had. My rushing around had damped down my excitement about the evening, but the anticipation was rising up again.

He turned off the light and started the engine.

"So you squeezed in more demolition today?" He headed through town.

"I did. It's so satisfying. I was trying to finish ripping out the front wall and totally lost track of time. I'd just realized how late it was when I found something incredible in the wall. Something creepy. That's why I'm late."

"All's well that ends well, as my Grampy used to say. So tell me what you found."

"A little cupboard set into the wall that was papered over. Inside, I found a book and a doll. It was a doll with a really odd face and a big pin sticking into her neck."

"Like a voodoo doll?"

"I guess. I've never seen one before."

"I have, when I went to New Orleans a few years ago," Abe said. "They're usually sort of small hand-sewn cloth figures with Xs for eyes and mouths."

"This isn't like that. It's a girl's doll, and not a baby doll, either. It must have a name, but I wasn't interested in dolls when I was little, so I don't know what kind it is."

"What was the book?" Abe asked as we turned onto Route 46.

"It said *Diary* on the outside, but I didn't have time to even open it. The room had been Maude's, I think, so it was must be her diary and her doll. Neither looked like an antique. I brought both of them, though. We can look together later if you want."

"Explore a mysterious find with my best girl? Can't think of anything else I'd rather do. Well, almost anything." He laid his warm, strong hand on my knee with a promise of that other *anything*.

We rode in comfortable silence up and down hills on the curvy state route. I thought about what we might read in the diary. Had Maude written about boys, slumber parties, and teenage angst? Maybe she'd expressed doubts and fears about being adopted and had jotted down thoughts of finding her birth mother. Or perhaps she dwelt on her schoolwork and world affairs.

I thought she was about forty, forty-five, which would put her teen years in the late 1980s. It would be fun to peruse the diary. I wrinkled my nose. Or should I simply hand it over to her unread? The presence of the doll complicated things. I wanted to see if she'd written about it.

Abe slowed and turned onto a smaller road, darker and without any houses dotting the sides, but it was well-paved. "Did you bring your crossword puzzle, too?"

"Oh, shoot."

"What?"

"I was in such a rush I forgot to bring the puzzle. And I didn't get the champagne out of the fridge, either. Darn it." I turned sideways to look at him.

He laughed. "Great minds think alike. I have a bottle of bubbly in the cooler in the back."

"You do? Perfect. We'll just have to have a second celebration later."

"Twist my arm, baby."

"You know, besides the obvious pleasure of getting away with you, it's awfully nice to get away from thinking about Charles's murder. It's really been on my mind all the time. Maybe forgetting the puzzle was my subconscious at work."

"You can use a break, then. Happy to provide it." He slowed and began peering at the side of the road. "The drive is along here."

Rain began to fall, at first only dotting the windshield and then letting loose a torrent, as if a giant was throwing out the bathwater.

"Looks like it's going to be a real frog strangler," he said.

"A what?"

"A frog strangler. You know, a gully washer." He pronounced *washer* with an *R* sound like many Hoosiers did—the word *war* followed by *sher*. "It'll be raining old women and sticks."

I could hear the grin in his voice. "I love the expressions around here. I'll bet you learned those from your Grampy."

"Bingo." Abe wrenched the wheel to the right all of a sudden and we began bumping down a decidedly unpaved road. After a few teeth-jarring minutes, he pulled up to a low structure the headlights showed to be a log cabin.

"It's a real log cabin," I exclaimed. "I've never been inside one and I've always wanted to see what they're like."

"I'm afraid we're going to be soaked getting from here to there. It's about ten yards. I'll start up the woodstove once we're in."

I looked out at the rain. "It's just water, right?"

"Absolutely." He pulled a flashlight from under the seat and switched it on. I flipped up the hood of my rain jacket after he did the same, and clutched my small duffle to my chest.

"Ready to make a break for it?" he asked.

"After you."

Chapter 55

I rubbed my hands above the woodstove, which was beginning to broadcast heat. The stove featured glass in the door, so we could watch the logs burning. Our rain jackets dried on a rack on the other side of the stove. The cabin was a delight, furnished with sturdy simple furniture, lamps casting a warm yellow glow, and a braided rug in front of the stove. It was open to the kitchen at the back where Abe worked on our dinner.

I moseyed over and perched on a stool at the counter facing him. "This is a great place."

"Grampy built it by hand. We've fixed it up over the years, adding insulation and wall board, for example, and electricity. But it still has that feeling of being a log cabin, don't you think?"

"Absolutely." A utility porch extended off the kitchen with a door to the back of the house. A long bow hung from a peg on the wall of the porch. A quiver of arrows hung from the next peg. A bright orange hat occupied the next peg, and a heavy camouflage jacket the following one. Several

pairs of snowshoes were on a shelf above the pegs.
Narrow skis leaned against the wall.

Abe reached into the fridge. "Ready for a drink?"

"You better believe it." I watched him pour
Prosecco into two jam jars.

"The finest of bubblies in the simplest of glasses.
That's how we roll out here in Brown County." He
handed me one and raised his.

"Happy birthday," I said before clinking my glass
with his. "Mmm." I savored the smooth fizzy drink
as it went down. "So what are you cooking?"

"Sorghrum pork chops and mushrooms on fusilli
with sautéed asparagus."

"That sounds fabulous, Abe. You said you learned
to cook from your father."

"You bet. The O'Neill men like to eat well."

"Does Don cook, too?"

"Yep." Abe set out a basket filled with crackers, a
dish with a dark spread, and a bowl of tiny mari-
nated mozzarella balls. "Have some munchies." He
added a tiny glass full of toothpicks next to the
cheese.

I dipped a cracker in the spread. "Tapenade?" I
popped it in my mouth.

"Exactly. Homemade, too, from three kinds of
olives." He grinned. The dimple split his cheek and
a strand of his wavy walnut-colored hair hung down
on his forehead.

I swallowed my bite and held out my arms. "Come
here, you."

After he came around the counter, I pulled his
face in for a long deep kiss. "I like you," I said when
we came up for air.

"Mmm. More." He pulled me up to standing and we dove in for another kiss, body to body.

I was lost to lust, weak knees and all.

He pushed back a few inches and held me by the shoulders, looking straight into my eyes. "How hungry are you?"

"For you?" My breath came so quickly I was almost panting. "I thought you'd never ask."

He took two quick steps to the stove and turned off the burners. "Dinner can wait." As he led me to the long couch in front of the woodstove, the sound of the rain falling outside quieted to the tapping of frozen drops.

Chapter 56

I watched Abe—rosy cheeked and tousled—finish cooking. From my perch on the stool, I was feeling equally rosy cheeked and tousled. When dinner was ready, he set the round table with placemats and candles. The sorghrum-mushroom sauce, which included sautéed shallots, was exactly the right topping for lightly grilled pork, and the asparagus was perfectly done.

It was eight-thirty by the time we got to the diary. We'd finished the champagne and half a bottle of pinot noir, and sat on the couch nestled under a western-design fleece blanket in front of the woodstove. The tapping of ice needles continued outside.

"I hope the frozen rain won't be a problem in the morning," I said.

"If it is, it is. We have plenty of sand and salt in the shed, in case we need it, but I think it'll likely change back to rain later on."

I slid out from the colorful blanket and rummaged in my duffle, coming back with three items.

I laid the doll and diary on the end table next to me and handed him the tissue-paper wrapped wall hanging before snuggling in again. "Happy birthday."

"You didn't have to give me anything, Robbie." He looked pleased, nonetheless, as he carefully peeled off the sticker and opened the package. He held it up. "I love it. Handmade, right?"

"Jo Schultz weaves them. I thought the colors looked like you."

He leaned over and kissed my cheek, then sat back. "It'll have a place of pride on my wall. My bedroom wall, I think." He winked at me. "What else you got there?"

I hated to spoil the moment with the doll and the diary. Now I wished I hadn't brought them. "We can look at those things another time."

"No, I'm curious. Let's see."

"Okay." I laid the diary on his lap and then lifted the doll, about nine inches tall, in front of us. She had the look of a teenager, but not the extreme figure of a Barbie doll. Her wide black-rimmed blue eyes looked almost scared with thin raised eyebrows, and her smile was tentative. She had long blond hair flowing straight back from her high forehead and wore bell-bottoms, green go-go boots, and a multi-colored shirt. It was the heavy needle ending in a black pearl sticking out from her neck that was the alarming part.

"What do you want to bet that needle isn't part of the original packaging?" Abe asked. He turned the doll over and then faced her front again.

"Right. And why was she in that cupboard?"

Abe got a faraway look in his eyes. "I used to have

these books about a tiny Indian who lived in a cupboard."

"I read the first one, too. Loved it."

He lifted the diary. "Shall we read about the Girl in the Cupboard?"

"I wonder if it's Maude's diary."

"One way to find out." He opened the book and we began reading together.

The first dozen pages were indeed about the normal concerns of a teenage girl. Complaining about her hair, saying that Joey, a boy she liked, smiled back at her in geometry class, talking about going to the mall with her girlfriends. We read silently together, occasionally pointing to a funny passage or a sad one. One page was nothing but a curlicued heart in red ink with *MS + JB* inscribed inside and the two names spelled out below.

"Maude Shultz and Joey Beaton," I read. "Do you know any Beatons around here?"

Abe shook his head.

The next page was filled with all versions of Maude's imagined married name—*Mr. and Mrs. Joseph Beaton, Maude Beaton, Mrs. J. Beaton*, and more, written in various experiments in handwriting style.

"She's quite the dreamer," Abe said. "What is she, fifteen, sixteen?"

I flipped back to the first page, marking our place with my finger. "She didn't put a year on it, but she's got to be in high school if she's taking geometry. Between fourteen and eighteen, I guess."

"Who gets married that young?"

"Nobody, but I remember having a crush on a boy at that age and writing the same kind of thing."

The name *Lovey* started appearing on the pages more regularly.

"That's an odd name. It sounds like a nickname, an endearment," he said. "I've never met anybody named Lovey."

"I wish Adele were around. I could ask her. She knows everything about everybody."

One entry read, *Dear Diary. That idiot Lovey—who names their daughter Love, anyway—she's always tagging along. I know we used to be friends, but I don't like her anymore. You think she'd get the message.* The next read, *Pathetic Lovey asked if she can come over and study after school. I told her no way. She started crying. Double pathetic.*

I looked at Abe. "She's really cruel to that girl."

"Isn't that a trademark of adolescent girls? I mean, I wasn't one, and I only have a son, but to hear several of Sean's friends who are girls talk?" He whistled. "They're only in middle school but boy, can they be cutting to each other."

We continued reading.

"Ooh, look at this one." I pointed to the page.

I can't believe it. Joey ate lunch with Lovey today. And looked like he was enjoying it. She probably begged him and he felt sorry for her.

"What was that about?" I asked.

"If Maude is as cruel as she sounds, could be this Joey dude doesn't actually like her and is trying to get to know a girl who isn't so mean." Abe frowned.

Christmas cards were pasted on the next few pages, with notes from an aunt and a couple of friends. We reached a page where the writing switched from a blue ink to a heavy black pen, maybe even a marker, and everything was in printed capital letters. Across the top of the page was written L'S SCHEDULE. ADDRESS. PHONE. A class schedule, a street address, and a phone number followed.

"*L* must be Lovey," I said. "If Maude doesn't like her so much, why is she writing down all her information?"

"Maybe she made up with her." Abe shrugged.

The ramblings about daily life no longer appeared. I flipped the page.

She's not getting away with this was written in black letters surrounded by a black box. Below it was a newsprint picture of a diminutive girl with long blond hair walking hand in hand with a tall, dark-haired boy down a hallway lined with tall lockers. The heading read A LICK OF GOSSIP and the caption on the picture was *Junior Lovey Rogers gets lovey-dovey with senior Joey Beaton. Can marriage be far behind?*

Abe made a tsking sound. "They still had that ridiculous gossip column in the South Lick High student newspaper when I went there."

"So presumably Maude is also a junior. And can drive." I watched the stove glowing with embers. "I'm not so sure I want to turn the page."

Abe laid his arm across my shoulders and squeezed. "You don't have to, you know. We can just close it and go to bed. Which sounds like a pretty good option to me." He nuzzled my neck, sending a delicious shiver up my scalp and down to my toes.

"Me, too. But I think I have to know."

I turned the page to see *December 4*, a picture of a stick figure of a girl with long hair, and the words

Will it work? A thin line extended from the figure's neck.

On the next page she'd written *December 18. Apparently not.*

Pasted on the following page was a faded short piece from the *Brown County Democrat* about the record cold and how the ice on Crooked Lake was already a foot thick on January 8. Someone was quoted declaring the ice officially safe for skating and ice fishing, and that conditions were prime because of the lack of snow.

I swore softly and twisted to look at Abe. "Why am I getting a bad feeling about this?"

"What? Why?"

"Abe, Crooked Lake is where we found Charles dead. In an ice fishing hole."

"Hey, it's the closest lake."

"Why is a high school girl tracking the thickness of the ice?"

"Who knows, maybe she liked to ice skate outdoors."

"Maybe." *Or maybe not.*

I turned the page again.

I have a new plan.

Preparing was the only word on the following page.

Getting ready the entry on the facing sheet.

She'll never suspect on the next page.

Then we saw the word *Done.*

I swallowed hard and slowly turned to the next page. A newspaper article was pasted on the right-hand page but folded in half. I glanced at Abe and sighed, then opened it.

FISHERMAN FINDS BODY IN CROOKED LAKE was the *Brown County Democrat* leading headline in an extra-large font.

I read the first paragraph aloud. "'A fisherman found the body of a local teenage girl yesterday in an ice hole on Crooked Lake. Authorities appear to suspect suicide after a note was retrieved from her coat pocket. Identification is being withheld pending notification of the parents, who are currently out of town.'"

I closed my eyes for a moment then opened them, shivering but not from a caress. Abe glanced at me and hurried to add more wood to the stove, but I wasn't shivering from cold, either. He poked until they lit, then latched the stove's door and joined me as I turned to the next page.

Maude was back to her girlish blue pen. *She thought I was getting friendly with her when I asked her to go for a moonlight walk on the lake and when I brought her a mug of hot chocolate to drink. She thought I was sharing a secret with her when I gave her the note in that plastic bag and told her to put it in her pocket and read it later. She was as pathetic as always when I suggested closing our eyes and holding our breath and making a wish. I just helped her hold her breath long enough for me to get my wish.*

Chapter 57

Abe and I stared at each other. A log popped in the stove and a flurry of sparks went up.

I wrenched my attention back to the diary and finished reading the entry in a whisper. "'*Then down the hole she went. Now I'll get my love back without her interfering.*'"

On the last page another red heart decorated with *MS + JB* stared up at us.

"Abe, Maude killed that girl. The same way she killed Charles." I brought my hand to my mouth.

He closed the book and set it on the end table next to the doll. "It looks that way, doesn't it?" He rubbed my shoulders. "Why would she murder her own husband, though? Maybe it's all coincidence."

The irregular tapping of the frozen rain had not let up. Despite the heat from the stove, I was chilled at my core. "Jo said Charles was psychologically abusive to her and Ron. I don't know why she didn't divorce him, if that was the case."

"Certain people stay in dysfunctional relationships for years," Abe said. "Hard to know why.

Myself, I made the choice to get out of my marriage when trying to fix it wasn't working. But killing your husband to get rid of him?" He whistled. "Extreme measures."

"I can't believe it. She must have killed Charles, and then come into the restaurant for breakfast with her mother like nothing had happened."

"That's a chilling thought."

I thought for a moment. "I heard a noise upstairs earlier in the week. It must have been her in my passageway, hoping to get the diary out of the wall so I didn't discover it. I went up to look and must have scared her off."

"When was that?"

"Monday, I think. She never got it out earlier, when the store was for sale." I thought for a moment. "Now I remember. She said she and Charles were away for the year when Jo sold the store. Maybe she didn't feel the need to retrieve the diary until she killed Charles the same way."

"And until you started ripping out walls. Then after you secured the place, she wasn't able to get in," Abe pointed out. "If the police learn about the death of the high school girl and they put that together with Charles's death, they would want to watch her pretty closely."

"I'm sure she was the one who cut the padlock and left the threatening note. Something else must have interrupted her that time, though, because she never succeeded." I thought a bit more. "Yeah, and the thread I found in the passageway was red. Maude wore a bright red coat the day after Charles was killed, but she wore a black one when she came in today, probably because her red one got torn in the tunnel. Why didn't I put those things together?"

"Because it's not your job?"

"You'd think I'd be smarter than that. I consider myself as a puzzle solver, Abe. I'm usually better than the average bear at this stuff. I kept seeing people wearing red everywhere, so maybe that's why I didn't connect the thread with Maude." I stood and rubbed my hands together over the stove. I couldn't seem to get warm.

When I looked back at Abe, he'd picked up the doll. *Huh.*

I plopped back on the couch next to him. "We shouldn't even be handling these items, now that they're evidence against Maude, but it's too late for that. And that doll just jogged a memory. A teenage babysitter of mine used to bring her old dolls over. I think there was a series of hippie dolls. The Season of Love dolls or something like that. Let me see." I held my hand out. "They had names like Peace and Flower." I lifted the doll's shirt and turned her around. "Yep. I was right." I showed him the word embossed on her waist in the back.

"'*Love,*'" Abe read and shook his head. "So Maude stuck a needle in the neck of the doll with the same name as the girl she wanted to kill."

"I wonder if she believed in voodoo, thought that would make Lovey get sick and die. And when it didn't, she killed her herself."

"The diary backs that up." He picked it up and flipped through until he found the page with the stick figure on it. "See that line?"

"The pin. And after she says it didn't work, she

writes that she has a new plan." I narrowed my eyes at the open diary. "We need to call this in."

"Yes, but—"

I retrieved my phone from my bag and swore. Not a bar to be seen. "You don't get reception here?" I heard a note of panic in my voice.

"Not usually. Sorry, Robbie. There's one carrier that sometimes reaches out here, but it's not mine. Or yours, I guess."

"No landline, either?"

He shook his head slowly. "My parents never saw the need. We're usually out here for a getaway, and they like to be inaccessible. When I come out with Sean, it's good for him not to be able to text twenty-four hours a day, too. Come sit down." He patted the couch. "We'll call the detective as soon as we get into range in the morning."

I sat, but perched sideways so I could face him. "I guess. She won't be able to do anything without the diary anyway."

"Exactly. Do you think Maude's mother knew anything about what she did?"

I turned and snuggled into his arm. "I doubt it." I thought about my conversations with Jo. "She did say something about Maude having a rough patch in high school, though. And Maude told me she'd joined the military to . . . how did she put it? To get her act together and serve her country at the same time. Maybe killing Lovey had more repercussions than she'd expected.

"If Jo had known, I can't believe she would have simply closed her eyes to it." I remembered Jo had had that brief look of panic when I told her I'd found stuff in the walls. Maybe she did know.

"Imagine Maude living with that, knowing she'd ended a person's life, and on purpose," Abe said. "Can you imagine it for yourself?"

"No."

"When I was in the Navy, some guys returning from Afghanistan certainly had a lot of trouble living with their memories."

"You didn't go near there, right? Didn't you say you were sent to Japan?"

"Yes." He took my hand. "For some reason they needed a medic in Japan more than in the war zone. Go figure. At least I didn't have to use my weapon."

We sat in silence then with our thoughts, holding hands, staring at the glowing logs, listening to the frozen rain. Thinking of a ruthless girl who'd become an equally ruthless woman.

Chapter 58

Good thing for analog clocks. We'd set a small battery-operated alarm clock for five-thirty. When it jangled, Abe reached for the lamp, but it wouldn't turn on.

He groaned. "Ice must have knocked out the power."

"Oh, dear." It was toasty and cozy under the down comforter, but when I poked my nose out, the dark air was frigid. Frigid but quiet. The frozen rain must have stopped. I pulled him back under with me.

"You were the one who wanted to get up and out of here," he murmured from an inch away.

I sighed. "I know. And I should." The deliciousness of our melded skin was just too much to part with.

He gave me a long smoldering kiss, and then sat up before things got interesting. "I'll get the woodstove going. Luckily, the kitchen stove runs on propane, so I can still make coffee.

"Good," I muttered.

"I'll bring you a mug when coffee's ready, okay?"

"I'd rather have you, but okay."

"Sugar, we might have serious chipping and scraping to do. And I'll bet I have twenty emergency calls waiting for me. This isn't going to be our last night together, you know."

I smiled to myself as I pulled the comforter over my head. I was beginning to think I never wanted to have a final night with Abraham O'Neill.

Half an hour later I was dressed, complete with knit hat and boots. Abe tossed me one of his mother's down vests to put on over my sweater, since the house was still quite cold. He'd lit three gas hurricane lanterns for light. I stood in front of the woodstove with my fingers wrapped around the most delicious cup of coffee I'd ever tasted.

Abe was suiting up in snow boots, the camouflage jacket, and an orange hat. He pulled on warm gloves and grabbed a flashlight. "I'm going to see how bad it is out there." He went into the front vestibule and opened the door.

He hadn't even closed it when I heard a *whoop* and a *thud*. I set down my coffee and hurried over. Abe lay a few feet from the door on his back on a silvery surface.

"Are you all right?" I asked him.

The light from inside revealed a world coated in ice. The walkway to the car looked like a skating rink. Every branch, every shrub I could see was covered with a thick layer of ice.

"Yeah," he grunted as he managed to turn over. "Grab the snow shovel inside the door, would you?" When I did, he said, "Hook yourself around the door jamb and extend the shovel end to me."

I fit my right hand into the handle, grabbed the door with my left arm, hooking my leg around the frame, and got the end of the shovel to Abe. He pulled himself along until he could grab the doorway himself. A moment later we were both back inside with the door closed.

"That's worse than I've ever seen it." He smiled wryly at me. "I'm afraid we're not getting out any time soon."

"So it didn't turn back to rain overnight."

"Sure didn't." He shook his head. "I should have brought the jeep."

"You have another car?"

"Yeah, for weather exactly like this. Four-wheel drive, studded snow tires, the works. But I wasn't expecting the frozen part. The VW is not famed for traveling anywhere on ice, I'm afraid."

"You weren't hurt in the fall, I hope." I held his face in my hands.

"Nah. I have pretty good falling reflexes. It's slick out there. Could take a while to melt. Sun won't come up for another hour, if we even see it."

"I wish I could get word to Danna. She's competent, but she'll be confused about where I am. If she could even make it in to work, with all this ice. And I really, really want to deliver that diary to Octavia."

Abe squeezed my shoulder. "Sorry, sugar. I can't get word to my boss, either. Tell you what. Let's have breakfast. After the sun comes up, I'll start salting and sanding to at least make a walkable path to the van. The county crew usually gets to the road out there fairly promptly. Then it's only a matter of getting the van from the house to the road."

Chapter 59

I watched from the kitchen window as Abe scattered salt and sand on the back steps and the ground below. The sun was up now that it was past seven-thirty, but the light still just filtered through the trees. If anything was going to melt the ice, it was going to be the salt, not the sunshine. Not for a while, anyway.

He came in and headed for the front door carrying two small buckets he'd filled from the larger ones out back.

"Can I help?" I asked.

"Let me do the first pass. We'll give it a few minutes to start melting, and then, sure, you can help. We have at least two ice chippers around here somewhere, which we'll need to break the ice enough to walk on." He opened the door and stood there while tossing out cup after cup of salt, farther and farther down the walk. He repeated that with sand and closed the door.

The house was starting to warm up, finally. The

embrace Abe delivered after he shed his outer wrappings made me even warmer.

"What do you want to do while we wait?" he asked in his huskiest voice, the one that made me want to drop whatever else I was doing. "We have board games. We could play cards. Or we could head back to—"

A glint of light flashed through the wide plate-glass window at the front of the house, like a reflection off glass or polished metal.

"What was that?" He whipped his head to the right. "Hang on a second." He hurried to the edge of the window. "Someone's here." He turned toward me, frowning and beckoning.

I joined him. Behind his VW I saw the passenger side of a big dark SUV. The sun angled off its windshield, making it impossible to see the driver. An identical big black SUV had sat in Maude's driveway.

"A friend of Mom's sometimes parks here when she goes hunting," Abe said with furrowed brow. "But it's only small critter season right now, like rabbits and fox. And she wouldn't park me in like that."

"Abe, Maude drives a car just like that," I murmured.

"Why would she be here?"

"Uh-oh." I pointed. From beyond the van I saw the driver's door open on the other side of the SUV. A dark hat appeared above it.

With a loud crack the glass in the far side of the cabin's front window split open. A zing hit the wall beyond. Abe instantly pulled me away and to the floor. Shards splashed onto the area under the break.

"Was that a shot?" I cried. My heart hammered at my rib case.

"Yes. Stay down."

Another shot cracked over our heads and slammed into the back wall. Abe pulled me with him on hands and knees around behind the couch.

"That's a big gun. Military issue, I'd say," he whispered.

"Maude. She was in the Army. She must have trailed us or something."

He nodded, regarding me intensely.

"Are the doors locked?" I asked.

"Not a chance," he whispered back. "But with any luck she won't be able to get up the walk."

"How did she even get down the drive?"

"Car like that with studded tires can go almost anywhere."

I gasped when the next shot took out another window. At least it didn't sound like it was fired from any closer. The cold air was countering the heat of the woodstove at an alarming rate.

"Do you have a hunting rifle?" I asked, my voice shaking. What were we going to do?

"No. We're gun free around here." He squared his jaw. "But I'm a crack shot with the bow."

"I know you're both in there," Maude's voice rang out. "I want the diary."

My brain raced. She must have broken into the store last night, found the diary missing from the cupboard where she'd left it. "We can't give it to her," I whispered. "If we do, she'll get close enough to kill us. But let's see what she says." I cleared my throat. "I'm all alone here," I called. I hoped she hadn't seen us clearly through the window.

"Where's O'Neill?"

"He went out snowshoeing early to check his . . . fox traps. He's not back yet."

Abe nodded encouragement.

"If I give you the book, will you leave?" I asked.

"Give it to me first," Maude shouted.

"You have to promise you won't shoot me," I shouted back. As if that kind of promise would mean anything.

"Ha," she scoffed. "I can do what I want. I'm the one with the gun, remember."

"Is that how you killed Charles?" I called out.

"The bastard. He was going to tell my mother about her real daughter. I'd been taking his crap for years, but that put me over the top."

I stared wide eyed at Abe. I'd seen the resemblance between Jo and Zen. Charles must have, too.

"So?" I called. "She wouldn't have dropped you just because she found her birth daughter."

"Enough talking. I need the diary now," she yelled. "Did you read it?"

"Not yet. I was going to as soon as I did the dishes." I rolled my eyes, not sure where all these lies were coming from.

"Liar," she called.

Abe whispered. "I'm going to get the bow. I'll head out the back door and try to pick her off. You should come with me."

"No. She'd get suspicious. I'll keep her talking. But what about the ice?"

"I can crawl on my elbows and knees. Military training. I hate to leave you in here alone."

"It's okay." Not really, but it needed to be okay. "Be careful."

Another shot slammed into the house, hitting the front door. I swore.

As he coiled himself for his exit, I whispered, "Love you." Because that's what it felt like.

"Yeah." He flashed me a dimple and then scurried, back bent like a beetle, into the back porch.

"You going to give it to me or do I have to come in there?" Maude called.

"What's in it, anyway? I used to keep a sweet sixteen diary. Was that yours?"

She snorted audibly. "Right. It was a real sweet year."

I heard the back door click softly shut. A third window shattered from another shot. How many bullets did she have in that thing? Just our luck it would be one of those semi-automatic things with a zillion rounds in it that I read about with awful tragic regularity in the news.

Please don't let Abe be the next statistic. Or me. I sent my prayer out into the universe.

"In my diary all I wrote about was boys, school, and girlfriends," I called, trying to keep my tone light.

"That's pretty much what I wrote about, too." She barked a cheerless laugh. "Jordan, I need the book and I need it now. I'm assuming you don't have any weapons, but if you do, lay them on the ground and stand up in front of the window with your hands on your head. Now."

"No way. I'll toss the book out. You can take it and leave."

"Sorry. Do what I tell you or you're dead."

I didn't even know if my legs would hold me. My throat thickened. I pushed up to my feet and quickly got my hands on my head. I spied her standing behind the open car door about fifteen yards away, her head above the roof. She must be perched on the running board or whatever they called it. Abe was right. It was a wicked-looking weapon and she was pointing it with both hands straight at me, her arms resting on the top of the door. Thank goodness a few trees were between us, but they weren't big ones.

Where was Abe? I tried to look without moving my head, but I couldn't see him. I swallowed down my fear. "How can I give you the book with my hands on my head?" I asked.

"Where is it?"

"Right here next to me on this end table." My voice shook. I swallowed hard. There was nothing to prevent her from killing me and snatching the book. *Wait.* Of course there was. The ice. She couldn't get to the house. Unless she had cleats on her boots. But if she had cleats she'd already be in the house. And if she killed me and waited for the ice to melt to get the diary, she didn't know when Abe would come back and find her.

"Pick it up with your right hand."

"I'm left-handed."

"All right, already." Maude cursed. "With your left. Open the door and throw it toward me as far as you can. Flat like a Frisbee."

She was out of luck there. I'd always been terrible with any sport involving eye-hand coordination. I still needed to stall for time so Abe could get in position and take aim. He'd have only one chance.

"I have a terrible arm. There's a shovel near the door. I'll put the book on that and shove it across the ice to you."

"No. Throw it. I don't want you touching that shovel."

"I'm picking the book up now," I called, nearly screeching. I grabbed the book and moved into the vestibule as slowly as I could, trying to swallow down my fear.

"Hurry up!"

I swung open the door and stood there, relying on her being desperate to have the diary. My legs shook. I gulped in air. I readied the book, curling it toward me with a clammy hand. I got ready to dive back into the house as soon as I threw it. I didn't have a shred of doubt that she'd kill me as soon as she held the diary.

A branch cracked. A brushing noise whistled. It was followed by another and then by the crack of gunshot. But the shot wasn't aimed at me.

Maude disappeared. Abe cried out.

"No!" I screamed.

Chapter 60

I waited. No more shots. "Abe!" I called.

"Here, Robbie." His voice was weak and came from the woods to the right of the driveway.

Had Abe hit Maude? "Can you see Maude?" I called.

He didn't answer. Had she shot him? Maude didn't speak, either. Was she feigning injury with her silence? Would she kill me if I went to him? I had to risk it.

I looked around. Little holes from the salt dappled the front walk. I dropped the diary and took a couple of stomping steps, breaking through the ice. I crunched down the walk to the drive as fast as I could. Crossing in front of the VW, I stepped into the woods and looked all around, searching. I couldn't see Abe, but at least there were no more shots.

"Where are you?" My voice wobbled. "Abe, talk to me!"

"Here."

I whipped my head to the sound and finally spied

him behind the wide trunk of an old oak. I hurried to him, crunching through the icy crust and into the snow below. Still wearing the camouflage jacket, he was curled up behind the tree, clutching his thigh. The bow lay discarded a yard away. The snow around his leg was tinged with red.

"She shot you! Let me see." Kneeling next to him, I tore off my hat.

When he took his hand away from his leg, blood oozed through a hole in his pants near his groin. I pressed my hat on it and leaned into it with both hands.

"Where'd you learn to do that?" he asked with a faint smile. His face was as pale as linen.

"Never mind. You must have gotten her. She stopped shooting." How was I going to get medical help to him or get him to a hospital? *Think, Jordan, think.*

"I blew it," Abe said. "Stepped on a branch. She saw me and got off a shot. She missed, almost. I didn't."

"You didn't blow it. You're alive, aren't you?" I lifted my cap, dismayed to see new blood seeping out. I pressed again. "We have to get you out of here. Can you keep pressing on this? I'm going to run in and get something to bandage the wound. And a blanket."

"Okay." His strength seemed to be ebbing fast.

I swallowed away the despair threatening to close up my throat. I guided his hand to the wound, then ripped off the down vest I was wearing. I laid it over him and snugged it around his neck. "Please keep your eyes open. Sing to yourself or something."

I heard faint traces of "Staying Alive" as I dashed

to the house. I tore a pillowcase off a bed pillow and found a pair of scissors to start the rip. The scissors slipped from my hand as it shook from the cold. I dashed to the back hall and shrugged on a wool coat that smelled of wood smoke and Abe. Blinking back tears, I focused on making bandages as fast as I could. When I was holding a half dozen long pieces of cotton, I grabbed the blanket off the back of the couch and headed for the door.

"No. Phone," I told myself and scrabbled in my bag until I found it.

Abe's eyes were closed and his hand had fallen away from the wound. "Abe. Sweetheart." I knelt again and patted his cheeks. "Wake up, please." The blood-soaked hat lay damp on the snow.

His eyelids fluttered open. "Just tired."

"I know. Tell me the alphabet. Count backwards from a hundred. Anything." I folded one strip of pillowcase a bunch of times and pressed that against his wound. At least the bleeding was ebbing.

"Ichi. Ni. San. Shi. Go . . ."

"Counting in Japanese? That's good," I said as I wrapped the leg tightly three or four times, tying off the final ends. "Keep going."

"Roku. Shichi. Hachi. Kyu . . . Jyu."

"Good. Now we're going to have to walk to Maude's car. I'm driving you to town, or at least to a cell signal." I slid my arms under his armpits. "Come on now, sit up with me. Put your head on my shoulder. That's it." I managed to get him sitting. "Now brace yourself. I'm going to stand and pull you up. Okay?"

"Okay," he whispered.

I let him go and got to my feet, then draped the

blanket around his shoulders. Bracing my feet, bending my knees, I extended both hands to him. *Thank goodness for biker's thighs.*

"Up you go." I almost fell over backwards, and I cringed at his cry of pain, but a second later he was up. I maneuvered myself next to him, slinging his arm over my shoulders, my arm around his waist. "Hop if you have to."

The SUV seemed impossibly far away. We were going to have to steer around trees. I marveled that Abe had figured out how to get an arrow into Maude without hitting any obstacles. Ice still coated every branch of the trees, no matter how tiny, and sun lit them up like a forest full of twinkling glass. How could it look so beautiful when we'd both nearly lost our lives? Maude apparently had lost hers or at least her ability to kill us. We'd see in a minute.

Finally I could see the driver's side of the SUV. Maude lay face down on the ground. Her feet remained hooked over the edge of the open doorway, and the thick weapon had slid beyond reach of her fingers. She had to be dead.

The car was still running. The quiet clean air smelled of exhaust. Like it had when the police snowmobiles had arrived at Charles's death.

Abe made a sound deep in his throat when he saw Maude. He swayed.

"Come on," I urged. "We're almost there. And she's beyond help." At least that's what it looked like. I moved him past Maude and opened the back door of the SUV. How was I going to get him in? "Can you grab the top of the doorway?"

He nodded. It looked like it took the last speck of his strength. He stepped up with his good leg and swung himself in, the blanket sliding off his shoulders. He collapsed in a near fetal position on the wide seat. I covered him with the blanket and closed the door.

I turned toward Maude. Reaching down, I touched her neck. No pulse. "I'm sorry, Maude. I'm sorry your life was so horrible you felt you needed to kill people. But right now I'm taking your car." I unhooked her feet and slid her legs aside so I wouldn't run over them backing out. I climbed into the driver's seat and moved it forward so I could reach the pedals. Before I closed the door, I heard the insistent knocking of a Pileated woodpecker echoing through the trees, setting the tempo, telling me to hurry.

Chapter 61

Because of the ice, I drove slowly on the access road. The last thing we needed was to end up in a ditch or a snowbank. Right before I arrived at Route 46, I pulled over and checked my phone. *Yes, bars!* I jabbed 911. When a dispatcher answered, I ever so briefly outlined what had happened and where we were.

"Do you feel you are still in danger, ma'am?" she asked.

"Not from our attacker, but Abe O'Neill needs urgent medical care. Please tell them to hurry." My words ended in a sob. I had to stay strong for Abe. "Should I keep driving or stay here where they can find me?"

"Please stay where you are. Help is on the way. Is the victim breathing?"

"Just a sec." I left the car in PARK but kept it running with the heat on its highest setting and climbed into the back with Abe. His chest rose and fell regularly, and under the blanket my makeshift bandage was still holding despite blood seeping through it. He was barely with me but opened his eyes, then they drifted closed and stayed there.

"Yes, he's breathing but kind of going in and out of consciousness, I think."

"Keep the call open, ma'am. Alert me to any change in his status," she instructed.

"Okay." I snugged the blanket around him and waited, my hand stroking his shoulder. Tears burned my eyes and threatened to close my throat. I shook them off. I had to stay present and not wallow in worry.

An ambulance pulled up several minutes later, followed by Buck and Octavia in separate cars. I jumped out and pointed to the backseat. "He's in there. Hurry."

I watched as the paramedics tended to Abe, finally strapping him to a wheeled gurney. "One second, guys." I leaned down and kissed Abe's forehead. "You're going to make it. I'll see you there."

"Love you," he whispered.

"Yeah." I sniffed and wiped my eyes as the guys slid him into the back of the ambulance. The doors closed and the vehicle rolled away, lights flashing and siren screaming. I leaned my back against the SUV, closing my eyes. If the ground hadn't been frozen I would have slid to sitting and stayed there for a long, long time.

Someone cleared their throat next to me. I reluctantly opened my eyes to see Octavia standing in front of me with folded arms. "Who shot O'Neill?"

I swallowed. "Give me one minute, okay? I have to tell Danna why I'm not at work."

When she nodded, I texted Danna. Really sorry. Trapped by ice, then Abe shot in leg. Hope to follow

him to hosp. I didn't add, After the cops get through
with me.

Seconds later she responded.

No! You OK? No probs here. Phil helping. But
store window broken overnight.

I wrote back. I'm fine. Talk later.

Maude must have broken the window and gotten
in that way.

I slid the phone into my pocket and straightened
my shoulders. "All right," I told Octavia.

I'd told dispatch there was a shooting and
Charles Stilton's murderer was dead, but nothing
more. "Maude Stilton tried to kill us both. Abe got
her with an arrow."

"Is she alive?" Octavia's eyebrows went up and
stayed there.

I shook my head.

"We need you to show us the victim and the
cabin, Robbie. And you shouldn't be driving this
vehicle."

I glared at her. "I had to! Maude blocked Abe's
van. She was trying to kill us. Did you want him to
die out there in the woods? There was no cell reception, no landline."

"Sorry. Not blaming you for anything. Just come
with me, all right?" She pointed to her vehicle.

Buck ambled up. "Want she should ride with me?"

"Can I?" I asked.

"No. But please follow us, Buck, so you can give
her a ride back." Octavia ushered me into the front
seat of her car, a small SUV that looked plain until

I noticed the police-type dashboard and the light on top of it.

"Turn around and go back down this road," I said. "It's still icy, though."

"Already in four-wheel drive. Please tell me what all transpired."

"I'd spent the night with Abe O'Neill at his family's cabin." Despite the heat blasting through the vents, my teeth chattered. "We couldn't get out this morning because of the ice. Maude Stilton showed up—"

"How did she know where to find you?"

I thought for a minute. "Yesterday in the restaurant I mentioned to Danna where I was going. Maude was there and overhead me. She probably knew the O'Neill family. Or Googled their vacation house. I really don't know."

"Please go on."

"Maude showed up this morning and started shooting at the house."

"Why would she do that?"

"Right before I left with Abe yesterday I found a diary in an upstairs wall of my building. It was Maude's from when she was a teenager. Abe and I read it last night. And get this. In the diary, she confessed to killing a classmate. Exactly the same way she killed Charles."

"In an ice fishing hole."

"Exactly." I stared at Octavia. "In the diary, it sounds like she suffocated the girl. How did Charles die? Buck told me there wasn't any water in his lungs so he was dead before he went in."

Octavia rolled her eyes a little. "He knows not to share that level of detail. That said, you deserve to know. It doesn't matter now. We found Rohypnol in his blood."

I wrinkled my nose. "What's that?"

"It's a sedative like Valium, but it's sold on the street. One of the so-called date rape drugs. Made in Mexico. They call it *roofie* or *roach*. Maude could have given it to him in a drink then walked him out onto the ice. He would have been too sedated to resist suffocation. Maude was enough bigger than him to pull it off."

"Drugged." I turned to stare at her. "Maude said something the other day about how Georgia could have drugged Charles and shoved him into the hole. I didn't notice, but now that I think of it, there certainly hadn't been mention of drugs in the news about his death."

"Absolutely none. Too bad you didn't think to tell me."

I opened my mouth to object, but Octavia held up her hand. "Please. I'm not blaming you, Robbie."

I stared out the front window. "I wonder if Maude could have given her teenage victim a similar drug in the eighties." In the hot chocolate she gave Lovey.

"Certainly possible. Many of the sedatives were developed in the sixties."

"Maude had to be my passageway intruder," I said. "She must have been desperate to get the diary back. She grew up in the house so she obviously knew about the tunnel."

"I'm surprised she didn't get it out before you bought the building."

I nodded slowly. "On Saturday morning she came for breakfast with her mother, Jo Schultz. Maude mentioned she'd been away on sabbatical with

Charles when the store sold. Until she heard I was renovating up there, maybe she thought the diary would be safe in the wall. Since she'd just used the same method to kill Charles, she had even more reason to want the diary back."

"Sounds plausible."

"She tried to retrieve it last night sometime after I left at six-thirty. Danna said a window was broken in the store this morning. Maude found the diary gone, and came over here to get it back."

"So she threatened to kill you and Mr. O'Neill, too."

"Yes. She shot out half the windows in the front of the house. The path was so icy she stayed standing in the open door to her car."

"Then what happened?" Octavia asked.

"Hang on a minute. I think our turn is coming up." I peered at the side of the road. Abe had found it in the dark, but I wasn't sure I could locate it even in daylight. "There it is. Go slow, now." Last night in the downpour I hadn't seen the rustic pointing hand made of wood with the words *O'Neill Paradise* carved into it.

After she made the turn, I said, "Abe snuck out the back door. He's an experienced bow hunter. I told Maude he wasn't there and that I hadn't read the diary. She kept demanding I throw it to her."

"Did you?"

"Wait. Stop here." I caught sight of Maude and swallowed hard. I pointed. "There she is." I glanced at her still awkwardly positioned body and then looked away. I didn't need to see any more. I gestured toward the house. "There are all the shot out windows."

"You weren't kidding about that," Octavia said. "I'm guessing you kept Maude talking while O'Neill approached from the woods?"

"Right."

Sliding a bit, the vehicle stopped in time to not run over Maude's body.

Octavia faced me. "Go ahead and finish your story."

"I was about to throw the diary when Abe got Maude with an arrow, but he cracked a branch right before he did and she managed to hit him in the leg."

"How did you get him out, wounded as he is?"

"It wasn't easy, but I needed to. So I just did."

"The diary still inside?"

"Yes, and a voodoo-type doll that looks like the girl, whose name was Lovey."

Octavia nodded slowly. "The presumed suicide that recently came into question. Interesting. Thank you for those details. Officer Bird will take you home."

"Can I at least get my bag out of the house? Maude was never in there."

Octavia thought for a moment. "Okay."

"Thanks." I opened the car door.

"One more thing. Did you touch the body, move it at all?"

I shivered. "I had to move her legs. Her feet were on the car door opening. I didn't want to run her over."

"Got it. Nice work, Robbie. You did a couple brave strong things here, both of you."

I sat in silence for a moment reliving what had happened less than an hour earlier. The glass flying.

The gunshots. Abe's bravery. His marksmanship. My anguish at his bleeding. My desperation to get him help. "We just did what we had to do."

"I'm sorry we didn't get to Ms. Stilton before you did. She was up there on our suspect list, certainly. Not a scrap of alibi. Lying about her son didn't help, either."

"Where did Maude say Charles had been that night?" I asked.

"She told us he'd gone to his new mistress's house, that she didn't know who it was this time."

"All fabrication on her part?"

"Yes. Convincing her son to lie about seeing Ms. Perlman on the lake just topped it off. I'm only sorry Ms. Stilton can't be fully prosecuted for both murders, and a couple attempted ones, too."

Despite the lack of prosecution, it seemed to me Maude had received the ultimate punishment.

Chapter 62

I sat by the window in Abe's hospital room. He hadn't gotten out of surgery and recovery until about one o'clock. Buck had taken me home from the cabin. He'd taken one glance at me and patted my knee, then drove in blessed silence. I was all talked out.

Once we'd arrived at my store I'd asked Buck who would tell Jo and Ron about Maude's death, and he said he'd do it personally. He also said he would contact Abe's parents.

I'd briefly checked in with Danna and Phil. Phil had boarded up the broken window and the restaurant was full of locals who could walk there.

Then I'd slowly driven my van to Bloomington, grateful for the salt and sand trucks, which were out everywhere.

I watched Abe sleep. His injured leg was elevated and an IV trailed out of his arm, but he was otherwise unencumbered by machines. Color had blessedly returned to his face and his hair was tousled like it had been last night. *Only last night.* The morning had felt like it had lasted a week.

But he was all right. I was all right. And Maude would never kill again.

He opened his eyes. When he caught sight of me, a shadow of his dimple dented his cheek. He patted the bed next to him. I walked over and gently kissed his lips, then perched at his side, taking his hand.

"You did awesome, Robbie. Keeping her distracted like that, rescuing me. You must have medic training. And braveness training, too."

"Girl Scouts. I always loved wrapping up wounds, both real and imagined. You were the brave one, though."

"Stupid, more like it. Didn't see that branch. I'd have an intact leg if I had. I spent my childhood trying to walk 'like an Indian.'" He surrounded the last words with finger quotes. "Probably not supposed to say things like that any more, but you know, walking without rustling leaves or stepping on noisy branches. Guess I'm out of practice."

"Doesn't matter now."

He gazed at the window. When he looked back at me, the lines at the edges of his eyes had deepened. "I killed her, didn't I?"

I stroked the back of his hand. "Yes. I don't know how you shot so accurately, but you did."

He let out a sigh. "I know it was self-defense. More important, it was defending you. But it's a tough thing to live with."

"You're going to be okay." We could get him counseling if he wanted. Later.

I heard my phone vibrate in my bag and retrieved it. "It's Jo," I told him.

His mouth turned down. "You should talk to her."

"I know." I waited another ring before connecting. This was going to be hard. Abe had killed her daughter.

"Robbie, Buck came over with the news," Jo said. "I wanted to tell you how sorry I am for Maude's actions. I feel responsible."

"Please don't, Jo. Hey, okay if I put you on speaker? I'm in the hospital with Abe."

After a moment of not speaking, she said it was fine and greeted Abe, who said hello back.

"Anyway, Maude was responsible for herself," I said. "But I'm sorry you lost her."

She sniffed. "I'm sorry, too, more than you know. The poor dear always was troubled and I never figured out how to fix it for her."

I flashed on that brief look of panic on Jo's face when I said I was demolishing the upstairs. "Did you know what Maude did as a teenager?" I asked.

What followed was a silence so full I thought it might burst.

"Buck told me about the diary. I knew Maude and that girl were friends, and then they weren't. When I heard about the suicide, I asked Maude about it over and over. She insisted she didn't know anything about the matter. She'd been at another friend's house—or so she said—and I let it go." Jo cleared her throat. "The police never came asking. Now I know I was somehow complicit in Lovey's death by not going to them. I never saw the diary, though, and I didn't have any proof. It was just a sense I had."

I glanced at Abe. He shook his head slowly, sadly.

"Maude had a tough time with all kinds of things as a teenager," Jo went on.

"It must be hard to raise a teen," I said.

"I can vouch for that," Abe added.

"Joining the military seemed to straighten her out, give her a purpose," Jo said.

"So you didn't know about the diary in the wall upstairs at my place?" I asked Jo.

"No. I'll tell you, though, Maude was upset when I sold the building during the time she and Chuck were away. Anyway, that's all done now. I'm going to miss my girl terribly, as difficult as she was. But at least I have Ronnie, and I'm glad for that."

"I'm glad he has you," I said.

"Yes." Jo sniffed again. "I wanted to tell you that Zenobia and I had a brief reunion last night. It was awkward, but I think we might find our way to getting to know each other at last."

"I hope so." Too bad Zen and Maude wouldn't get a half sister reunion. Given what happened with mine, and what kind of person Maude was, it might not have been so wonderful. Actually, they weren't blood half sisters after all, I thought, because Maude was adopted. Water under the bridge, anyway.

I glanced at Abe, who was pointing at his chest. I nodded.

"Jo, may I say how terrible I feel that things played out the way they did?" Abe said.

"You poor thing, Abe. To be threatened like that."

"I never wanted to kill Maude. But she gave us no choice."

"I know. I know that better than anyone. And if it means anything, I forgive you." Jo fell silent

"I appreciate that," Abe said softly.

Jo cleared her throat. "I'll let you two visit now. I need to go find my grandson."

We all said good-bye and I disconnected the call. After a moment of quiet, I said, "She forgave you before you even asked."

"She's got a big heart." He shifted in bed and winced.

The door flew open, and Sean hurried in. "Dad!" He reached the other side of the bed in two loping teenage steps and threw his arms around Abe's neck.

I let go of Abe's hand and stood.

Abe grinned at me even as his eyes filled. "Hey, buddy." He stroked Sean's back like he was a toddler.

Sean finally straightened, wiping the corners of his eyes. "They called to say you were shot. And that you were awesome brave."

"I wouldn't say that, exactly," Abe said. "How'd you get here, anyway?"

"Grandma brought me. She's parking the car. So you shot that person?" Sean's eyes were wide in his skinny acned face. "With the longbow?"

"You do what you have to do, son. Right, Robbie?" Abe's dimple was back in full force.

I smiled at both of them. "Right."

Recipes

Warm up Your Tootsies Omelet

Serves four.

Ingredients

4 corn tortillas
1 tablespoon butter
4 eggs, beaten
½ cup pepper jack cheese, grated
2 tablespoons roasted red peppers, drained and
  chopped
Sour cream, to taste
Salt and pepper, to taste
Jalapeno salsa, to taste

Directions

Wrap tortillas in foil and warm in oven.

Melt butter in a non-stick skillet on medium low
heat. Pour in eggs and swirl around to coat pan.
When it starts to set, gently lift the edges and swirl
uncooked egg underneath. Sprinkle on cheese and
red peppers.

When set, fold in half and remove to a plate. Spread
two tortillas on two other plates and top each with a
quarter of the omelet. Add a dollop of sour cream,
salt and pepper, and salsa to taste.

Sullo Scio

Serves four.

Ingredients

 4 fat cloves garlic, peeled and minced
 2 tablespoons olive oil
 1 tablespoon minced fresh rosemary
 1 large can whole tomatoes, rough chopped in
   the can
 1 15-ounce can chick peas (garbanzo beans)
 1 quart chicken stock
 1 package tagliatelle
 1 teaspoon kosher salt
 Black pepper to taste
 Parmesan cheese, freshly grated

Directions

In a medium saucepan, sauté the garlic in the olive
oil until soft. Do not brown. Add the rosemary,
tomatoes, salt and pepper to taste, and chick peas.

Add the stock and bring to a boil. Add the tagliatelle
and cook until al dente according to the directions
on the package.

Serve hot with fresh grated Parmesan.

Grits with Cheese
(Used by permission from the
Grit Girl, Georgeanne Ross)

Serves six.

Ingredients

    2 cups chicken broth
    ½ cup whipping cream
    1 cup Original Grit Girl Stone Ground yellow
       grits
    2 cups grated white cheddar cheese

Directions

Combine broth and cream in a large sauce pan;
bring to a boil.

Stir in the grits, stirring constantly. Cover the pan
and reduce the heat. Simmer ten to twenty minutes,
stirring as needed. Stir in cheese.

Serve with shrimp, eggs, sausage, or whatever you
like.

Pork Chops with Sorghrum Sauce
(With inspiration from NYT bestselling author
Sheila Connolly, used by permission)

Serves two to four.

Ingredients

    2 boneless pork chops
    Salt and pepper
    2 tablespoon olive oil
    2 tablespoon butter
    8 ounces mushrooms, sliced
    1 tablespoon minced garlic
    1 tablespoon flour
    ½ cup Sorghrum (a liquor distilled from
        sorghum, or bourbon if you can't find it)
    1 cup chicken broth
    1½ teaspoon finely grated lemon rind
    1 teaspoon thyme, dried or fresh
    1 tablespoon lemon juice

Directions

Dry the meat with paper towels and sprinkle with
salt and pepper.

In a large skillet over medium-high heat, heat one
tablespoon of oil until it shimmers. Add the pork
chops and cook until they are browned on the
bottom and are slightly springy when you touch
them, not stiff. Turn and brown the second side.

Transfer to a plate, cover and keep warm.

Swirl one tablespoon of butter and one of oil in the skillet. Lower the heat to medium-low, add the mushrooms, and sauté until they begin to exude juices.

Add the garlic and a bit more salt and cook until the garlic softens (about one minute). Add the flour and cook, stirring, for another minute (to cook the flour).

Remove the pan from the heat and stir in the alcohol. Return to the heat, raise it to medium and simmer, stirring to incorporate the tasty stuff in the pan. This is where you burn off the alcohol in the whiskey, in case you're worried.

After about a minute, add the chicken broth and whisk. Simmer, stirring occasionally, until the liquid is reduced to about ½ cup (it should thicken slightly).

Add the lemon juice, lemon rind, and thyme, and heat through over medium-low heat.

Add one more tablespoon of butter, then taste for seasoning. Add salt and pepper if desired.

When you serve the dish, spoon the sauce on the meat and serve immediately. Spoon extra sauce on noodles, rice, or potatoes as a side dish if desired.

Please turn the page for an exciting sneak peek of
Maddie Day's next Country Store Mystery

BISCUITS AND SLASHED BROWNS

coming soon wherever print and e-books are sold!

Chapter 1

The banner outside Pans 'N Pancakes read, "Join Maple Mania!" The Brown County Maple Festival's logo of a grinning bottle of syrup beamed its invitation, but the look on Professor Elissa Genest's face would have frozen butter on a tall stack of hot flapjacks.

I'd hung the banner across the wide covered porch of my country store restaurant and had stepped into the road to check the level. Instead, I watched as the middle-aged scholar glued her fists to her hips and glared at a portly man in a perfectly tailored suit with sharply creased trousers. He'd just climbed out of a silver Lexus and hadn't said a word so far.

"How dare you?" she snarled, not trying to keep her voice down. Elissa, a long-time resident of our little town of South Lick, Indiana, and a regular at Pans 'N Pancake, had just finished a full breakfast inside.

The man clasped his hands in front of him and sort of smiled, but his top lip curled, making him look like he'd tasted curdled milk. "My dear, can I help it if my grant proposal was funded and yours wasn't?"

"I'm not your dear." She spoke each scorn-laced word distinctly.

They must be continuing a prior disagreement. I abandoned my banner examination and approached the pair. "Good morning, sir. I'm Robbie Jordan, owner and chef here." I extended my hand.

"Ah, Ms. Jordan. I was just coming to sample your menu. Your restaurant is quite the talk of the conference." He patted his expansive stomach and talked through his smile, his tiny eyes almost disappearing in the flesh of his cheeks. "I'm Warren Connolly."

I shook his extended hand. The academic conference on maple tree science was on a parallel track with the Maple Festival, which aimed to bring tourists to town in March, a normally dead time of year for local businesses. The festival schedule included opportunities to learn about sugaring off, fun events for children, a Native American maple syrup demonstration in Brown County State Park, and themed culinary cook-offs. This afternoon was the breakfast event, with area chefs competing to produce the winning maple-favored breakfast item right here at my restaurant. I hoped I was ready.

But I'd never really trusted people who talked and smiled at the same time. Elissa looked like she didn't, either.

"Nice to meet you, Mr. Connolly," I said. "Are you at Indiana University or from out of town?"

"It's Professor Connolly. I teach and do my research at Boston College."

"Research." Elissa surrounded the word with finger quotes. "You call accepting money from climate-change deniers and then countering well-established facts with some environmental fantasy research?" She shook her head and turned away, her words sizzling the frosty early-March air. "Great breakfast, Robbie," she called as she headed for her car.

"Thanks," I answered, but I wasn't sure she heard me. I shivered, since I wasn't exactly dressed for forty-degree weather in my jeans, long-sleeved t-shirt, and blue store apron. The sun promised to warm the day later, though. Cold nights and warm days created perfect conditions for inciting maple sap to run in the veins of trees all over Indiana's most heavily forested county. Since it was only eight o'clock, we were still in the chilly part of the cycle.

"How about that breakfast?" I said in a bright tone to the professor.

He laid a hand on the railing. He nodded slowly. "Excellent idea," he said, but his now unsmiling gaze was on Elissa's sedan as it disappeared down the road toward the center of town.

My new employee, Turner Rao, gave me a frantic look. Danna, my tall and able assistant since I'd opened last fall, was away at a volleyball tournament and I'd apparently been outside a few minutes too long. Turner was frantically flipping whole wheat banana walnut pancakes, turning sausages and bacon, and rescuing an almost burnt pair of toasts. Across the room a customer with an empty platter waved his hand in the air like he wanted his check, while another held up her coffee mug signaling for a refill. I pointed Professor Connolly to a table for two in the corner, mouthed "Sorry" to Turner, and grabbed the coffee pot.

I'd restored order in a couple of minutes, grateful I'd found the slim twenty-two year old to help out, since Danna and I had agreed we really needed a third worker. Turner was a good enough short order cook to man the grill, and despite his recent college degree he didn't mind waiting and busing tables or doing cleanup. Danna and I also wore all hats around here, although I was the only one who did the books and paid the bills. It was my business, after all. I'd purchased the run-down country store over a year ago, and had used the carpentry skills my late mother taught me to do the renovation work myself. I was the proud proprietor of a popular breakfast and lunch restaurant that also sold vintage cookware and a few other odds and ends, including my Aunt Adele's gorgeous yarn from her nearby sheep farm. I was almost done renovating the second floor of the building into several rooms I planned to rent out as a bed and breakfast. The village of South Lick in scenic hilly Brown County was now this native Californian's home—my apartment conveniently abutted the store at the back—and I couldn't be happier.

It would all fall apart, though, if I didn't keep my customers happy, too. I delivered a menu to the professor and asked if he'd like coffee.

"Sure." He gave the menu a once-over glance and handed it back. "I'll have the Kitchen Sink omelet, with biscuits, plus bacon—crisp—and hash browns."

I waited for the "please." When it wasn't forthcoming, I said, "You got it."

"I don't suppose you serve Bloody Marys, do you?"

"Sorry, no liquor license." I decided not to mention I had a BYOB policy in place. I didn't advertise it, but regulars knew they could bring a bottle of wine or a couple of beers to lunch to celebrate special occasions. The state restricted the practice to wine and beer, only, and I wasn't allowed to pour it. Someone occasionally showed up with a bottle for Sunday brunch, but never for breakfast on a Thursday.

"I didn't think so." He pulled his mouth in disappointment. "What's the best bar in town?" He drummed his puffy fingers on the table. A gold ring featuring an embedded diamond dented his right pinkie.

I glanced at the big old school clock on the wall—he wanted a bar before nine in the morning? "The Casino Tavern, on the other side of town. Actually it's the only bar in town." A casino in South Lick had flourished over a hundred years ago, in the heyday of the mineral springs, but the present-day bar was a casino in name only. "The conference is in Nashville, right?" I'd lived in Brown County for four years. By now I said the name of the colorful artsy county seat like the locals did, swallowing the last syllable instead of pronouncing it like the first vowel in "villain," like I'd learned it growing up in Santa Barbara.

"That's correct."

"The bar's on the road out of town heading that way. You probably passed it on your way here." I saw Turner make the hand signal that meant an order was ready. "I'll go get your food started."

Apparently "please" wasn't the only word missing from this Bostonian's vocabulary, since he didn't thank me, either. I gave Turner the order, delivered three platters to some South Lick residents, and poured Connolly's coffee. He didn't even look up from whatever he was doing on his phone.

Back at the grill, I asked Turner, "Want to switch?" We tried to change jobs once an hour or so to avoid boredom—and to give each other a break from rude customers.

"Sure. One second."

I watched Turner's long smooth-skinned fingers deftly wrap around the handle of the pitcher holding the pancake batter. His mother, Fern Turner-Rao, was a local girl but his father, Sajit, had been born in India. The family owned a maple tree farm in the county and Sajit was also somehow affiliated with the university over in Bloomington. After pouring six pancakes worth of batter into identically sized disks, Turner pulled off his apron and donned a fresh one from the box.

I was checking the status of the current orders on the lined up slips of paper when the bell on the door jangled.

"What's he doing here?" Turner muttered under his breath.

His father hurried toward us. He wore a fleece vest over a blue Oxford button-down. "Turner, I need your help at the farm." His accent wasn't a strong one, but his son's name sounded almost like "Durner."

"*Baba,* I told you." Turner kept his voice low. "I have a job, I can't just leave."

"But we have much to prepare for tomorrow. You know we are hosting the sugaring-off demonstration for the Festival." His hands flew through the air as he talked.

"I can't." Turner, at six foot two a couple of inches taller than his father, put his face right in front of his father's. "Robbie would be alone here. I'm not leaving."

Sajit made some kind of exclamation. "You are a smart boy. What are you doing cooking for your job? We paid for you to earn your degree. You should be using it, not doing women's work making American breakfast."

I sniffed, and tore my gaze away from the pair. Just in time I flipped the cakes before they burned, and scooted four crispy sausages to the cooler end of the grill. Turner had told me his father wasn't particularly happy with his son working for me, but I hadn't realized Sajit felt so strongly about it.

"You didn't pay much," Turner said. "You know I got free tuition because of your IU affiliation, and I lived at home."

"I have sacrificed much for you. You are my only son."

"And Sujita is going to graduate school. Your only daughter will be a doctor one day. That should make you happy. Me, I love to cook," Turner said, loading his forearms with four orders. "I want to be a chef. This is great experience for me. Please don't make a big fuss, *Baba.*"

"It will be on your head if a hundred people come tomorrow and we are not ready." Sajit turned away with a huff of air.

I ladled out an omelet's worth of beaten eggs, but out of the corner of my eye I saw Sajit freeze. Now what was wrong? I sprinkled sauteed green peppers, mushrooms, and onions onto the egg base, added capers and a handful of grated cheddar, and looked up to see what the problem was. Sajit stared with narrowed eyes at Warren Connolly, who shot him the curled lip under flared nostrils for a second. Then Connolly plastered on a fake grin and waved to Sajit with one pudgy hand.

"Dr. Rao. Join me, would you?" the professor called.

This time whatever Hindi word Sajit muttered sounded a lot more like a curse than the earlier expression of frustration, but he made his way to Connolly's table.

I exchanged a glance with Turner. He only shrugged. As he delivered his plates to their destination, I turned half of the omelet over onto itself, hoping the men's interaction wasn't going to turn into a display of in-store fireworks. That was never good for business.

After a super busy hour, which was exhausting but always great for the old bottom line, ten o'clock brought a total lull in business. Also great was the lack of a blowup between Sajit and Warren, contrary to what I'd thought was going to happen. Sajit had sat with the other professor and talked for about ten minutes. Every time I glanced their way, Sajit hadn't looked happy, but neither man had raised his voice. Turner's father left without saying goodbye to his son, which seemed to relieve the young man. Maybe I'd been wrong about the look Connolly and Sajit had exchanged.

"Sit down for a few while you can, Turner," I said. "And make yourself whatever you want to eat, first. If it's like earlier, we won't have a minute for lunch until we close at one-thirty." I was still trying to ensure he both felt welcome as my employee and paced himself on both rest and eating. The last thing we needed was one of us passing out from low blood sugar. I threw a slice of sharp cheese on top of a sad-looking unclaimed pancake and topped it with another, making myself a goofy sandwich. I brought it and a glass of milk to a table and sank blissfully into a chair.

He joined me a couple of minutes later, with a plate full of an egg-meat scramble and some overly crisp hash browns.

"I didn't realize your dad felt so strongly about you working here," I ventured. "I hope it's going to be okay at home."

He swallowed a bite of potato. "It'll be fine. But it's time for me to move out. Dad grew up in India, and the expectations for first sons—and especially only sons—are pretty different there, even now."

I wanted to ask what his mom thought, but I also didn't want him to think I, his boss, was prying into his personal life. His dad had brought the issue to my grill—that one was fair game. Then he answered my unasked question anyway.

"At least Mom's got my back. She's always said Su and I could do whatever we wanted with our lives, as long as it was legal and we could support ourselves." He scarfed down his eggs while I finished my pancake sandwich. "Are you all set for this afternoon?"

I shot a quick look at the clock. "I think so. I'm really glad I decided to close an hour early today. The judges and officials will be here by two-thirty, so we'll have plenty of time to clean up and get the place presentable. I'll have my biscuits all ready to pop in the oven fifteen minutes before the entry deadline."

"The doors open at three, right?"

"That's right, and the judging is at three-thirty. I hope we pack the place."

"The contest is just one locally made breakfast item, I think you said."

"Exactly, and it has to include maple. The county doesn't have a multi-cookstation facility like they set up on those cooking competition shows, so the cooking won't be live." I cringed a little. Murder had entered my life more than once since I'd opened the store, and I'd become just a teensy tiny bit sensitive to phrases like *live*. "I'm doing maple-flavored biscuits—but they'll include your secret ingredient. The judges are going to love them."

"Who's judging?" He stood and cleared both our places.

"Some of the scientists at the conference, I think, and maybe some locals, too. I don't know who." I joined him in the kitchen area. "I'm going to prep the dough now. It'll bake up better after a couple of hours of chilling."

"Good idea."

"I don't really care if I win the contest or not, even though they're lumping chefs together with amateur cooks. But it's great exposure for the store and restaurant." I measured out flour, baking powder, salt, and the touch of both curry powder and cayenne that Turner had added, with scrumptious results, a month earlier. As I cut in the butter, I asked, "Do you know that professor who was in this morning? The man from Boston?"

"No. The one Dad was talking to?"

"That's the one. His name is Warren Connolly. They didn't exactly seem to be best buds."

"I've never seen him at the house. But my father knows all kinds of people professionally who he doesn't hang out with for fun."

"What's your dad's exact occupation again?" I added the milk mixed with syrup to the flour-butter mixture and gave the dough a quick knead.

"He's a research biochemist." He finished setting up the last table for the next round of customers just as the little cowbell on the door set up a jangle. "He's tacked into climate change waters recently. Mostly because he's seen the change in the trees on our farm."

A tall thin figure in uniform pushed through the door. "Hey, Buck, come on in," I called to our lanky police lieutenant as I wrapped the thick disk of dough in plastic. "Are you a sailor?" I asked Turner.

His dark eyes lit up. "You bet. Me, a sailboat, Lake Monroe? It's the best."

"I used to sail off the Pacific coast back home."

"You did? That's one of my dreams. To be executive chef on a touring yacht. I want to see the world, but from the water." His eyes were dreamy, focused on a faraway horizon.

"You should totally go for it." I carried a menu over to Buck.

"I hear y'all talking 'bout sailing?" he asked, laying his uniform hat on the small table he preferred at the back of the restaurant, where he could eat and keep an eagle eye on the town, too.

When I nodded, he went on.

"You might could sail a boat all the way to China through the hole in my stomach right about now. I'm that hungry."

No wonder. He was only about six foot a hundred—or at least a foot taller than my own five three—and as skinny as a twig. "You must have a metabolism like a hummingbird, Buck." I smiled fondly at him.

"Welp, I got me a appetite like a horse. Can I get one of everything?"

"For a change?" I snorted.

"Shucks, Robbie. Anymore, I don't even know why you ask."

A couple of minutes I carried over a tray and set down three plates in front of him. He beamed at the sight: a tall stack of my signature pancakes, two over easy next to three links and a mound of hash browns, plus a couple of biscuits covered in creamy homemade sausage gravy. He tucked his napkin into his collar and his fork into the biscuits.

"You ain't seen no more dead bodies, have you?" he asked, laden fork halfway to his mouth, gravy dripping onto the pancakes.

"I'm happy to say I haven't." A shudder ran through me remembering the one my friend Lou and I had encountered this winter while we were out snowshoeing. The man had been murdered, and his killer had later come after my boyfriend Abe and me in a remote cottage in the woods during an ice storm. "Thank goodness."

"I sure don't know what it is with you and murder. You're like a flame to them moths."

Was I? It was true, I'd helped solve three murders since my store opened. I was the one who'd found two of the bodies, in fact, one right here in my store. But surely that was a coincidence. I had no intention of brushing up against even one more violent person. I loved my store and my town, I had a very nice relationship developing with Abe, and life was good. My plan for it definitely didn't include murder.

As it turned out, two of the judges that afternoon had been in the store a few hours earlier. At three twenty-five, two of my still-warm biscuits were displayed on a small white plate in the middle of the array of other entries. My plate, with both biscuits neatly halved, was identified only by "#8 - Maple Biscuits" on the typed white card in front of the plate. The biscuits had come out as close to perfect as was even possible, rising high and flaky with golden brown tops and a crumb you just couldn't wait to get your mouth around. I'd done a pre-taste, of course, and the combo of maple and Indian spice was exactly right, with a subtle zing following the hint of sweetness.

To my entry's left were dark heavy-looking maple donuts and then plump maple sausages, all on

identical plates. On the other side sat maple bars,
topped with a glistening icing, with a plate of maple
bran muffins beyond. The other offerings were
along the same vein, with only one, a pecan-topped
coffee cake, offered by another area chef. Most
looked way too sweet for my tastes, but I kept my
mouth shut. I was a contestant, not a judge.

I'd grabbed time to wash up and don a magenta
silk tunic for the occasion. I'd tried to tame my full
black curls with a couple of clips, and had thrown
on a dash of colored lip gloss. I was glad I had, as
a reporter from the *Brown County Democrat* had
snapped a photo of all the entrants lined up in a
row at the side of the contest table. He'd also taken
a couple of me alone, since I was hosting.

The store was packed to the gills with tourists
and locals alike. Since three o'clock they'd been
filing past the contest entries, pointing, murmuring,
but not touching. The organizers, one of whom was
my Aunt Adele, had stretched a cord in front of the
length of the table to keep viewers a couple of feet
away.

Now Adele stepped up to the portable PA system
they'd set up, not that this forthright senior citizen
really needed amplification. She tapped the mike.
"We're about ready to start. Can you shut your
sweet pieholes already?" She smiled to soften the
message and nobody seemed to take it the wrong
way. The buzzing conversation soon grew still. You
didn't mess with Aunt Adele.

"Thank you," she continued. "As you know, this
is the kickoff culinary competition for the Festival.
We're delighted to get such a great array of entries.
Our cooks are there." She pointed to our line at the

side of the table. "But they're not necessarily in the same order as their entries." The crowd clapped, and someone called out, "Let's hear it for links!" A supporter of the sausage maker, no doubt.

"Let me introduce our esteemed judges and they can get a-tastin'." Adele turned to the four standing behind her.

"First, we have South Lick's own top chef, Christina James."

My friend Christina, her long blond hair wore down for once, smiled and waved to the crowd.

"Next, our esteemed farmer-scientist, Dr. Sajit Rao."

Sajit held up a hand in acknowledgment, but kept a serious expression on his face. After Turner and I had finished the cleanup earlier, he'd asked if I needed him to stay, and I'd said I didn't, so he wasn't here to see his father judge. I kind of hoped the younger man had gone home to help with whatever needed doing for their demonstration tomorrow.

"From the Nashville Inn, up-and-coming chef Nick Fernandes," Adele announced.

A dark-eyed man looking somewhere near my own age of twenty-seven nodded, his hands clasped in front of his white chef tunic. He'd taken over Christina's spot at the inn when she was hired at Hoosier Hollow, the new gourmet restaurant down the street last winter.

"Finally, visiting from Boston, we have world-renowned scientist Professor Warren Connolly."

When the applause died down, Adele added, "I guess you might know a small little thing or two about maple up there in New England, Professor, am I right?"

"We most certainly do." He patted his stomach with both hands and rocked back on his heels, beaming, looking for all the world like the stereotype of a well-off businessman. His cheeks were flushed, though.

I'd be willing to bet Professor Connolly had studied a liquid lunch at the Casino in the hours since breakfast. Didn't he have conference sessions to attend? Oh, well. Not my circus, not my monkey. When a man climbed onto a chair way at the back of the crowd, my cheeks warmed. It was my hunky electrician, Abe O'Neill. He waved and blew me a kiss, then gestured with two thumbs up.

Adele handed each judge a pen, a small clipboard holding a score sheet, and a water bottle for clearing their palates between tastes. She instructed them on the procedure and the judging categories.

"Professor Connolly, you'll go first," Adele said.

"Oh, no. Ladies first. I insist."

Christina caught my eye and lifted one eyebrow as if to say, "Where'd they get this throwback?" but she proceeded to the first plate. I watched as the line of judges moved down the line of plates. They tasted, scribbled, tasted some more, marked the final grade, sipped water, and moved to the next entry. Somebody gave a piercing two-fingered whistle when Christina tasted the muffins, and my neighbor in the entrants' lineup folded her hands so tight when Christina came to the maple bars I was pretty sure they were hers.

I tried not to look too closely when the judges sampled my biscuits, but Christina managed to slip me a wink. She knew quality when she tasted it. The dark donuts next to my entry seemed to act to my advantage. To a one the judges grimaced after tasting them.

Warren Connolly, bringing up the rear, popped an entire biscuit half into his mouth as soon as he got to #8. No subtle rolling on the tongue for him. He coughed but it was a strangled sound, like he was choking on the bite. I watched as his eyes bugged out. His face turned even redder. He grabbed at his throat with both hands. Nick, just ahead of Connolly in line, turned and stared, eyes wide, but he didn't move to help. Was he paralyzed? Why didn't he whack Connolly on the back? This was terrible. Choking was no joke. Too many people stood between us for me to try to reach the professor. The entire crowd seemed rooted to the floor. The professor's water bottle thunked onto the floor.

"Help him!" I cried.